This Life is Beautiful

By Lamia Islam

Edited by Gabriel Headington

www.thislifeisbeautiful.com

Contents

"Do not grieve over past joys.
Be sure they will reappear in another form.
A child's joy is in milk and nursing, but once
weaned, it finds new joy in bread and honey.
Joy appears in many different forms. It moves
from place to place. It may suddenly show in the
falling rain or in the rose bed. It comes now
as water, now as beauty, or as nourishing bread.
But suddenly it may show its face and destroy
all idols that prevent you from seeking the divine.
In sleep when the soul leaves the body you may
dream of yourself as a tall cypress or a beautiful rose,
but be warned, my friend, all these phantoms dissolve
into thin air once the soul returns to the body.
Do not rely on anything but your heart."

Rumi

Part 1

Between Darkness and Light

Chapter 1
A Day like Any Other

"The mind is its own place, and in itself can make a Heaven of Hell, a Hell of Heaven."

John Milton

I was totally disoriented, unsure of who I was or why I was lying in my parents' bed. One night of sleep had felt like an eternity. The unnerving stillness and silence of the room in which I lay was broken only by the steady ticking of a clock, hung high on one of its four white walls. I would have assumed this was a day like any other, except for the numbing fear and confusion I felt that seemingly came out of nowhere.

Everything around me seemed normal enough. Everything in the room was set just as it usually was. The thick, green velvet curtains were drawn, inviting the morning light to seep in through the large windows. The air was still and undisturbed, its silence broken only by the steady ticking of the clock, signaling the morning to come. A white fan whirred gently from the high ceiling as I lay in my parents Burma teak wood bed, with its crescent moon shaped headboard. Matching night tables sat on either side. To the left was a wall with four square windows and a wooden door that led to a terrace. Across the large room, was my father's desk with a neatly arranged row of books – mostly self-help books but a few were on religion and psychology. A beige rug was strewn on the white marble floor in front of the bed. Everything was perfectly in its place. And yet something was different.

I sat up shakily and looked around the room, my eyes finally rested on a photo frame beside the bed. A picture of two little girls, all smiles and giggles, dressed lavishly for a wedding, holding up their syrupy sweets, like prizes won from the food table. Samama. I let go of a breath I did not realise I had been holding. This is what is different. This picture was not here before. I was surprised to find that my sense of relief was immediately followed by that cold numbness again, spreading all throughout my body. I felt suddenly sick and groggy. Why had I woken up in my parents' bed? I was 22 years old. It's not as though I just went and climbed in their bed anymore because I had a nightmare. Why did I have this unidentifiable fear sweeping through me? And why had I woken up so late in the morning? And still felt dazed enough to need three cups of coffee to get me going?

I sat for a while, trying to clear my head when I noticed my mother peeping through the crack in the door. When she realised I had seen her, she came inside, cautiously, with a smile that was just a bit too cheery to be normal.

'Mum, are you okay?' My mother was a bit taken aback by the question and laughed awkwardly.

'Of course, honey.' She leaned a little closer. 'Are you okay?' Her large smile was still pasted on, but her slightly furrowed eyebrows betrayed a sense of worry.

'Mumm, what's going on? I feel really strange. And you seem…different.'

'Different?' My mother just kept that smile fixed in place and acted completely oblivious to the strangeness of her own behavior.

I looked out the window toward the sun rising high in the sky, then quickly turned back to my mother.

'Why am I in your room?'

My mother faltered only for a second. 'Well, its nice isn't it?'

'Well, yes but—'

'How about you come and join us for lunch?'

Lunch? I had apparently under-estimated how late I had woken up. I rose from the bed somewhat shakily with legs like a new born deer. *Just how long have I been lying here?* Once I'd showered and dressed, I made my way to the dining room for lunch. As I approached I could hear many voices chattering softly.

When I entered the dining room I was surprised to see so many people seated at the table, the conversations immediately stopped and all heads turned to greet me: my mother, my father, my sister, my Aunt Sabera and her son Maher. Whilst the fact that my extended family were here for lunch was nothing new – we shared meals regularly and had at one time shared the same house – what was out of the ordinary was the almost deathly silence as I entered the room and the fixed grins everyone had pasted on their faces. My aunt Sabera, with whom I had always had a special bond, attempted to break the silence.

'Hello Aalinna, come sit, join us. I have brought your favorite dish.' It was a trigger, everyone else round the table came to life, they all began commenting at once and looking at each other with each comment, as if looking for assurance that they had not said the wrong thing.

'Yes, 'said my mother and father in unison, 'your favorite. How kind of your aunt.'

'Doesn't all the food look wonderful, Aalinna? Screeched my sister Maryam, rising as I approached to sit in the seat next to her.

'Yeah let's dig in!' chipped in Maher, his normally deep voice sounding a few octaves too high.

Now I really knew things weren't right. Family lunches normally consisted of copious amounts of food, laughter, teasing, chatter and trying to get a word in over the din. While it was unusual to be invited to sit next to my aunt, and to have my mother gushing, and thanking her for bringing my favorite dish, it was normal for family, especially my aunt, to bring dishes when they came for lunch. My younger sister Maryam even noticed the effort that had been made to prepare and lay the copious amounts of food on the table. As for cousin Maher, normally he would tease me instantly or make jokes when I walked into the room, but he was behaving like a nervous boy on a first date.

The meal carried on in much the same way, with me being the focus of everyone's self-conscious attention.. I can't remember if I spoke or replied much. I think apart from the feelings of grogginess and disorientation, I was stunned at everyone's behavior and a little frightened.

*

The rest of the day went in much the same way. My mother and father seemed just a little bit happier than normal. Everyone talked with me just a little bit too kindly. My younger sister tried to joke with me just a little more than usual. Everyone changed the topic a little too quickly when I asked why they were acting so strange – or why I felt so strange. My whole family was extra nice and caring, yet they all seemed to have concern and worry etched on their faces.

In the late afternoon, I retired to my room and sat down on the plush red couch at the foot of my bed. I felt so confused and couldn't wrap my head around everyone's strange behavior. After a while my best friend Yushra surprised me with a visit. She peeked her head into my room and then sat next to me. I felt relieved to see her. Her birthday had been the day before, and we had made plans to go out. Though, now that I thought about it, I couldn't remember what those plans were, or what we actually did. I probed her with questions. *Why did I feel so strange?*

Why was my family acting so strange? But it soon became apparent that Yushra was also acting as weird as the others and trying to come off as normal.

She sat next to me on that big red couch the rest of the day, as though she never wanted to leave. My mother brought us a cup of tea, and for the first time I noticed my tongue felt extremely heavy. I attempted a first sip and recoiled at the stinging that shot through my teeth and gums.

What the hell was going on? I excused myself from the room for a moment, under the pretense of getting something to go with our tea. If I could get anyone to answer my questions and shed some light on what was going on, it would be my father. I found him in his study, surrounded by four different newspapers – t*he Daily Inqilab, the Daily Jugantor, the Bangladesh Observer* and *the Independent*. This was finally something normal – my father could not read just one newspaper. He had to know the news from here to America and to read the same news in two languages was an added bonus.

'Dad—' before I could ask him anything, I stopped short. I glanced at the headline on the newspaper unfolded in front of him and noticed the date – September 10, 1998. September 10th? How was that even possible? The day before was September 4th, Yushra's birthday. You would think that the *Bangladesh Observer* would not make such an elementary mistake in its printing. I stifled a laugh but it confused me enough to draw my attention to another newspaper, the *Daily Jugantor*. Once again, the headline said the date was September 10, 1998. I knew that the day before was September the 4th. Six days cannot vanish into thin air. My heart caught in my chest, I was holding my breath. I reached for another newspaper and was almost exploding with anxiety by the time I reached for the fourth – was the world not aware that nearly a whole week had transpired between yesterday and today? Or was *I* the one who did not realise it?

I reeled, completely disoriented. Had the world gone mad? I suddenly felt I didn't know who I was. Confused and panicked, I was terrified that I could not remember what Yushra and I had done for her birthday.

My father, who had been watching me anxiously from his overstuffed leather armchair, became aware of what I had noticed.

'Come-Come Aalinna, sit with me.' I fled.

I rushed from his study to the telephone and called my friend Tahira.

'What day is it?' I demanded of her as soon as she answered.

'Oh yeah, hi, Aalinna. Date? Well it's September 10th,'she replied.

I shook my head in disbelief, unwilling to surrender to the fact that I had lost six whole days of my life. I rang two other friends, asking the same question and getting the same reply. A sensation of complete anxiety made my chest tighten. It was hard to breathe. Was this some sort of a prank? I had never felt so scared. For the life of me, I could not recall where I had been or what I had done for, what might have been, an entire week.

As I looked around, my eyes darted back and forth, desperately grasping for any clue that could help me piece together the mystery of the six missing days. My own sense of confusion and disorientation gave rise to an increasing panic. I could not wrap my mind around even what was familiar. In fact, I realised my mind was the main problem. I could barely concentrate and every detail was foggy. Every memory was distant and incomplete. I could hardly connect any two thoughts in my head, much less analyze what was happening to me.

I glanced over at my father, who had been standing at a discreet distance listening to my calls and watching me grow more frantic with each one. I could see the tension mounting in him as well. My mother came to his side, then he quickly suggested I go lay down in my room. My mother approached to take my arm. I recoiled, both at her, and at the suggestion. If I lay down any longer I might fall asleep again and wake up only to find another week of my life missing, or maybe not wake at all.

I turned from my mother and rushed down the stairs. *I just need a breath of fresh air*. I stopped short of the bottom of the steps. I toppled my weight onto the railing, stared at the front door, and remembered.

Chapter 2
Happy

"I do not exist to impress the world. I exist to live my life in a way that will make me happy."

Richard Bach

It had been the end of summer and my friend Zoha was leaving for the United States to get her master's degree. Nadra, now married, was heading to New Jersey to join her husband, and Yushra's birthday party was imminent, for which I had bought myself a gorgeous outfit. I'd arrived home from my friend's house in an uncontrollable state of elation. For the last month I had barely slept, spending most of my time out with her and other friends playing poker, hanging out, drinking wine and smoking pot. Although my parents probably suspected what I was doing, they didn't say anything about my lifestyle, and in my rebellious independent streak I didn't really care what they thought.

Feelings of happiness surged through every part of my body. I was on top of the world. Though I can't recall the specific words coming out of my mouth I know I was saying things that made no sense. Talking rubbish to anyone who would listen – all the while feeling as if I was in total control. I called my friend Zoha, I was so excited and impatient I resented the time it took for me to dial and she to answer, the ring tone was agony.

'Hiiiii,' I screeched barely caring if it was her at the other end or not.

'Hey,' replied Zoha with laughter in her voice, "someone's happy today. How are you? You looking forward to Yushra's party tonight?"

'Hell yeah I'm on top of the world. Oh, Zoha I am so pleased for you, going to the States to study is only going to be the beginning for you,' I gushed.

'Oh thank you, Aalinna, you are so sweet. I'm pretty nervous so I hope you're right,' Zoha said with a nervous giggle

'Hope! Hope? Come on, Zoha, we are friends. You know my skills and the power of insight I have. This is why I'm calling, I have deemed that you will pass your studies with flying colours and go on to do many important things! I have seen it… these things I know! Have I not told you this before?' I'm a little indignant, surely she knows it is me that she is talking to?

I chose not to let it bother me. *After all*, I thought, *she's my friend and it isn't her fault that she's not as intelligent and important as me*,

Yes, Zoha must have thought, *you have told me such things before but this is getting out of hand.* . I was calling her more and more often, talking weirdly like this. At least it wasn't 2.00 or 3.00 in the morning this time, talking persistently in that high pitched voice about any up and coming event and how great it would be, 'especially' when she was attending. Zoha had initially put this behaviour down to a joke or drunkenness, given my antics lately, but now she was actually worried and nervous at the sound of my voice.

'Thanks Aalinna. I will see you at Yushra's party,' she said as she hurriedly hung up.

*

I had a level of confidence so intense that even I was surprised. I talked too much, laughed too loudly and rambled on unnecessarily and uncontrollably. I blurted out my strange dreams and thoughts to those around me, whether they wanted to hear them or not. I was open and free with anyone who wanted to talk – or didn't – and was just a bit too bubbly and excited over everything.

I began writing pages upon pages of my thoughts in a new diary—even if there were no actual people around, I could still express myself in a journal. Any outlet for this surge of emotions was a welcome release. I was needlessly happy, and exhausting to my friends and family.

My parents were dumbfounded by my behavior. They were aware of my nights of walking around the house chattering to myself at all hours, pestering some poor soul on the phone, waking them from their slumber, only to tell them how wonderful everything was. And if it wasn't wonderful for them? No problem, I could fix it. I was like a caged animal with all this euphoria and happiness inside me. I needed to be living life no matter what hour of the day or night. Often my mother grew exasperated and rose, sleepily, from her bed to tell me to get off the phone as I was keeping up the whole house up.

On one occasion she confronted me: 'Aalinna get off that phone, have you seen the time?'

'Ok,' I'd said brightly – quickly saying goodbye to the person on the other end. I headed downstairs, when my mother, who was slowly walking back to her room with a worried frown, turned and exclaim in a hushed whisper, '*Now,* what are you doing?'

'I'm going out,' I replied incredulously, thinking *'what's her problem?'*

'Oh Aalinna, no, please come to bed its 2am.

I took no notice, carrying on down the stairs towards the front door. My mother soon caught up and even overtook me, pushing past on the stairs.

'You can't go out alone at this time of night! Still, I didn't listen, I couldn't, I needed *out,* I could not stay cooped up in this silence when I had so much to say and share.

The silence turned deafening. I tried to get past my mother who was now blocking the door, stunned and frightened. After a flash of arguing back and forth, she realised that I was determined. She couldn't stop me.

'Ok, ok,' my mother sighed, "but only if I can come with you. Please just let me quickly dress and I will come.' I agreed, and watched as she took the stairs two at a time in her haste to change and get back, before I opened the door and disappeared into the night alone.

On entering the bedroom, my mother saw that my father was wide awake and staring at her, he had obviously heard the whole commotion.

'This has got to stop, she is getting worse, she is flirting and talking with anyone in the street that catches her eye – calling her friends at all hours of day and night, rambling on about how wonderful life is and how she has the power and knows the true way of things... and as for confronting her aunt and bringing up past upsets in the family?'

'Shh! Please!' Said my mother as she breathlessly tried to get dressed, swinging the door closed so I would not overhear.

'We will talk of this, but for now I need to get back to her,' she continued, struggling with the buttons of a cotton jacket.

My father readily conceded, not only because he too saw the wisdom in my mother's words but also because he hated the effect 'All This' was having on his wife, who was always worried what Aalinna would do next. He loved his beautiful, inquisitive, social and friendly daughter. But this wasn't right, chattering expressively, and dramatically displaying her emotions with no thought to anyone and everyone, without inhibition or thought as to how she sounded, or even if her words offended or hurt. Even poor Maryam was not only becoming increasingly weary of her big sister's outbursts, she was having to ignore strange looks and whispers from others too.

I wish I could tell you what happened on the 'night walk' with my mother, but I can't remember, other than it wasn't the first or last time it happened.

*

On that fateful evening, I had donned my lavish new dress and set of earrings that I had just bought, ready for an adventurous night out with Yushra for her birthday. I smiled flirtatiously at my reflection in the mirror and called goodbye to my parents.

'You have to stay home,' my mother said, standing by the door. "You're not going out," my father added, jaw set and eyes slightly narrowed.

I naturally assumed they were joking, and waved them aside. As a very independent 22-year-old, living in my parents' home, they did not stop me from coming and going as I pleased – until now.

Looking over at my parents, standing side by side like two sentries in front of the door, I thought *what is going on?* They were looking at each other for support and nodded slightly at each other. I was baffled. There had been no fall out or misdemeanor over the last few days that could come back to haunt me, warranting my parents to attempt to 'ground' me at 22 years old.

'What are you talking about? Why? But it's Yushra's birthday party tonight – you know that.'

Still, my parents just stood there resolutely, blocking my exit. I noticed from the corner of my eye Maryam, sitting half way up the stairs looking nervous, with her arms wrapped round her knees. She bowed her head when she caught me looking, this was all too weird. At a loss for words, I just stood there, the faint notion that something was really wrong now taking over. The more they persisted and refused to move from the door, the more aggressive and furious I became.

'Seriously, what is going on? What is wrong with you all? How dare you? This is bullshit!' When not even my harsh words and foul language moved them I knew it was hopeless. Furious, I stormed off down the hall and into my bedroom, slamming the door so hard that the windows shook, locking it firmly behind me.

They must have sensed something about the trouble to come, like the wind that picks up a bit before an impending storm. They knew my uncontrollable state wasn't normal or natural. My parents did not have a clue as to what had turned their naturally easy-going girl into a non-stop talking machine.

My parents tried relentlessly to coax me into opening the door. I heard them telling Maryam to try talking to me, but I only heard her run down the corridor stifling a cry after I had screamed at her, calling her a traitor. No matter what they said, I wouldn't let them in the room. Finally, as the hours blurred, they stopped trying.

Congratulating myself on my victorious defiance, I fumed in frustration, furiously flipping through the magazines on my nightstand. Hours later, there was a quiet knock on the door. A gentle, unassuming knock that I somehow knew didn't belong to any of my family members.

'Please open the door.' It was a man's voice, very kind, and vaguely familiar. Cautiously, I opened the door a crack, and peered at a man, casually dressed in slacks and a polo shirt with sandals. Dr. Chowdury. I recognized our family physician instantly. He had helped to safely deliver me and two of the most important people in my life, my little sister Maryam and my best friend Samama. Throughout my childhood, any time I or a family member was sick, Dr. Chowdury would faithfully drive over to our house, take care of us, prescribe medicine or do anything necessary. He was very kind and more like a family friend than our physician. I felt I could trust him when I was sure everyone else had gone mad.

Dr. Chowdury asked if he could come in. My mind in a frenzy from the evening's events, his calm demeanor was welcome and comforting. I allowed him to take my hand and lead me to the plush red couch, oblivious to my worried parents and sister, anxiously listening from outside the room. He spoke quietly and told me to close my eyes. Moments later I felt drowsy and light, as if I were floating in the air.

At that time, I didn't realise that Dr. Chowdury had given me a sedative. All I knew was that my nerves had calmed. I soon fell into a deep slumber, and became lost in the enveloping darkness.

For a week I lingered in this obscure blackness. Sleep was deep, and unavoidable. When I awoke, I barely knew I was awake. It was just like that first minute when you rouse from a dream. You remember some of what happened, but you try for a full minute to determine if the dream was real or not. For that one minute, you are utterly confused and you try desperately to determine if your next move will be based on the events of your dream or the realities of your life – and which is which to begin with. It only takes that dream minute, though, to emerge from the confusion, but this time was different. The dream minute took an entire week.

I never knew the hour, the day, the moment. Each day evaporated around me until it was lost completely. Sometimes it was day and sometimes night.

My parents came and left but I hardly knew. Amidst this fog, someone gave me medication, tiny pills in a little paper cup. I hid the pills under my tongue for all those days. I did not know why I did not want to swallow them. It was not until I got a serious tongue infection that anyone realised I was hiding the pills. After that, the doctor was much more diligent in ensuring I swallowed them.

I can't tell you what came first or what came last. Sometimes I thought the phone rang – maybe I answered it. I heard voices, sultry and familiar, though I hardly knew if the voices belonged to friends from long ago or if one of them was my own. And just when something began to make sense, I drifted into sleep or I sat on the bed, hazily staring out the window, locked into a moment in time, unable to pull my mind or body away.

Most of the time, I simply dreamed. Sometimes the dreams were disturbing, and sometimes they were sweet memories of halcyon days long ago.

Chapter 3
Born With Wings

"You were born with potential. You were born with goodness and trust. You were born with ideals and dreams. You were born with greatness. You were born with wings. You are not meant for crawling, so don't. You have wings. Learn to use them and fly."

Rumi

Only a few weeks before my hazy slumber, I'd attended my Aunt Rida and Uncle Amer's party to celebrate their 15th wedding anniversary. The whole event was beautiful and was held in a rental hall in the bustling city of Dhaka, Bangladesh, where my family and I lived.

We had shown up over an hour late, as the city's flooded streets prevented cars, cattle and even determined rickshaw peddlers, from going anywhere. The outside of the rental hall was covered in long strings of tiny, bright-blue lights, hanging from the rooftop. It set the dark street aglow and invited guests to a warm evening inside – hinting of fantasy. As beautiful as it was, it could never compare in my mind to the actual wedding it commemorated. That day truly was a fairy tale, a childhood memory I would never forget — a memory captured and framed in the picture next to my parents' bed.

*

Chapter 3

Perhaps the memory of my Aunt Rida's actual wedding day was so special, because nothing out of the ordinary happened! It was a very typical Bangladeshi wedding. It lasted a full week, and was marked by friends and family coming every day to the large three-story house in which we grew up together.

The house had been decorated in millions of tiny bright lights, strung all the way up to the roof, draped down the sides and front of the building and canopied across the trees in the yard. The cook we shared between our families prepared lavish meals for all the guests, whilst contending with chasing myself, and my cousins, Samama, Rabab, and Maher from the kitchen. Brandishing a ladle, cloth or whatever came to hand, she would growl at us and threaten us with a slap. We in turn would run screeching from the kitchen, loving every moment, our stash of stolen treats falling through our hands.

Samama and I had sat huddled together two little girls in matching dresses, our fingers and lips tacky and sugar coated from the huge tray of sweets we shared. Female family members and married women, who we considered ancient, had been transformed into beautiful butterflies with their colourful, flowing saris. We watched in awe as they flitted around, laughing, chattering, and adorning the bride with mehndi, using the traditional yellow turmeric. Their faces looked so different to us, not only because of their meticulously applied make–up, but by their laughter and carefree exuberance, at the joy and excitement of the whole occasion.

My father, normally reserved, was amongst the throng of men chatting and laughing with my uncle. No business talk today, as they watched the antics of the women and children good naturedly.

I had never enjoyed myself so much in all my life as I did at that wedding. It was not simply the lavish meals, plates piled high with sweets, and colourful saris that made the event so memorable. It was because it represented all the love and closeness our family shared throughout the year. The laughter and light-heartedness of that week was not out of the ordinary. The smiles on our faces, the hugs and teasing, our hopeful and exuberant spirits — all of these things were normal for us. The only thing the wedding really added, was a lot more decoration, a lot more sweets, and perhaps a little more time with family. Although we were always with family, always giving love and taking support; always sharing meals together. The closeness of our family was so tangible that day, my heart filled to the brim with a sense of safety, love and security. I was, as I usually was — happy and carefree, confident and bubbly, a people-person who loved meeting new acquaintances and making new friends. Neither a care, nor worry in the world to dampen my spirits.

The three-story house in which most of the wedding took place was also the home that I grew up in for the first nine years of my life. My aunt, who was only a teenager when we moved out, lived with my grandparents on the first floor, where you could also find the kitchen, dining and living rooms. My grandfather's two sons, my father and uncle, with whom he shared the family business, lived on the second floor. My mother and father had a room on one side, while my aunt and uncle had a room on the other, divided by another common area in the middle. The third floor might as well have been my own clubhouse. There, my cousin Samama, her twin brother Rabab, their older brother Maher and I each had our own room, my little sister Maryam still sleeping on the same floor as my parents. Our four rooms encircled a large common living area with a TV.

My cousins and I, who for all intents and purposes, were my

sister and brothers, spent endless hours together on that third floor: playing hide and seek, whispering our secrets, arguing senselessly, and giggling away the evenings. Often when we played hide and seek Samama and I would hide and the boys would seek.

'Where do you think they could be Rabab?' Maher would say, pointing at the cupboard with a wink. Samama and I hid crouched down, arms wrapped round each other, getting tenser by the minute.

As the door flew open we would let out a long scream and bury our heads in each other's necks. This normally lead to us being dubbed sissies and Samama and I chanting back 'Cheaters, Cheaters' – all trying to shout over the top of each other.

The game normally ended with either an adult shouting up the stairs to keep it down or if it was one of our late night escapades, as it so often was, a loud banging from the floor above would signal that, if peace did not ensue, one of our parents would come and scold us all. If we weren't on the third floor, then we could easily be found on our beautiful rooftop garden or in our enormous backyard, swimming in the pool, climbing trees, playing soccer or badminton.

Samama and Rabab especially, were always by my side. Upon returning from school each day, before we'd throw our backpacks aside and head for our bikes, Samama would coax me to stay with her for a while. We would sit in her room and she would produce the day's lessons that she had meticulously written down for me. Whilst we munched on biscuits, she would explain the lessons to me in a way that only she could be sure I would understand; in school I could not seem to take it in or make sense of what the teacher was writing down nor the point she was trying to make. I had to endure long lectures, not only from my teachers, but also from my parents, once they had heard about my 'lack of effort and interest' in a terse phone call home. I loved Samama, not only for the kindness of this act but for her ability to see and accept me for who I was. I don't think I would have made it through those school years without her.

From mansion to tin-roofed shanty, we knew everyone, and everyone knew us. We could pedal our bikes and meet up with friends. The dirt paths and paved roads never held a stranger, and we were always happy to pick up a game of cricket or visit with a friend's grandmother, standing on our tip-toes behind a throng of men at a local tea stall to watch the World Cup on their TV. We'd crowd around a street vendor to buy his pitha snacks and share with each other. Our favourite place to ride our bikes, by far, was the local park. It was always kept very nicely, and many of our friends would go there to play basketball, have a picnic by the pond or saunter around its tree-lined walking paths.

Samama and I loved to take a spin on the merry-go-round, or hang out at the slides and monkey bars, gossiping and giggling and then, when the group dispersed, we would sit close whispering our secrets and concerns. Nothing could have made me happier than to stay in that three-floor house, with our family so close, and my own little club-house shared with my cousins on the third floor. When my parents decided it was time to move into a separate home, once Maryam was old enough to need her own room, I was devastated.

On the day we officially moved, Samama and I cried incessantly and gave each other many tearful hugs goodbye. My mother merely watched us and stifled a small laugh over the drama — we were only moving a few streets away. Still, Samama and I would not be on the same floor anymore, which I was sure would mean the end of the world.

However, we still sat together, each morning on the big orange van that took us to school every day. As loyally as ever she would take notes and share them with me. We had plenty of sleepovers at each other's houses, often with Rabab and Maher in tow, whom I swear, only came to tease and pester us.

Whilst we no longer ate lunch together during the week, as we had done before, we did so on Fridays, without exception, one week dining at Samama's house and the next at mine. Aunt Sabera, Samama's mother, laden with dishes of food would burst through the door.

'Come, come, let's get this lot to the table,' she would shout over her shoulder to my uncle, whom she had also burdened like a camel with yet more containers, often filled with my favourite dishes and sweets. I had a special bond with Aunt Sabera which was expressed through an awful lot of spoiling. This relationship would strengthen as I got older and would become invaluable during my adolescence.

I found that I really enjoyed our new set up. I enjoyed coming home to the quiet of our small family of four. I spent more time with Maryam my little sister, who was not so little anymore; whilst I had loved her from the day she was born I was often so busy with my cousins that she got left out. Sometimes, when Maryam hung around with us, I would become impatient with her getting under my feet, or exasperated when she spoilt our games, like 'hide and seek', by telling the boys where we were hiding. I could now sit with her playing games or chasing her through the house whist she filled it with her giggles. I was enjoying being the big sister.

We were also only a ten-minute bike ride away from my mother's side of the family, a place I loved to go any time I had the chance. My mother had a younger brother and sister who were both married with children. I loved playing with my cousins, and even my father, normally quite reserved, became extremely cheerful and funny around his in-laws.

This was the part of his personality that I enjoyed the best. I also loved listening to my mother's older brother, who never married because he did not believe in the concept of marriage. Everyone saw him as the odd-bird of the family, but I always found him fun to be with and thought his point-of-view on many things in life, extremely interesting. His bohemian, hippie sort of life-style, quite uncommon in traditional Bangladesh, fascinated me.

My mother and father set a beautiful example for me in this. Our family was quite well off, especially considering the poverty found all throughout Bangladesh. Our money and our lifestyle, however, never altered their view of other people. While many other well-to-do Bangladeshi families, too easily lifted their noses and looked down haughtily on anyone of a lower social class, they never cared how much or how little anyone had. They often invited people of various backgrounds to our house, and all of us could easily chat away the evening with anyone who's race, social class, or anything else was different from our own. In fact, my parents and I found their differences intriguing.

My mother, however liberal she may have been, was very Bangladeshi minded when it came to education. I loved my mother and respected that, as well as having her children when she was only 20 and 25 years old, she also managed and ran a large household and its staff. Like most teenagers I always assumed it was my mother's mission in life to eliminate every ounce of fun in life, and replace it with work, study, maturity and dullness. I, the very personification of free-spirited independence, did not respond well to this. I, therefore, viewed my mother as imposing and dominating, with a very short temper. I was not exactly the best student in school, and my mother did not have high expectations for me, so she made sure to carve out time every day after school to provide a little extra educational support for me.

The tutoring sessions that would begin with sweet words of encouragement and hopeful anticipations, usually ended with furrowed eyebrows, folded arms, exasperated sighs, and unnerving silence. I was not particularly bothered by my poor performance, I enjoyed school, I was popular and had a wide circle of friends and no matter how mediocre my input, I always managed to *get by*. This perhaps contributed to my mother's exasperation!

'Really, Aalinna? Sometimes I wonder why I bother, I do not think you have listened to one word I have said,' as she caught me staring off into space.

'Go just go,' she'd screech, brought to her wits end by my lack of interest.

Adolescence has a way of unravelling even the best of family relationships, or at least fraying their edges a bit, disagreements and issues that were kept to a simmer in my childhood now bubbled and boiled over without inhibition in my adolescence. Issues came to the surface, like my poor performance in school, also my hesitancy toward prayer and to our family's religion, which I had left unquestioned in the past. Before, I had been the obedient, peace-making child but now I was unwilling to blindly accept.

My mum could not content herself with my mediocre performance in school or lackadaisical commitment to religion. Her response to me ran the gamut from coaxing and scolding, to encouraging and demanding. I must do better in school. I must be more religious. The more she pressured me, the more I resisted. Often I would make statements just to antagonize her.

Her scolding did not improve my grades and they certainly did not encourage any sort of piety in me. More often than not, during these times I would turn to my Aunt Sabera. To be honest, as a child I thought loved her more than my own mother. There was just something about the way my aunt treated me that was different from any other adult. On the days that she would find me on her sofa – of which there many throughout my adolescence – she would turn from her stove in the kitchen on hearing me storm through her front door yelling denouncements of my mother.

'I can't take it anymore! What is her problem? She never listens, Aunt Sabera she just wants to talk at me, criticizing and shoving her precious opinions down my throat.'

Then the tears would come and she would turn down the light on her stove, wipe her hands and come to where I sat, stoop down on one knee, look me straight in the eye with the gentlest smile, and listen. She didn't act like I was a bothersome child; she was truly interested and would not become distracted or irritated no matter how much or for how long I rambled. Aunt Sabera always remembered every detail and kept any secret I shared.

At times this closeness between us could cause friction between Samama and I, she being a teenager herself was as moody and rebellious as me, but the fact that Sabera was her mother meant they could not talk as I and her own mother could.

On one occasion, when she walked in to find her mother with her arms wrapped round me and hushing me with affection she startled me, muttering 'Oh, hi Aalinna. When I saw your bike outside I thought you'd come to visit me. How silly of me.' She headed across the room to the arm chair.

'Hi. Yeah. Sorry, that mother of mine has been driving me crazy again so I came to let off steam,' I sniffed.

'How nice for you. I'm glad my mother has the patience and understanding for someone round here, pity she couldn't try it out on her own daughter.' The room fell silent and I moved out of my aunt's arms now fully aware of the animosity in Samama's tone.

'Oh really Samama,' said my aunt as she stood up and headed for the kitchen.

'You see, Aalinna!' Samama shouted jumping of the chair with arms flailing. 'Now you see her true colours. One word from me and she either screams or walks away, no cosy little chats on the sofa for me, oh no! I don't know what you see in her but she obviously sees something in you worth caring about – unlike her own daughter'. She shouted so her mother could hear her from the kitchen where I could see she was now standing hands on her head.

I was not put out by Samama's outburst, more so I felt guilty. This was not the first time she had become frustrated with the closeness between her mother and I.

Once when we had been sitting in my room huddled on my bed, inconspicuously whispering and laughing I flopped back on the pillow and began to complain about my mother. This was nothing new, Samama and I often had these 'discussions' around our frustrations with our parents and had even taken to calling them 'our mother bashing sessions'.

'Ugh," she started today again, 'apparently I am not praying enough or listening when she's reading the Koran to me, she always has to find something to get at me.'

'Huh' said Samama companionably, 'they're all the same. Mine was going on at me much the same earlier, why do you think I'm here?' She smiled.

'Ah no, Samama your mum is great, be nice.'

Samama jumped off the bed hands waving and hair flying, 'No she is not. You don't understand she drives me crazy some days and I've no one to talk to.'

'Oh, honey don't say that, of course you have, you have me don't you?'

'That's exactly my point I don't feel like I do, anytime I complain about her or try to talk to you, you see her point of view and gush about how nice she is, you're meant to be on my side, you're meant to agree with me, you're my friend not hers Aalinna,' Samama cried, the frustration evident in her voice, as she plonked exhausted and sobbing onto the large cushion on the other side of the room, her head now hung low and her fingers picking at her nails.

I felt awful, I got of the bed and went to kneel by her she didn't look up as I began to speak I caught her peeking through her hair at me. 'I am so sorry I didn't think.' No response, 'Come on Samama we share everything, our hopes, dreams, fears, the future. No-one could ever mean more to me than you!'

As Samama looked up to my surprise she began to giggle, 'Ok, ok, no need to go all drama queen on me, just don't do it again,' she grabbed me in a hug and we fell giggling to the floor.

'Hey, I have an idea,' I said as we lay on the floor breathlessly, "you could always confide in my mum if you want'....... this sarcastic comment earned me a pillow to the head.

All was well between us once again.

Over time, I'd started having a mind of my own when it came to religion. Quietly brewing questions I knew I wasn't supposed to have, nor had the courage to ask my mother for fear of getting scolded. However, I found ways to silently rebel, satisfying my independent spirit. When she read scriptures to me and encouraged me to pray, I was determined to not hear her. I wore a façade that declared that I did not understand anything.

I had to admit that my father was always my favourite. I so wanted to be like him when I grew up. He was quietly confident, religious but not strict. Playful and spirited. Most importantly for me, though, he was patient and understanding. Even though he was a very busy businessman whose work required him to travel frequently, he always seemed to make time for us. Before leaving for a business trip, he would always take my mother, sister and me out for dinner. When he was home, he was never above having a tea party with my sister, sitting cross legged amongst her teddy's sipping from a bright red plastic tea-cup: he would let me beat him at badminton when he took us to the Gulshan club, he played in the pool with my sister and I, never growing tired of our squeals of delight and our constant mantra "please just one more time dad". A genuine and honest person who has never, criticized me, imposed his opinions on me, or interfered in my life. He never talks for the sake of saying something. Instead, he has his own gentle way of expressing himself.

When I was in my twenties I went out a lot. I think my father suspected that I was doing things like drinking alcohol, taking drugs and going to late night parties, but he didn't reprimand me or confront me harshly, two things that would have pushed me away. Instead, he gently said, 'Take care of yourself, Aalinna. There are a lot of bad things out there and you should stay away from them.'

Of course, he was right, and I should have, but I didn't.

While my parents and I managed to survive the rocky years of my adolescence, mostly unscathed, with the strong ties of love and affection ever holding us together, college life brought an entirely new array of adventures to experience.

Though I lived at home, I immersed myself in college life. None of my high school friends, or anyone I knew, attended the same college as me, which was something I loved. It was a new environment with all new people, never having had a fear of meeting new people; I relished the excitement of it all. I made friends easily, and did so within the first month. People's differences had always intrigued me, and I was able to easily move between different social circles.

Nights, weekends, and even school hours were filled with moving from one social scene to the next. At that time there was nothing questionable about my behaviour, other than the enormous lack of time and attention I devoted to my studies. My friends and I spent endless hours of fun together, whether it was movies and popcorn at someone's house, going for long drives or eating out at restaurants. Initially there was the ever-so-seldom, occasional cigarette that a friend had normally swiped from her father's stash, which we'd secretly smoke, dragging deeply and coughing loudly – then light candles, swish mouthwash, and spray cans of air freshener to cover our tracks.

*

Eventually, my excitement in making new friends led me to acquaint myself with a different sort of group.

These new friends were quite adventurous and didn't hesitate to experiment with alcohol and drugs and now, at the mature age of 20; I felt I was ready to do the same.

On the night I first tried drinking I was at a party at my friend Farina's house. In those days young people in Bangladesh would normally have parties during the day, it being considered inappropriate for young girls to be out at night unchaperoned, never mind with boys. We would make the house as dark and shadowy as possible, closing curtains, lighting candles and playing music, trying to make it seem like a night out. On this night Fariah's parents were out of town and she had stolen a bottle of Smirnoff from her father's bar, which we planned to replace by the time her parents returned.

I tentatively took a few sips, this wasn't so bad I thought, and before I knew it, I was absolutely wasted. Fariha and my other friends knew that there was no way I could possibly go home in the state I was in. Being drop-dead drunk did not exactly mix well with my parents' piety. Fariha, therefore, wisely called my mother hoping to convince her that we had an assignment due in two days that we desperately needed to work on.

'Hello Auntie, yes, yes, all is fine,' she said as my mother answered the phone, turning furiously to wave me away as I, in my drunkenness decided it would be a goodtime to talk to my mother.

'Hey,' I shouted from the background, 'is that my mum, let me say hello.' Whilst Fariha covered the mouthpiece, I was unceremoniously dragged to the next room by some other friend.

'Yes Auntie, I will ensure she calls you in the morning No she's fine, she's upstairs making notes and did not want to break her concentration,' Fariha lied, fingers crossed on the receiver. 'Ok, Salam and thank you'. I will never know how she managed it, maybe it was that my mother was so pleased I was finally showing an interest in my studies, or she was simply stunned by the fact that I was. It was a family rule that I could not stay at anyone else's home for the night, and so it was unusual for my mother to not even get to speak to me and dissect the whole situation, but my mother miraculously agreed.

In my early college days, I knew a few people who smoked pot – I never gave it even one curious passing thought. However, my new-found friends, had apparently relaxed my personal standards more than I'd realised. While hanging out at Faraz's apartment one day, I decided to give it a try. Faraz was a guy I'd met in college. I remember the first day I saw him – we were all in a coffee shop that we used regularly, constantly crowded, smoke-filled and the worst food ever – we loved it! It was close to the college and more importantly, was only frequented by other students and people our own age. The last thing we needed were our professors or visiting parents listening in on our conversations, or, worse still asking why we'd been there for three hours rather than at lectures. Faraz was what most girls would have wanted as a boyfriend, fun, independent, popular; we had a lot in common I thought. Heads turned when he entered and he was immediately greeted by everyone and offered a seat from various groups. He had a smile that let people know he was genuinely interested in what they were saying and mingled confidently and good naturedly with everyone.

That day in his apartment the three of us smoked a joint, we chatted and laughed for hours. How much of it was the effect of the joint, I don't know but we soon found ourselves crouched on the floor sharing stories and laughing at our adventures and mishaps in life. Smoking pot was still a little out of my league, and I was so paranoid for two days, I couldn't leave my house. Faraz and I found ourselves spending more and more time together. I knew he liked me a lot and I began to take interest in him as well.

Eventually, we began the phone conversations that spiralled late into the night. We saw each other all the time within our group of friends, but began making excuses to meet up with one another alone as well. It gradually became obvious that we liked one another. One day we went out for a drive and he asked me out. I said 'yes' and we officially began dating. During one of our drives together I told him all about Samama and her family, how much they meant to me, and my close bond with Aunt Sabera and how I was missing not having her and Samama around so much. I would not say that I loved Faraz, but I did really like him. When we first started dating, it was a lot of fun, with every get-together felt like a new adventure, and every new experience was filled with excitement. Over time I started to see a different side to him.

He began to become very possessive and controlling, always telling me what to do and what not to do, where to go or not go, and always requiring me to answer to him. On one occasion we ended up in a huge fight. Faraz and I had arranged to meet and, as usual, he came and picked me up from a friend's apartment. This time, I was upstairs on a call to Samama.

'Hi' I heard him shout upstairs,

'Oh, hi,' I yelled back. '"I'm just on the telephone – grab a drink or something.' I continued with my conversation laughing, joking swopping stories and filling Samama in on all that had been going. From my vantage point lying on the bed twirling the telephone cord, I thought I saw movement by the door. 'Hang on Samama… Faraz! Is that you?' As there was no reply I carried on chatting for a bit longer, said my goodbyes, and with one last quick look in the mirror and squirt of perfume I went downstairs to join Faraz. As soon as I stepped into the room I knew something was wrong. Faraz stood tall and stiff with his back to me smoking a joint, blowing his smoke out the glass doors.

'Hi, we ready to go?' I said coming up behind him and wrapping my arms around his waist hoping to avoid an argument.

'I was ready to go hours ago,' he said not turning or responding to my touch.

'Oh come on,' I said with a shaky half laugh, 'I wasn't that long, we had a lot to catch up on.''Yeah, I bet you did.'

'Not this again, please…'

Faraz was having none of it, this wasn't the first time he had got upset or angry at not having my undivided attention.

'You knew I was down here waiting for you and *we* are due to go out,' he said huffing like a child.

'I know but I've told you how much I miss them all.''Yeah well, I've told you you've got *me* now,' he said, whirling round to confront me, 'so I don't see why you have to be on the phone to her – I heard you telling her our business.'

'Wow, hang on, that was you at the bedroom door? God, Faraz were you spying on me and listening to my private conversation?' I screeched.

His complaining and possessiveness was bad enough but creeping about, listening in on my private conversations, that was a step to far! Faraz knew by the look on my face that he had over stepped the mark; he marched to the car with me following him and we drove in silence to the party. All my life, I had been independent and free-spirited, and resentful toward anyone who tried to control me.

Even after that night Faraz demanded more and more of my attention. I found his behaviour toward me incredibly suffocating but he seemed to see it as normal. I realised he felt that he owned me now because we were together, and my independent, outgoing nature that had attracted him to me in the beginning was now his nemesis and something he felt he had to curtail. *This is no fun anymore,* I thought. The arguments continued and so did my resentment.

Over time, I realised that we were glaringly different from each other. Our relationship was falling apart, and a break-up was inevitable.

It wasn't until I finally broke it off I realised how stifling our relationship had become to me. Now I was free to take as long as I liked on phone calls, arrive and stay as early or late as I wanted, mix, mingle and talk to whoever I pleased without fear of upsetting him, it was good to be me again, and I felt free. My feelings of freedom and elation, however, were not mutual. Faraz was miserable after the break up, finding it hard to see me when we were at the same occasion, laughing and joking. I'd often catch him watching me with either a sad or angry look on his face, depending on his mood. He started doing drugs and drinking much more frequently. Our friends, wanting to eliminate any awkwardness, and hoping to restore the easy-going friendship we all used to share, tried to patch things up between us but I was adamant, about not getting back together.

To avoid the awkwardness and also in the hope that distance would help Faraz move on, I decided to no longer socialize with any of our mutual friends. This was no sacrifice on my part, as I was in many other social circles, besides, breaking off a few relationships was easy, and I certainly didn't lose sleep over it. At that time, I wore strength and confidence like a crown, and nothing could stop me from doing what I wanted. I had a level of confidence that was off the charts.. I loved meeting new people anyway and as always, made new friends easily. For me, there was nothing that I couldn't do.

With those destructive relationships now behind me, it seemed I was back to being my normal, independent, care-free self. Or so I told myself, but a new pattern was developing in my life. Throughout my difficulties with school, doubts over religion, light skirmishes with parents and experimentation with drugs, I was becoming rather adept at hiding my thoughts and emotions. I was learning all too well how to suppress any negative sentiments, stuffing them away and never really dealing with them, hoping they would be forgotten.

Chapter 4
Samama

"We're all islands shouting lies to each other across seas of Misunderstanding."

Rudyard Kipling

When we were 20 and 21, Samama's father and my father, who were brothers and partners in the family business, had a huge falling out over a deal. The details of their argument have long remained a mystery to me, but what was once a prosperous partnership had turned into a disaster.

They had lost a large amount of money and each one blamed the other. Their disagreement exploded one Friday evening when we were supposed to have dinner with Samama and her family. I couldn't wait, especially because Samama said she had some fun news to share. On my way upstairs to put the finishing touches to my make-up I heard angered hissed talking, I was stunned to realise it was my father's voice. This was so uncharacteristic of his normal calm nature and soft spoken ways. I crept towards their bedroom door where I could now hear both their raised voices.

'They are our family let's not make a rift that may never heal. Please reconsider; I do not think this is the way,' my mother pleaded tearfully, 'Let us go as a family and you and your brother can take the chance to talk privately after dinner, I'm sure this can all be sorted, I'm sure it is all a misunderstanding,' sounding more like she was trying to convince herself than him.

Her ramblings were cut short by my father, who raised his head out of his hands and exploded, 'Well I'm glad you're sure because I'm not sure of anything anymore! Talk you say? Reconsider you say? You do not know what you're talking about!'

Silence. Then only the sound of my mother's sniffling could be heard. My father moved next to where she was sitting on the bed.

'Please, sweetheart, just do as I say' he said with a huge sigh. 'Now go tell the children we will be staying here for dinner tonight I need to think'.

On hearing my mother's footsteps across the shiny granite floor I flew from the door and made for the stairs, making out I had only just come up. My mother emerged, her face tear stained and her whole appearance a bit disheveled, she forced an air of confidence and declared, 'We're eating dinner at home tonight.'

'What?' Even having listened in on the argument I was stunned. We never cancelled plans with our relatives – especially Samama's family. 'Why?'

'We'll talk about it later,' my mother said. My normal reaction would have been to question, argue and whine, but I knew after hearing their argument, that something was very wrong.

'Now go and tell your sister. Please.' For the first in a long time I obeyed without question.

Dinner was a chore. Maryam sat sulkily huffing and puffing to show her disdain, and whined, 'Well, I don't understand why we can't eat with the rest of the family.' Refusing to let up even when I kicked her under the table – my examples of insufferable moodiness had made its mark on her. My mother rambled insistently, as was her way when nervous, trying to talk over Maryam to ease the tension and the look of thunder on my father's face.

I rushed to call Samama as soon as dinner was finished. I was relieved when it was Samama who answered the phone. Even this felt weird; I used to love a chatting with my aunt anytime I got the chance, even the normal teasing I got from Rabab when he answered one of my calls to Samama would have sounded good right now. Him shrieking in his best girly voice: 'Oh, hello Samama I'm so in love! Oh, Samama come see my new dress and beautiful shoes!' Until eventually Samama's voice would be heard shouting, 'Give me that phone! You are such a pain.'

'Thank God it's you,' said Samama bringing me back to the present. "What the hell is going on? First my parents have a huge argument and then we're told you and the rest of the family won't be coming to dinner. Father nearly bit the boys' heads off when they tried to question him about what had happened."

'Yes, yes, it is much the same this end,' I said, 'but do you know what has gone on?

'No, I was hoping you could tell me!'

The moments ticked by as we both fell silent.

'This is ridiculous they're meant to be the adults – falling out like children at their age. I'm sure it will all get sorted and they will feel silly by tomorrow for causing all this fuss.'

'Yes I'm sure.' I agreed, knowing neither of us deep down truly believed it.

*

Initially Samama and I tried to remain close. We swore we wouldn't let our fathers' business problems come between us. We still made plans when we had free time and on the weekends, but something had changed. I didn't feel comfortable when I went to Samama's house anymore. My beloved aunt began slowly pulling away from me. She was never cruel or unkind;

she just wasn't herself. She never looked me in the eye anymore. The warmth that had characterized all of our interactions was now gone. The special feelings evaporated. It was a distancing that hurt so deeply, compounded by the horrible timing of it all, as these were my college years My parents didn't seem to understand me and I relied on my aunt to talk to. It was very difficult for me to accept that our two families were falling apart.

Eventually, the fissure in our tight-knit family seeped into my relationship with Samama, like a crack that starts at the ceiling and slowly spreads toward the floor. In a heated moment, she'd say something about my father that would hurt, I'd retaliate with something ugly about hers. We barely knew what we were talking about but could hardly throw aside the loyalty we felt toward our own parents. One afternoon, we got into an uncomfortable discussion about how things had changed.

'It's your father's fault,' she blurted out, all this is his fault.' I didn't say a word, but after that I knew I'd lost my best friend, my first friend, my sister. The resulting grief was like that of a death in the family. I remember lying in my bed for days, feeling a gaping hole where my relationship with Samama had once been. I'd never known life without her. What would it be like?

Six months went by. We barely saw Samama's family, at social events, or extended family get-togethers. My side of the family would sit at one end of the room and theirs at the other. All present knew of the falling out but not why. I couldn't even look at Samama or I felt my heart would break.

The hurt, however, was soon replaced by anger when the family argument dealt an insidious blow to my pride. Upon my meeting a new girl from a neighboring town one day at college, she, with a tinge of surprise in her voice, casually commented about how nice I was.

'Why wouldn't I be?'

'I heard all these horrible things about you'

'Like what and from whom? I growled. I was standing with a group of friends who had now all stopped chattering to listen in.

'Well, that you were spoiled and irresponsible, she said, not so confident for seeing the look on my face.

As she went on and on, sharing all the things she'd heard about me. My anger dissolved and the tears came. My humiliation was complete, the realization seeping in to my numbed brain; the source of these horrible words had to be Samama – there were details in her stories that only she would know. The more this new girl told me, the redder my face brightened, and the wider the wound opened. The ugly things they had circulated about my character were unbelievable, and hurtful to say the least, and I swore never to talk to anyone from that family again. Eventually, my anger got the best of me and I began circulating rumors about them, as well. I knew it was not right, but my sense of hurt and betrayal was overwhelming.

About a month later, I got a call from Samama. I had just returned from a night out with friends and was tired but happy. We had hung out at a friend's apartment where I had met a lot of new people. Now that I didn't have to contend with Faraz's possessiveness I'd enjoyed chatting with as many different people as possible – ever the social butterfly. I froze in shock on hearing her voice on my answering machine. We had not spoken to one another in over six months. I replayed her message over and over again, her familiar, though uncertain, voice awakening sweet memories of our love and friendship for each other. Part of me wanted to dial her number right away; telling her how much I'd missed her; how sorry I was for the things I'd said. But the side of me that was so hurt, so angry and disappointed with all that had happened reared its ugly head; the more I thought of all that had happened the more I began to seethe. I thought to myself that she was the one who should be apologizing and saying she missed me but all I get is "Hello, Aalinna, it's me can we talk?" I finally let my hatred overwhelm me and deleted the message.

I lay in bed that night convincing myself that I didn't care about her or her phone call, refusing to acknowledge that it was all I could think of. A few weeks later, she left another message telling me that soon she and her twin brother Rabab were leaving to go to graduate school at the University of Toronto.

'I want to talk to you before I go, Aalinna please call me.'

I don't know why this second message infuriated me; looking back I think that whilst I was still very angry and hurt by what had happened I realised I had missed a chance for us to make up and now she was going away. How could she do this? How dare she do this? This time, I called her back. Samama had little time to say anything before I immediately confronted her with the nasty rumors she had spread. Being accosted by my aggression immediately put Samama on the defensive and we soon found ourselves engaged in another fruitless argument. We fervently insulted one another, and our arguing escalated into shouting. I finally screamed into the phone, 'Go to hell, Samama!' and slammed the receiver down. I could barely breathe; I buried my face into my hands and cried myself to sleep.

*

Two weeks later, my mother woke me in the middle of the night. Through bleary, sleepy eyes, I could see my mother was trembling, working hard to steady her hand on my own.

'Samama was in a car accident,' she said, tears in her eyes. 'She is dead.'

I watched the tears stream down my mother's face. I watched her bury her head in my father's shoulder. I made it to the bathroom before I vomited and passed out.

*

That night we heard the news, we went immediately to Samama's house. Our twos families began to heal the rift that had so insidiously worked its way into our lives. The wounds had cut deeply, but our reunification was almost instantaneous. The house was surrounded by extended family, friends and neighbours who had gathered on hearing the news, wishing to help and comfort by bringing offerings of food, prayers, transport or anything else that may be needed.

The journey to the house was a blur. I think we were all in shock, but we were soon shaken out of it once we entered the room where the family sat. My aunt was a statue: stiff, grey and frighteningly still in her armchair whilst the Imran sitting next to her prayed, trying to give her comfort. Everything and everyone seemed to be in slow motion; even the dust caught in a beam of light coming through the darkened room seemed to hesitate.

My mother immediately went to Aunt Sabera, crouching next to her, taking her hand and crying her sympathies into it. My aunt neither looked up nor for that matter acknowledged anyone round her. She sat dried eyed, and just stared. My father went to the other end of the room where the men were gathered, huddled together whispering and murmuring. My poor uncle in the middle was looking bewildered, never seeming to grasp what was going on.

From where I stood frozen at the entrance to the room, a movement caught my eye. It seemed out of character with all else that was going on in the room. This movement was robotic but determined. It moved from the kitchen across the room to the balcony, a note book and pen in hand, it was Maher, Samama's older brother.

The sight of him brought me out of my trance and my next thought made me feel physically sick and the room began to swim. Rabab. Where was Rabab? He and Samama were together at university. My mind raced trying to remember what my mother had said when she gave me the news. Rabab – car accident in Toronto – Samama dead… that was it. I couldn't remember anything she'd said after that. I could now see Maher on the balcony, with his back to me. He put the notebook and pen on a nearby table and held on to the railings for support. A friend I did not know patted him on the back. I rushed across the room causing everyone to turn and look but I didn't care. As I pulled the balcony doors open Maher turned to look at me we both knew that the moment we touched or hugged it would make this whole thing real and that would bring us to a place we may never come back from.

Hi,' said Maher in a soft voice.

Hi, I replied rooted to the spot. 'Rabab?' I said with a plea in my voice, 'he was in the car too.' I felt my body sway.

'No.' Maher said, putting a hand out to steady me, but pulling it away quickly and keeping his composure. 'He is hurt but not badly, well physically anyway.'

Maher's friend Zayef who was standing at a polite distance took me by the arm and guided me into a chair next to him.

'What the hell happened?'

'We don't have all the details, they crashed, and Rabab is in the hospital. I've just got off the phone with them. I can bring him home in a day or two. I will fly out there and bring them both home.' He said determinedly.

'Are you sure you're up to this'"

'Look at them, Aalinna. He said turning to look through the glass doors at his parents.

'Mother has not said a word or moved since we sat her in that chair, and father just mumbles and stares. I have to do this, it is my responsibility, we are a family, that's what we do – look after each other.'

I hadn't been much of a 'family' to them lately, and my last words to – *no. Stop*, I warned myself. Don't go there not now.

'Yes of course you're right and you must allow me to help, anything that needs doing just tell me.' 'I have a meeting in the morning at the Canadian High Commission, to sort out flight arrangements. I want to go as soon as possible. It will be easier to organise certain things from that end – getting the body back being the main one."

I thought, *'God, give him strength.'*

'I want to be with Rabab, he is all alone and sick in a foreign country and grieving for –' he couldn't say it. 'All that has happened... he continued business like, 'there are the police to talk to and endless paper work and the college to deal with.'

'Sorry Aalinna, this is my friend Zayef,' said Maher as his friend drew closer, feeling his distress, "he has flown in from America where he is studying. He will come to Canada with me."

I had a fleeting image of me and Samama being chased through the park by Rabab, Maher and Maher's best friend, Zayef, with their football in my arms that we had stolen to tease them.

'Off course, I'm sorry, I didn't recognize you, it's been a long time and we've all grown quite a bit,' I said embarrassed.

'Please, it's no problem. I'm not surprised under the circumstances, and as you say we've all grown up.''Do not worry, brother,' said Zayef putting a steadying arm round Maher. 'You are family; I am here for you. We shall go together.' Yes, that's what friends do, they are there for each other in times of need.

'Thank you," 'said Maher. 'You are a true friend.'

I felt like I was suffocating, choking on my own envy and guilt, watching these two friends together.

'I shall go now and see what I can do inside and allow you to get on. I said as I rose from the chair.

'I'm so sorry, Aalinna, said Zayef, 'I know how close you and Sa … you both were.' He changed his mind about using her name when he seen both myself and Maher flinch.

Maher broke the tension. 'Thank you, Aalinna. I will call you tomorrow and let you know how things are going and if there is anything you can help with. Rabab will be so pleased that you and the family have come.' His words of kindness were like physical blows, if only they knew.

I went through the sliding doors and back into the living room. The scene was much the same, like a bad play in and old theater. The characters in the same positions, the sound muffled and out of sync and faces either void of emotion or overly animated trying to convey their grief in their own idiosyncratic ways. The sound of a quiet sobbing, the raw emotion, the only thing in the room that seemed real. It was Maryam – I had completely forgot about her. I couldn't even remember her being in the car with us on the way here. I thought back, in my mind's eye I could see her now in the background as I stared straight ahead from the back into the rear view mirror of my parent's car. Yes, she was there, sitting knees hunched up to her chin, physically shaking, looking directly at me. She beseeched me with her eyes to help explain, to reassure. As usual I had been too wrapped up in myself to notice.

*

I was determined to give myself as hard a time as possible. I would not allow myself to grieve; I deserved no understanding for my own deep loss, the emotions that came with it and the shock I was going through.

I felt paranoid and self-conscious when I ran into our mutual friends. When they gave me their condolences or we talked about fun times we had all had, I wondered if they all knew and were only doing it to hear and see my response. It was torture but I knew I deserved it.

Over the coming days we spent most of our time at my Aunt Sabera's helping out where we could or just being there for the family. My aunt and uncle's grief had consumed them; Aunt Sabera hadn't said a word and allowed people to guide her from task to task, washing, dressing, even encouraging her to walk a little. It seemed that if left, she would never have moved from the chair. No food passed her lips, only sips of water that the other women coaxed her to drink As for my uncle he did as instructed, taking his lead from the advice of the other men, shuffling along with a vacant look in his eyes, my father was therefore going to accompany Maher and Zayef to Canada to represent my uncle and support what the elder men classed as the 'young boys'.

Rabab was now physically well enough to travel on the same plane as Samama. Maher confided in me that Rabab was distraught, blaming himself and cursing that it should have been him not her. He had refused to, in his words, 'allow her to fly back all alone'. Each time I spoke to Maher he sounded more and more exhausted and increasingly concerned about Rabab's well-being.

When my father gathered my uncle and aunt together to tell them that he Maher and Zayef would be flying out to bringing Rabab and Samama home, their eyes lit up and for the first time since getting the news. Colour came to their faces, then the realisation dawned on them what the words really meant; Samama would not be travelling up front between her two brothers, mercilessly teased but alive and giggling. Once again they wore their masks of grief, all hope gone.

We all went to the airport to meet the plane, the airport in Dhaka is a bustling place always busy inside and out; crowds gather continuously and guards try to control the tide of cabs, trucks and tuktuks as passengers get dropped off. The air was stiflingly humid, the heat piercing and as always shouts and tooting of horns was continuous. We were kindly allowed to wait in a private room that had a view of the tarmac and where we would be able to see the plane land and its passengers disembark.

It was strange us all being together in this room. It felt like it should be a time of joy and excitement like a family wedding or the excitement before a holiday. Samama and I would have been off in the shops trying on all the duty free make-up and perfumes, returning to the departure gate smelling like a chemical factory having combined so many scents, and our faces like two painted dolls laden with makeup. I almost began to giggle; the cool breeze from the air con humming above my head brought another thought: does she have air conditioning? Is she cool enough stuck in the hold of that plane all alone in the dark? Is she frightened? Oh God, can she breathe? My head was spinning

I gaped for air myself, she will suffocate! The sane part of my brain knew these thoughts were crazy, I had to s accept that she was dead and would never breathe again. Once again I made it to the toilet in time to throw up.

A small aircraft had been chartered for the last leg of the journey, carrying only Samama, Rabab, Mayer, Zayef and my father. An official looking man approached my uncle and Aunt Sabera:

'Sir, the plane will be landing in ten minutes, once landed it may be best if you proceed to the passengers lounge to greet your son,' he said at tentatively. My mother immediately understood that the gentleman was trying to get us to move to another room so that we wouldn't see the coffin being unloaded. .

'Yes of course,' agreed the Imam, who was sitting next to my uncle, on seeing that he had not looked up. 'I will gather everyone and we will move to the...'

'NO!' said a strong deep voice, it echoed across the room and everyone turned to stare. It wasn't a particularly loud or angry statement more so because it was my uncle who had spoken.

'I will wait for both my children and see them both back into their country's soil where they belong.' My aunt next to him gave a small bob of her head; this was the first response she had given to anything or anyone. My uncle took this rightfully as her agreement and we all sat and waited, determined to support them.

The steps of the plane where attached and the door stood open. The first to appear at the entrance were my father and Zayef who proceeded to walk down the steps of the plane and head for the arrivals lounge head bowed, next was Maher. *My God*, I thought, *was it possible to lose so much weight in such a short time*? The clothes he wore practically hung on him and his eyes sunk into his sockets. His neck was lost in his collar; he put his hand back and supported Rabab as he came out. At first I thought I'd made a mistake, this must be another passenger, a sickly old man, pale and gaunt, scratches on his waxy face, his head bandaged and leaning on a cane in evident pain. It was Rabab, a shadow of his former self. As they both made their way down the plane steps, Maher in front walking sideways for fear of Rabab falling, two men in suits came trundling along the runway pushing a long steel gurney, going to the back of the plane where a large hinged door began to open. My aunt and uncle stood up and approached the window holding each other for support and not saying a word. We all followed, gathering round them in a protective crescent. My knees began to buckle as the coffin was lowered out of the plane and onto the steel gurney. The silence was broken by the sobs and moaning that escaped from the women and the silent muttering of prayers from the men. Still not a word or movement from my aunt or uncle as the gurney was pushed pass Rabab and Maher as they stood either side of it and accompanied it into the airport and out of view. My aunt and uncle turned and walked silently from the room, leaving the rest of the men and women to do their crying and praying for them. Their children were back home and they needed to be with them.

My father now took control of organising the final arrangements for the funeral and went straight from the airport to the Mosque accompanied by my mother and me. I simply sat stunned, I can barely remember the journey. The sight of the white wooden box had stunned me. I knew it was coming. I'd imagined it so many times. Now I'd seen it, this was really happening.

When we arrived at the mosque I waited alone in the car. Maryam had not come with us that day, it would have been too much for her. I secretly think she was glad when my parents suggested she wait at my aunt and uncles' house until we got back, with the excuse that she could be helpful in looking after the smaller children.

I barely noticed as the car heated up in the mid-day sun and took no notice of the poor who tapped on the car window asking for money; this is a tradition in the Muslim faith especially on a Friday, when, after prayers, better off people give to the poor. Normally persistent and not easily deterred, on seeing my blank face staring out the window, they gave up, appearing frightened by me, and moving away. When my parents returned to the car a short time later, having made the final arrangements, my mother became angry on opening the car door:

'My God Aalinna, it is stifling in here! What are you thinking of not putting on the air conditioning? You will suffocate.'

She was becoming increasingly concerned at my behaviour and how I was dealing with the whole thing. Unbeknownst to me, she and my father had spent nights discussing the best way to deal with me, as well as help me. "Come, drink this," she said, passing a bottle of water to me in the back with one hand, and distributing money to the crowd that had gathered at her car door with the other.

We drove in silence to my aunt's house with the air-conditioning on full and my parents exchanging worried looks the whole way. My parents had purposely not gone straight back to my aunt and uncles' house as they knew the tradition followed that the coffin would be brought to the home and the body removed and washed down by the female family members. When we arrived most of the women were upstairs attending to Samama and the men were gathered in the living room. As I entered I saw Rabab slouched in a chair, a cup of tea by his side untouched, he lifted his head at the sound of the other men greeting us:

'Slamalaikum.'

'Oalaikum Assalam, we replied, a traditional Muslim greeting.

A thought stuck me. This could be where everyone found out

what I was really like, had Samama told him? Had she come off the phone that night crying and ran to her brother for comfort? Why not? He was her brother after all. Her twin brother. They were even living in the same apartment. Would he confront me here in front of everyone, his raised voice attracting the women, making them come down to see what was going on? My poor parents humiliated and my Aunt Sabera – I would not be able to bear her look of pain and disgust.

Rabab rose from the chair leaning heavily on his crutch, pain etched on his brow. 'Aalinna, it is so good to see you,' he said quietly and sadly. I ventured a smile and put my hand on his arm, stroking it slowly. Feeling guilty at the relief that flooded my body, she must not of told him, my sweet Samama faithful to the end. My father, realising the need for us to talk and be alone, suggested we get some air on the balcony. Rabab looked at him thankfully and we slowly made our way out.

As soon as we had closed the door Rabab turned to me, grabbed me in an embrace and began to sob. I held him and listened as he blamed himself over and over and apologised; he was sniffling so badly that I couldn't make sense of what he was saying so I just tried to comfort him. Even though his hold was like electric shocks through my body, I could feel my resolve getting lower and the well of emotions creeping from my stomach, threatening to escape from my throat in huge sobs and a string of apologies. I cannot do that. I do not deserve to feel relief. The least I can do is to be strong for him after what I've done – deep down I think I was too afraid that if I let go I would sink to my knees and never get up.

'Please Rabab calm yourself, let us talk about it calmly I am sure it is not all as you think, please tell me what happened.' He wiped his eyes drew in a long trembling breathe and told me all.

*

Rabab had been invited to a party that night, he had been very pleased with himself, whilst he wasn't shy or short of friends, 'This was the party of the year,' he'd gushed to Samama as she sat over her computer trying to ignore him while she worked.

'You see what a clever handsome brother you have?' he teased to the back of her head, trying to coax a reaction out of her, wanting to share in his excitement and good news – unaware that Samama was grinning widely and enjoying making him suffer.

'Bet you're jealous,' he said, grinning and throwing a pair of socks at her that he had found on the bed. Actually he had a plan up his sleeve; he wanted Samama to come with him, not that he would admit it to her. He loved having her around, he was proud to be seen with her and he missed her when she wasn't near him. Plus having his good looking, clever sister around wouldn't hurt when he needed introductions to the girls. So he invited her.

'Actually,' said Samama, throwing the socks back at him, 'I am invited too but I won't be going, I have work to do.'

Rabab said they had bantered back and forth, him determined to make her go and her determined to get her work completed. Kind hearted as always she gave in, scolding him the whole time she rushed to get dressed, while he, as he put it, went and cleaned out 'that damned car'.

They travelled along to the address they had been given, him driving and Samama attempting to read the map. Both laughed at her attempts to keep the map together as it flapped in the wind from the open window.

*

'The last I remember is her screaming my name and pointing, something flashed across our path in front of the car. I swerved. I remember nothing after that only waking up in hospital calling her name. They told me it was a deer that ran in front of us. A bloody deer, Aalinna. I killed her to save a bloody deer. May God forgive me?' Rabab sobbed, hands on his head. "Why did I have to go on at her? Why couldn't I just have left her to get on with her work, her own life?" he screamed as he ran from the balcony, through the living room and out the front door. I made to go after him but my father stopped me, taking my arm. 'Let him be, let him get it out'.

I am ashamed to say I was relieved, I couldn't deal with his guilt and pain as well as my own. I went back out to the balcony, glad to be away from everyone but not able to get away from my tumbling thoughts. I didn't hear my mother slide open the doors and come to stand in front of me. As I opened my eyes she attempted to shush me and told me to go back to sleep. I looked at my watch I had only been here half an hour, had I fallen asleep? It didn't feel like it though, I wouldn't have been surprised, I couldn't remember the last time I'd slept.

'I'm fine,' I said to my mother's worried face. 'What is it? Can I do something?' I said, standing ready to do as asked – anything to stop me thinking. 'No, no,' my mother said quietly, easing me back into the chair, 'I just thought I'd let you know we had finished upstairs and if maybe you wanted a few words with her…'

I knew this moment would come and I was dreading it, I knew what my mother meant when she said they'd finished upstairs, the ritual of gently washing and praying over Samama's body was complete. 'This is your chance to say goodbye,' my mother ventured.

My slow accent up the marble stairs was surreal, I could not admit to myself what I was about to do. I practically burst into the room for I knew if I hesitated at the door I would run down stairs and out the door. I owed her this, I needed to apologise.

Nothing could have prepared me for what was in front of me; she was beautiful and looked so peaceful. This didn't make sense; she had been in a car accident. Where were her injuries? I later found out that she had been wearing her seat belt and had remained upright and practically uninjured but her neck had nonetheless broken with the impact.

'Oh, my beautiful friend I am so sorry, please forgive me. I didn't mean it, any of it. Please come back to me.' Now that I was here in front of her, knowing I would never see or speak to her again, I felt my heart rip. My grief was coming in waves, threatening to engulf me. I knew the tears, and moaning, that were stuck behind my eyes, and choking my throat, would be a welcome relief, but I did not feel entitled. I deserved to suffer, I knew deep down that if I gave into it I would never recover. So I did what I do best I swallowed it down, hid it deep and stored it away.

'How can you do this to me? How can you be so selfish? Look at the state everyone's in, your poor mother and father, oh please...' I rambled and my despair turned to anger. How am I to cope you are my cousin, my sister, my best friend? Who am I to turn to? We share everything, clothes, secrets, everything. How can you be so selfish leaving me behind, not allowing me to apologise?

Finally, a few tears dropped as I kissed her beautiful brow. I took one last look, wiped my eyes, and left the room.

It would not be until much later that I would remember the exact details of the funeral. I realise now that I was honing my skills at blanking out what I could not deal with.

Chapter 5
Breaking Point

"Of all the liars in the world, sometimes the worst are our own fear."

Rudyard Kipling

I threw myself into my college work. Before, college life had been fairly relaxed and easy; I had been in no hurry to finish, previously I hadn't attended many classes anyway, always too busy enjoying and experimenting with life and friends. Now though trying to deal with emotions I couldn't express, I immersed myself in study. I felt pressure to live life to the full, accomplish as much as possible in the hope that if I kept busy with this immense work load I would have no time to think, no time to let Samama's death take hold.

I did not initially find college stressful, yes, I could barely keep up in class and I couldn't follow lectures because nothing made sense. As always, the words in the work sheets, texts books, novels just seemed to dance in front of me and no matter how hard I tried, I could not connect phrases or transform their significance to make anything meaningful. Taking notes was impossible, and writing no easier.

I mainly spent my days totally confused, regularly receiving two types of punishment for my considered lack of interest and effort; either being made to stand in the corner of the class room or outside in the corridor. I wasn't ashamed of this. I was fascinated by other people; I was quite happy to watch their interactions going on around me. I had plenty of friends and my poor grades and reprimands from teachers did nothing to shake my self-assurance.

Admittedly, phone calls from my teacher to my parents, and the resulting lectures I would receive, were always an uncomfortable and a slightly scary event. I accepted my inability to do school work as part of my nature, and had no intention of doing any better, nor any conception of doing better. I'd had tutors from the first grade, a quite common occurrence in Bangladeshi life, in fact, back when I lived in the big house with Samama, Rabab and Maher, most of us had tutors. So what was the problem?

Mother tried desperately to help, once again taking time to tutor me personally. I only saw her attempts to support me, as interference. I didn't think there was anything wrong with me and it certainly never occurred to me that I may have any kind of learning difficulty. In those days learning difficulties were neither well known nor diagnosed and didn't even have a name yet. I simply thought I needed to study to do better and as I wasn't doing that – well, what could I expect? Somehow I managed to pass all of my classes, while doing or understanding very little. Things began to go wrong, however, in the final months of college. I did so poorly on my exams I nearly failed the year, in fact I did fail two subjects, but much to my relief and appreciation the school somehow allowed me to continue. For the first time in my life I realised I had to put some effort into my school work and I began to care about my education.

I never put in 100%; it was more like 40%. This was still 40% more than I'd ever done. I still could not read well, concentrate in class or translate the blur on the whiteboard into anything stimulating. My notebook stayed blank. I didn't really understand what the teacher was trying to teach either, but instead of seeing it as a problem I figured out strategies to get around my learning issues.

My friends were there for me. They would help me with my lessons in class, summarise the lectures, give me their notes to copy and briefly explain what was being taught. Once when a major test was pending at 4.00pm, I had not a clue what would be on the test. On the morning of the exam I ambushed a friend as she entered the school gate.

'This exam this afternoon, I have no clue what is going to be on it. Can you give me some help?'

We went out of the gate together to a local café where we sat for two hours, she explained the exam content to me by sharing and reading her notes and I listening intently, taking in as much as I could with gratitude and caffeine. I actually got a better grade than she did, something I never ceased to tease her about. It was not to last; the extra courses I had taken on were simply too much for anyone to cope with. While reading and comprehension were way beyond me, I actually discovered during this time that I was quite good at mathematics. Also, to everyone's surprise, especially my own, I did very well on my grade 10 board exam. The school announced those results in front of the whole class. I was stunned to hear my name announced, more so when they said I earned one of the top five highest scores. Everyone lovingly cheered for me. It was an amazing feeling. My sense of pride and my parents' joy that day were inexpressible.

Aside from this brief triumph, the characteristic difficulty witch I navigated through school began to have ill effects. My parents didn't understand the normal course schedule and thus did not realise the immense workload I had taken on and the pressure I was under. Neither did I confide it to my friends. It was during my final months at college that my learning difficulties really started affecting my confidence. I didn't understand anything that I was studying or what my teachers were saying. Before that, I'd always been able to get by and even though I wasn't a top student, I had confidence. I started comparing myself to friends and would always find myself lacking.

I graduated, and whilst I did not flunk, I felt like the stupidest person on earth. I had worked diligently to finish my courses and passed them in record time, but the pressures of college life had dampened my high spirits and confidence, allowing what I'd been trying avoid all this time, to creep into my thoughts. The anxiety and raw pain that was bottled within was brimming. The end of college life was an important milestone. But rather than revelling in my accomplishments, I was fixated on the uncertainty of my future.

Really, I had three choices. Continue my education and study for a post grad, work in my father's company or get married. Working for my father wasn't really an option; I wanted to be independent and live independently from my family. Finding a husband and getting married was seen by my parents as the next natural step and they had often, during my college years, attempted to match me up. In fairness, this was a natural occurrence in Bangladesh, normally from the ripe old age of 18 years. It was common place for mothers to begin trying to find suitors for their daughters, on many occasions I would go with my family to a dinner party only to realise that it was I who was being served up and admired – not the food. Once the initial introductions had been made and a bit of chat had been allowed to dilute the situation we would all sit down to dine. I would be, oh so, coincidentally placed facing the suitor in question and the mothers would get into full swing.

'Oh, Aalinna, did I mention [I don't remember his name]'s father has his own company and now that he has finished his studies he will be joining the company. As a director, no less!' Said my mother all smiles and nodding to my prospective mother-in-law, who was in turn bobbing her head in agreement.

'Yes,' she responded, 'my son is also very handsome, don't you think?' I and the poor guy in question either seethed with embarrassment or looked at each other knowingly with a smirk and a raised eyebrow. This was generally fine and just occasionally amusing, it only got tricky when the said guy was interested; following me around all night trying to impress me and later trying to find ways to bump into me. One such suitor, after I had told him that I was not interested in him, just happened to turn up at the mall one day when I was shopping with friends. This, I initially put down to a coincidence but when he turned up a few days later at the cinema I was at, I began to suspect my mother's involvement. I would let my mother know in no uncertain terms to butt out – I didn't really mind these attempts at match-making and understood my mother's need to be seen to be ensuring her daughter was matched to a fitting man. It was an important role in the Bangladeshi culture for a mother, alas, she could be talked about or scorned for not being seen to be doing so.

Now that I had finished college my mother seized her chance to start again. This was one more pressure on top of what I was already feeling and I truly had no interest in getting married. I felt too young and wanted to do more with my life. Admittedly, I wasn't sure what I wanted to do, but being married wasn't it. As I often told my mother, what was the point in banging on for years about the importance of education, getting me tutors and pressuring me to study, if all I was going to do at the end of it was get married?

This time I was not so laid back and reacted strongly. This culminated in me cutting my hair off to make my point and to put off prospective suitors. My behaviour was beginning to get noticed. My mother was horrified but backed down and I agreed that once I had completed my undergrad we would consider it again.

I opted to continue my studies and do a post-graduate degree. Unfortunately, I had no idea how unprepared I was. I enrolled in a GRE course just because there seemed nothing else worth doing. The result was a disaster. Early on in the course, I realised that I was not equipped, mentally or academically, to keep up with the demands of study. Whatever effort I did make was clearly not enough. I attempted the first set of exams and walked out of them. It confirmed in my mind the gnawing suspicion that something was terribly wrong with me.

My self-esteem and my spirits took a further downward turn. Did I learn anything in college? I had passed seventeen courses, hard courses at that, but my brain hadn't registered one single thing.

Even socially, I began to feel like the outsider. My friends were happy and confident, looking forward to and planning their futures

'Well, Nadera,' Zoha remarked one evening. 'How're the moving plans? Are you all sorted?' Nadera, having finished her studies, would shortly join her husband who was in New Jersey.

'I don't know about sorted, but I've done all am going to do; I haven't stopped these last few weeks,.' she laughed. 'I can't wait to see him and America I'm so excited.'

'I bet you are,' said Yushra. 'As soon as I get some time off from my new job I'm coming to visit, so get my bed ready.' Everyone laughed. I smiled trying to hide my envy.

'Don't forget us two hard working, clever students. We need holidays too you know. Isn't that right, Aalinna?' Yushra continued, including me in her comment with a good humoured wink.

The camaraderie continued but that was the problem; I didn't feel included. They were all so happy and confident I was becoming envious and resentful of them. In my heart I knew I was being churlish and it was just one more reason for me to hate myself – I did want the best for them and I didn't want to begrudge them and their happiness and futures but what about me? What was wrong with me? I felt I had lost my last crutch, the confidence and the friends that had always kept me going.

During the day I would surround myself with people but at night I was unable to sleep, lying awake battling insomnia. Not sleeping because I was so anxious and becoming more anxious because I couldn't sleep, in a vicious circle. My eyes burned, my mind was tormented with distended thoughts, sapping what little energy I had left leaving me in a daze the following day. Soon, each day that passed seemed to blend into the other and I began losing track of time.

I went on with life mechanically, doing by rote, the things that I was used to doing. My behaviour towards my friends deteriorated; even in front of them I was beginning to lose control. To my shame, one day when we were all in the car with me driving, Yushra in the front and Zoha in the back, I completely 'lost control'. Happy and excited, they were once again talking about their plans but I couldn't bear it. Without any conscious thought, I began banging my hands against the steering wheel, my hair flying through the air as my head moved in tandem with my fists. I stopped abruptly, seeing the look of sheer confusion and astonishment on their faces. Yushra literally jumped and moved back from me, glancing worriedly back at Zoha who, I could see in my rear view mirror, had stopped mid-sentence to gawp at me.

'Shit, Aalinna, what was that about?'

Trying to make a joke out of it I gigged and simply carried on driving while pretending not to notice Zoha and Yushra's furtive looks. The anger and frustration that was going on in my head was now coming out in my actions. I was frightened of myself and what I would do next. The one person I would have confided in was gone.

*

My anxiety about my future left me hopeless and anxious all the time. I couldn't eat or if I did it either churned in my stomach or came back up. I lost a huge amount of weight and was continually active, moving around instead of sleeping. Exhausted, my moods grew more erratic. Although my feelings of inadequacy plagued my days, I needed to keep my evenings and nights full and surrounded by people.

My long term friends like Zoha and Nadera were the opposite of my new college friends who drank and partied late into the night. My new friends were essential to me, not because Zoha, Nadera and my other friends were boring, in fact they were great fun – but I needed company. I couldn't spend one more night alone with nothing but my constant thoughts, either wandering round my room trying to hide from myself and my feelings, doing menial tasks, listening to music – trying to deny the fact that I hadn't slept in days. Therefore, I would hang out at late night parties whenever I could, to avoid being alone. This led to me being caught up with things and people my friends didn't agree with and knew were wrong.

One day I decided to invite Yushra along to a party I knew was happening that evening.

'Come on, don't be boring, let's go. It's going to be a great night. We can meet them there at ten o'clock and I've even managed to get some booze.' Yushra just stared back at me.

'What is with you these days, Aalinna? You know that's not us! Sneaking out from college in the afternoon to go to a party and listen to some music is one thing, but this!'

'Hiding in a friend's flat with blanked out windows and listening to music, is not a fucking party, never mind that we were usually home by nine o'clock,' I spat.

'How are you even going to get there and back at that time of night?'

'It's not that far, I can walk.'

'What are you crazy? Apart from how vulnerable you are as a woman on your own, you know what this place is like. Someone we know is bound to see you, your parents are bound to get to know.'

'I don't care,' I told her. 'They need to butt out, I'm a woman, not a baby.'

I immediately regretted my outburst when I saw the look on Yushra's face.

All smiles and calm demeanour now, trying to cover my tracks, I took Yushra's hand.

'I'm sorry. I didn't mean to snap at you. Forget I mentioned it.

This was the final straw for Yushra. She had watched me untangle for long enough, frightened by my behaviour and risk-taking, as well as my erratic moods, she decided to call my parents. My mother and father, having experienced some of my behaviour and now hearing even worse stories from a worried friend, decided it was time to intervene. Later I would discover this had been the reason for my grounding the night of Yushra's party a few weeks later, when I eventually broke.

My grief and guilt over Samama's death and our senseless falling out, the pressure of failing academically and having to decide what to do next with my life, had finally overwhelmed me. I'd caged in my emotions, all the while unknowingly nurturing an environment for my illness to well up and take over.

Chapter 6
Comfortably Numb

"To live is the rarest thing in the world.
Most people exist, that is all."

Oscar Wilde

Now lost and mentally ill I had no idea how I had got here. Whilst a drug fuelled sleep for six days had initially managed to calm my constant, bumbling ramblings I did not think that anything else was wrong with me. I tentatively began to shake the whole wretched memory away. Within a week I was returning to my old chatty self again.

Unfortunately, as the days went on, I was becoming a bit *too* chatty, I could not see what others could see and was progressing quickly to becoming hyper again. My parents, who were still in shock, were clueless as to what had really happened and were also hoping to put the whole thing down to a one-off episode and move on. They soon realised that something more pernicious was still at play and they became increasingly alarmed by my behaviour. I was still just a little bit too talkative and my sense of inhibition seemed to have left me. I just wasn't right.

'Hey, I'm just off out, see you later.' I'd called over to my mum as I swung on her bedroom door, she was tending to some potted plants on the balcony adjoining her room. My mother loved gardening which was just as well, as we had a huge garden that took a lot of design and upkeep. Our house being on the corner of the street, had gardens on all sides which my mother had filled with the most beautiful array of flowers every colour and texture.

'Where are you off to so early? 'She asked, looking up from some pansies. 'You were up half the night, I could hear you p…,' she stopped mid-sentence. She took her eyes of her watering can for the first time.

'Aalinna! You can't go out like that!' I didn't see the problem; I had checked in the mirror enough times I looked great. My mother was lost for words and given recent events was still cautious when she spoke to me for fear of me having another 'bad turn' as we all now cautiously referred to it. We were all happy to deny the extent of what had happened and try to move on.

I stood there grinning, unable to see the problem. My mother realised this and tried a different tact. 'Where are you off too honey, are you going with someone?'

Duh, 'Yes, Mum, I'm meeting up with Zoha and Nadera. We're off to the mall to do some shopping, actually I think that's them arriving now.'

'Hi.' Came a shout in unison through the front door. I swiftly turned from my mother and ran down stairs with my arms open for a hug, ready to greet them – as if I hadn't spoken to them just last night and seen them the day before.

What they saw coming towards them looked more like a cross between a character from a bad Bollywood movie and a raunchy teen from an American TV drama. My hair was backcombed so high and off my forehead that a flock of birds could have quite happily, nested in it, unseen, for a whole winter. My face was caked in make-up, I had so much eye liner and mascara on – I looked like a cross between daisy the cow and a scarecrow. My lips were the same red as the scarlet low cut top I wore, leaving little to the imagination and the shortness of my skirt was only emphasised by the height of my matching red heels.

As Zoha hugged me she made eye contact with my mum over my shoulder. 'What the hell? 'She mouthed, so stunned she forgot to curb her language. Fortunately, my mother was thinking along the same lines and took no notice. Behind my back, she put her hands on her head and shook it, trying to convey to Zoha that they couldn't let me go out like that.

Zoha got her meaning and was in total agreement but before she could make a tactical move Nadera spoke. 'I'm not going out with you like that,' her shock at how I looked had made her speak before she engaged her brain. My head whipped round like it was on a coiled spring, I glared at her.

'And what is that supposed to mean?' I snapped, ready for an argument. The room froze, Nadera, realising her mistake looked at my mother while I in turn scowled at her, I was furious.

Once again, Zoha saved the day, 'Yeah,' she said, 'I'm not going out with you either like that. Look at me and Nadera, we're in our jeans you will show us up, it's no use, you're going to have to drop the beauty down a few notches' She laughed nervously stealing a glance at Nadera, urging her to play along.

Zoha knew me so well; if there is one way to get me to do something, manic or not, it's to tell me I'm doing it for a friend. As I visibly relaxed so did the rest of the room.

'Awh, don't say that. You are both so beautiful, but hey. No worries. If it makes you feel better I will change. I know!' I screeched, anger replaced by euphoria, "I will put my jeans on and we will all look like sisters." I skipped off up the stairs.

*

Confused about what to do, my parents turned to Dr. Chowdhury. But whilst he was a wonderful family physician, treating this was a bit outside of his normal realm of colds, flus and low blood pressure. Mental health problems in Bangladesh at this time were not only frowned upon but considered taboo, people could become social outcasts and they and their family's labelled as crazy and to be avoided. There was no literature available or programmes to turn to for advice, let alone any facilities or hospitals. My parents did not let this deter them, whilst they didn't plan on screaming it from the rooftops they were determined to stick by me and get me the best treatment possible, no matter what.

It was Dr. Chowdhury who first suggested that my parents take me to America. 'Salam' he said in greeting to my parents, who sat nervously in the sitting room.

'Salam,' replied my parents in unison, my father stood to greet him.

'I will come straight to the point,' he began 'I agree with you; I too believe that Aalinna is on a downward spiral. Having spoken to her and witnessed her – shall we say – demeanour and the behaviours you have told me about, I think she needs further treatment.'

Whilst my mother knew in her heart this was coming she was still visibly upset. She bowed her head and began fiddling with the handkerchief in her hand. My father saw her distress and squeezed her hand gently and spoke:

'Yes, this is what we feared, just tell us what we can do to help her.'

'Well, having spoken to my colleagues and done some research, I know of a place in New York that could offer her the most up-to-date treatment – and as you have your apartment there, I thought this would be best solution. It will give you both the opportunity to, shall we say, monitor and focus on Aalinna, as well as being away from prying eyes. You don't need me to tell you what this country is like for gossip.'

'No you don't,' said my father gloomily, 'for Aalinna's sake I want her to be able to get well without any outside pressures and with none of her behaviour coming back to haunt her in the future.' When my parents announced that we were taking a trip to New York for vacation, I welcomed the idea of an adventure. I didn't think anything was wrong with me and my parents' determined laughter and high spirits to make everything normal, did not betray otherwise. Maryam would stay in Dhaka with our Aunt Sabera for a little while. I hated to leave Maryam—she was a teenager, of course and would be fine.

As we prepared for the trip to New York, I remained in a state of extreme elation. It was not only my parent's nerves that took a hammering during this time, so did their credit card, I would jump from idea to idea, one day I'd decide I was going to be a photographer so would go out and buy all the latest equipment, I'd speak for hours with the shop assistant talking wildly and laughing loudly causing other customers to either stare or make a hasty exit. I think even the assistant wasn't sure whether to make a run for it or stay and take the cash. He was more than happy to put up with my ramblings given the amount I was spending though. The next week I might see a picture I liked in a gallery and I'd decide I just had to have it, and some brushes and easels as well. *Yeah! I'll paint and show everyone how much I have to share.* I spent hours in the gallery giving the poor assistant my valuable critique on all the paintings whilst oblivious to him sneering at the crazy lady and only listening because of the money he was making. My parents grew more uneasy and somewhat financially disadvantaged.

The money wasn't the issue, these incidents only increased their belief that they were doing the right thing, but for me it was fun. I felt I was on top of the world, I had no inhibition, I felt completely and utterly free.

My euphoria only escalated on the 22-hour plane ride from Dhaka to New York. I somehow convinced myself that everyone was looking at me because I was famous and that they wanted to know me. I talked endlessly to anyone who paid attention or simply made the mistake of looking my way, dominating every conversation; I captured the air stewardess as she stopped to offer me a drink.

'I love your uniform, you look great in it, so cute!' She thanked me smiling awkwardly at my compliment. 'I love fashion, I'm going to be a designer, well if I don't keep up with my photography that is – I bought a Super 16 in Brooklyn, what do you think? Her smile began to dwindle as she realised something wasn't quite right. I continued to ramble on as my mother tried to intervene, smiling, saying that the stewardess needed to get on as she was serving drinks.

'Oh don't worry, they will understand, of course the stewardess would want to chat to *me* for a while.' I knew how obnoxious I must have sounded but I truly believed I was being friendly and that people thought it was great to be around me *and* I was being kind giving them my time. I felt each person's glance on me and it seemed that without me the world would stop revolving. I was above everyone.

Of course, I was the only one who enjoyed that flight. I was completely unaware of the other passengers' thoughts, my parents' stress or their cheeks coloured bright red in embarrassment. My mania was such that I felt a deep connection to everything around me. I listened to music like John Lennon and Pink Floyd feeling so connected to each song that I played, playing them over and over. Those feelings were so intense that even today I cannot listen to the same music for fear it will take me right back there, I don't blame Barret and Gilmore.

Looking out the window of the plane I watched the sunlight stream through the wispy clouds and felt connected to every single yellow ray. It seemed like the entire world was at my feet.

Once in New York, my exhausted parents got us a taxi to their apartment. My parents sat together in the back of the cab, my father gripping my mother's hand as she lay with her head on his shoulder drained from the journey, and me.

'Thank God we brought her, we need her to see a doctor and quick,' he intoned, whilst I oblivious, enjoyed the cab ride watching the world go by.

We had a few days before my first appointment and I knew exactly what I wanted to do. I really wanted to go to graduate school and in my manic state, was totally convinced that I could get into Columbia University on the spot, in an instant. Whilst I had been to undergrad school in Dhaka, I hadn't taken my GREs, hadn't filled out an application and was completely unaware of any of the admissions requirements. To me this was no problem, I was determined that it was possible, they'd be lucky to have me.

I adamantly insisted we go to look at the university, wearing my parents down until they finally gave in. Given that, by this stage, my parents would not even let me out of the apartment alone, my father and two of his friends drove me to the Columbia University campus to take a look around.

Again, just like on the plane, I was sure everyone was watching and noticing me as if I was somebody special. I spiritedly introduced myself to anybody and everybody, chatting away furiously about any topic that seemed relevant and even a few that didn't.

'Hi' I screeched, making one poor group of girls jump out of their skin. Initially they smiled and responded in kind but they soon became wary as I rambled on, not drawing breath or waiting for a response before I posed my next question. "I'm Aalinna what're your names? I'm going to be attending in the fall, what are you studying? Here have my number let's stay in touch!'

Their long stares and quiet giggling whispers I just knew were admiring gazes and excited recognitions of my presence. I thought for sure I would get into the school. I could not wait to buy new clothes and a backpack for the first week of classes.

*

The day of my doctor's appointment arrived. I remember little about the ride to the city, except that my father's friend drove us about 20 minutes from our apartment into Manhattan. Along the way, we passed by the Long Island Zoo. I wished we could stop in for a little while. I don't know why but the thought of those strong, bold animals locked away in the cages caught in my gut. I wanted to ride in on my steed, break the locks on all their cages and set them free. Free to rampage through the streets of Manhattan, to soar over the great Statue of Liberty. It felt detrimental that I was restrained to my seat in the car and thus could not help them.

When we finally stopped we were at Cornell Hospital, world renowned as it was, it was situated in the well sandblasted corner of the Upper East Side. I was excited, as I stood on the kerb watching my father help my mother from the car, oblivious to her anxiety as he gave her arm a reassuring squeeze. Placing his hand on her back he guided her towards the hospital's sliding doors.

We were escorted to a consultation room and introduced to a doctor, she practically assaulted me with seemingly useless questions, about everything from my exercise and sleep patterns to my feelings about the car ride over to the hospital. My mind was bursting with thoughts and emotions I so desperately wanted to express but couldn't. I was trying to explain the emotions inside of me but I felt like I wasn't making any sense.

I got it into my head that the doctors were going to hypnotize me and was quite pleased with the idea. *I'll be able to get it all out, that will make me feel better*. I tried to remain patient and answer as many of their questions as possible. Eventually though, I became frustrated sitting in the incredibly uncomfortable hospital chair opposite the doctor. My head began to ache and I anxiously fidgeted as I watched her go in and out of the room, whisper to nurses, gathering and filing papers. After what seemed like an eternity, with no sign of a hypnotist in sight, I finally blurted out indignantly.

'Aren't you going to hypnotize me?'

The doctor glanced over at my parents with a puzzled expression and looking back to me without saying a word. She gave me a look of pity and shook her head. My stomach sank, I looked at my mother and saw the look of horror she gave my father, and he put his head in his hands. I realised they had no idea what I was talking about and in that moment I knew something was terribly wrong.

'You're going to stay in the hospital.' The doctor told me.

'What? I'm not ill so why would I need to stay in a hospital?' I couldn't wrap my brain around what she was saying. I started crying. *There's nothing wrong with me,* 'I don't want to stay!' I screamed at my mother, certain she would say that she was taking me home.

'You have to,' she said. 'Just for a little while.' Then she left. All it took was a second. She was gone and I was alone.

I was furious with her for putting me in the hospital; how could she do this? Bring me here to have me locked away! When will she be back? How long was I to stay here?

I had no idea what was going on. I had never stayed in any hospital before in my life. I was terrified by this new experience – one I didn't want to have. Now, in this utterly foreign environment, with my mum gone, I sat alone in the cold and sterile room with no one for company but strangers and my own senseless thoughts. I wore a pale, worn hospital gown and sat on the high cot-bed with its cold steel frame and sides that could rise up to imprison me further. Had I been abandoned?

I later learned that my parents had no idea I was going to be admitted either. They had simply taken me in to see a doctor. Once I started talking, it was clear to the doctor that something was seriously wrong and something more than a meet-and-greet would be necessary.

As I walked numbly behind the nurse, who had collected me from my room and briskly informed me that I needed to come along with her, a feeling of trepidation began to work its way from my numbed brain, throughout the rest of my body, to my feet, where it seemed they were working on their own, trailing along, moving me to where I needed to go.

'Get on the scale please, the nurse said to her clipboard, once we had arrived at the consultation room. I was confused by even this small request and looked at her for reassurance but none was forthcoming. She simply repeated the request to her clipboard. I stepped on and 'though I was still wearing socks, I could feel the scale's cold metal beneath my feet. A chill ran through my spine. The nurse moved the weights on the scale back and forth in rough, jerking movements until finally it was balanced.

'Ninety-four pounds.' She announced. *Ninety-four pounds? I'm dying. I haven't weighed ninety-four pounds since grade seven.* Still, it was plenty less than 105lb. My stomach twisted into knots and heaviness filled my chest. Once again, I lost all sense of time, the next thing I remember was being alone in my hospital room, having woken from a deep drugged sleep. I was wearing faded jeans and a checked, button-down shirt that I didn't recognize. Whilst I did not know if it was day or night or even what day of the week it was, I did know one thing, I had never experienced anything like the overwhelming sadness that shrouded me in that moment. It enveloped me completely, holding me down with its gravity, wrapping me in its thick and gloomy fold. My interesting, bubbly, adventurous personality had suddenly been muted into a colourless, lifeless soul. When I finally began to emerge from my dream-like state, the world was a mass of confusion. For the first time in life, I wasn't sure about anything and nor did I care. Everything in the room was cold and foreign to me. The walls were painted beige, cracked and chipped in some abstract pattern. The metal bed with its sides that could move up and down. The mattress was so thin I could practically feel the metal beneath me. I was lying on top of a worn grey sheet covered by a light, woven blanket. The air was sterile and stale. The adjoining bathroom had the lingering scent of disinfectant. This was a far cry from the smooth Burma teak wood, soft green velvet curtains and the comforting memory of Samama and me photographed and framed, full of life and carefree, in what seemed like a lifetime ago. Nothing was warm. Nothing was welcoming. It was the last place I wanted to be.

No matter how hard tried, I could not understand or make sense of what had happened to me; worse still, I could barely remember who I was. The previous 22 years of my life seemed to have completely disappeared and were now a remote recollection of scattered thoughts, blurred dreams and replays of past conversations. So much so, it was as if I was thinking about someone else's life. The slate seemed empty, it felt like a new beginning, a new life. My old Latin teacher would have said *Tabula Rasa,* I think. *Was I just being born?*

Even worse, the girl I was before – confident, friendly, fearless and happy was totally gone, just another distant memory. She was an acquaintance from my past. *So if I was no longer her, who was I?* I felt tired and unloved. Nothing seemed meaningful.

I lived like an animal caged at the Long Island Zoo. I wandered the halls of the hospital unit in a daze, always confused. I needed permission and help to accomplish even the smallest task. I felt so out of control of my own life. In the blink of an eye, I had become a child again. I had lost 22 years of my life. What the hell happened? I wondered. The emotions inside of me gravely contrasted the familiar confidence and independent spirit I used to know so well. These new feelings, unknown to me before, confused me, and frightened me to the core.

The other patients were a mix of different ages and ethnic backgrounds. No one stood out to me because I interacted with them as little as possible. In fact, I went out of my way to avoid them. There were plenty of girls around my age but I wanted nothing to do with them. Once I entered the hospital, something changed in me. Gone was the chatty, talkative girl from the plane. Gone was the ambitious applicant to Colombia University. Gone was the confident liberator of those trapped at the Long Island Zoo?

Gone was the manic side too. Suddenly, I was very quiet and withdrawn. Cautious. Just saying hello to anyone set my heart racing. My new-found shyness amazed even me, my confidence had plummeted to such a low that I didn't want to talk to anyone, especially a group of total strangers. I was convinced that whatever I said would be stupid, so why say anything at all? Wouldn't they just laugh at me? Every interaction was a struggle, I walked the corridors aimlessly.

After about a week, I cannot recall exactly I began one-on-one therapy sessions with a Dr. Simon. She was an extremely thin woman with dark curly hair and very sharp features, her demeanour and approach was formal and clinical.

Our sessions were aggravating. I would sit on the chair facing her numb, scared and confused, whilst she asked, 'So how are you today?' *I wish I knew.*

I tried desperately to keep my thoughts straight and find the right answer as much for her sake as mine, maybe a correct answer would stop her asking the same mundane queries over and over. Our sessions were always one-sided, I felt she was meant to be helping me, but I was the one doing all the work and I was always left confused and anxious.

During one out-of-the-ordinary session, however, my emotions managed to break free. Through my fog of despair and depression, just for a moment I felt my apathy leave me and a need to make a connection with the real world with someone. I was so lonely and lost, I desperately wanted to feel the comfort of my mother's arms and for her to stroke my hair and tell me everything would be okay. I felt maybe just maybe then there would be a point in talking to someone. I instinctively reached to touch her hand.

'No touching allowed in the hospital,' she said, stiffly, recoiling from me, scooting her chair back to avoid my touch.

'But I... I didn't finish my sentence, embarrassed and hurt I sat back on the edge of my chair hugging myself for comfort instead. Looking back now maybe I can understand the difficulties around physical contact between doctor and patient but there was no attempt at empathy or understanding, no explanation or, for that matter, further conversation at my attempt at connecting with someone; no eye contact, no smile, not even a pat on the leg or arm. Even a dog with a sad look seeking comfort would get more affection and understanding. *How can I connect with these people when this place is so cold?*

This was the vindication I needed and my depression wrapped round me like a comforting blanket. I was supposed to attend group therapy but after just one session I didn't go back. I couldn't explain what I was feeling to myself. How could I explain it to a room full of strangers? I had never been worried about what other people thought of me but in that room I felt like an idiot and especially after my previous attempt at reaching out to Dr. Simon. I felt that even if I could get my head straight enough to speak, anything I said or did would be wrong.

My only small release and solace was a once a day call I got to make to my best friend, Zoha, who at the time was in the graduate school at UT Austin. Cell phones were practically non-existent, so I'd call her collect. Struggling student that she was, she still accepted my call every time, an act of true friendship for which I was, and am still now, incredibly grateful. The only thing better than a chat with Zoha was receiving a call from my beloved baby sister. Hearing Maryam's voice when she called from Dhaka was another highlight of my week, though the joy was short-lived. The hospital, prison that it was, had restrictions on when you could use the phone and for how long. Still, these calls helped me keep a small grip on reality and contact with the outside world.

I cared little about the treatments I was receiving, much less those highly-anticipated therapy sessions twice a day. I'd line up with the rest of the patients at a counter in the corner of the communal area to get my medicine. A nurse would watch me take it out of the tiny paper cup, put it in my mouth and swallow it, monitoring my every move. Hiding pills under my tongue this time was definitely not an option.

There was no TV in my bedroom but there was one in the common area where the other patients would watch shows and the hospital would play old movies like *Grease* and *The Sound of Music*. There was also a Ping-Pong table, checkers and other board games, but I had little interest in doing anything. Instead, I sat on the thin, tiny bed in my room for hours on end, scared confused and all alone. I didn't read or listen to music. Instead, I sat there with my thoughts and this horrible weight that was buried in the centre of my stomach. To me it truly seemed like one-minute I was living my happy-go lucky life, confident and in control and the next I woke up in hospital.

To say I was depressed is an understatement. The sense of loneliness cut unbearably deep. It was like I was seeing my life before this, the old me, like a movie. I couldn't imagine being that girl. I was so eager to get out of that hospital, constantly asking my psychiatrist, 'When am I going home?'

'You have to stay a little longer.' She would answer. When I'd ask the nurse, she'd say, 'the doctor will tell you.'

'I want to go home;' I told my parents when they came to visit.

'Soon, 'they would say. Soon felt like it would never come. I might have been angry with my parents, if I could have clearly remembered the day they left me at the hospital. But by now my mind was a hazy mass of confusion. I could barely remember anything. All I knew was the horrible weight inside my chest dragging me further into the darkness and with each passing day I clung on trying to keep some semblance of myself and my sanity.

My parents' visits were a great comfort to me. My mother's hugs especially were soothing to my troubled heart.

These visits involved moments of awkward small talk, sharing little titbits of news from the paper or cheerful reminders of something funny Rabab and I used to do as children. My mother would bring a fresh set of clean clothes and exchange them for my dirty laundry. One thing I did care about, though, was gaining weight. I was petrified of how thin I'd become—I could barely recognize myself in the mirror! I hoped gaining weight would make me healthy and being healthy would mean I could leave that horrible place, but the hospital food was so bland I could barely palate it. My parents, unwilling to see me suffer, brought me take-out for lunch and dinner – sometimes Bangladeshi food, sometimes Chinese. I ate heartily in the hope of being released. My father and mother always put on a good face for me, acting strong and casual during our visits. Unknown to me, before seeing me they would meet with some of my doctors privately to see what progress I was making. They never asked me what was going on or how I felt. They tried to act normal as if they were just visiting me at a hotel or something, never once showing the deep pain they felt.

Finally, after some three weeks the weight began to lift off my shoulders, I began to think more clearly and I was able to finally loosen the shroud of depression that had been weighing so heavily. Hope began to seep into my tired heart and body like rays of sunshine, a nurturing nectar. By the fourth week I finally got the news I thought would never come: I was getting out. I buoyed through the hospital's glass sliding doors. I comforted myself with the assumption that the weight and memory of it all would evaporate completely, lifting off me and floating away like a bouquet of helium balloons. I would feel like myself again. Then next, would come the worst months of my life.

Chapter 7

Empty & Turned to Stone

"The world is very lovely, and it's very horrible – and it doesn't care about your life or mine or anything else."

Rudyard Kipling

When I got to my parent's Long Island apartment the initial euphoria I felt at my release dwindled and ceased within a few days. A horrible sensation filled my chest, one that I can't explain. It was heavy, foreign and suffocating. The horrible realisation that nothing inside of me had changed plummeted me into a debilitating depression.

It certainly did not help that my parents began treating me like a child, barely letting me out of their sight; yes, this had happened before but this time (like so many other things) it was crueller because I was now aware of it.

They brought me to all of my doctor's appointments and were in charge of ensuring I took all my medication, of which there were quite a lot. My father would hand me the medicine and watch me take it, just like the hospital nurses, making sure I didn't hide any pills under my tongue. Their distrust wasn't unfounded. Also, my mother was constantly monitoring what I ate since I had lost so much weight.

My parents, I knew, had only the best intentions: they wanted me to get better. Their constant supervision, combined with the fact that we were living in a small three-bedroom apartment, was however all the more suffocating. I missed the comfort of our huge house in Dhaka, familiar and spacious, where I had plenty of room and privacy.

In New York, there was too much interaction and they were afraid to leave me alone for a second. On the occasions that my parents would travel back and forth to Dhaka I felt like I could finally breathe a little. One parent would go to stay with Maryam and one would stay with me, then they would switch places. This provided a welcome break in the Long Island apartment.

What had happened to me? I had been an independent person, a mentally healthy adult. I had been very in control of my life and my emotions. I was strong. I was logical. Rational. I was the one that people turned to because I helped solve their problems. Now I had the problems and I needed the help.

*

They didn't say anything, but I could tell how concerned my parents were by the way they looked at me, by the glances that passed between them and in how eager they were to please. After all, my parents thought I was going to die so my consciousness was a bonus, regardless of its quality. They would have done anything for me. For example, before I became ill I used to smoke cigarettes, which my parents naturally hated. Having been locked away in the hospital for almost four weeks, I hadn't tried the comfort of nicotine as a remedy for my situation yet.

So in this new environment, where I had to ask my parents' permission for anything, I adamantly demanded that I wanted to smoke.

'I need some cigarettes from the shop.'

'You can't smoke,' mother said, her tone was weak, it was more like a question than a statement.

'Yes. I can.' I challenged but she didn't protest. Instead, my mother went to the store and bought me a pack of cigarettes. It was my parents' way of trying their best to give me comfort and my way of trying to gain some control.

Night-time was the happiest for me. It felt like it belonged to me and me alone. At night, life was not the burden it was during the day. I didn't have to face anyone, make conversation or pretend that I was the confident girl I had once been. I liked the quiet and stillness of the world and how the darkness outside seemed to match the darkness inside me. Strangely, I felt more in harmony with myself during those quiet moments. Nearly everyone was asleep and there were no rude intruders, no one to bother me, no one to interact with and feel like a total idiot in front of. I didn't have to face the world.

I was awake most of the night, but during the day, I wanted only to sleep. I would lie in bed, tossing and turning in a haze of various stages of sleep, blankets twisted around me, and the faint sounds of the world in the distance.

In the weeks and days after the hospital, the hyper, manic Aalinna was gone. Now I was very quiet and disturbed. I was like a zombie. Partly because I was taking so much medication.

Trying to 'snap me out of it' my mother would take me to places like Times Square the Metropolitan Museum or Broadway shows – obviously assuming that being around people and normality would be good for me but these situations were unbearable for me. I was under so much medication that I couldn't focus and my reaction time was slow. I felt like I was being mobbed by the crowds of people and the drills and engines and stereos were amplified. Being around people made me nervous, my heart would beat so fast I thought it would come out of my chest; my hands wringing with sweat I would long for the still of my room. I was so ashamed. I lived in fear that others would discover I'd been in the hospital or that I was ill at all.

*

In Bangladesh, being hospitalized for psychiatric reasons was hardly common and never to be discussed. It was natural to assume that I was the only person on earth who struggled with depression. At the time, I would rather have had people think I had a drug or alcohol problem than a mental illness. Maybe if I had attended the group therapy sessions, I would have realised I was not alone. How I wish someone would have at least told me how many people wrestled with this illness, how many smart and accomplished people of all ages, races, and classes that had not only wrestled with it, but had found ways to cope and live a fairly normal life. In some cases, even, a beautiful life.

Back then, I actually knew almost nothing about depression, or mania. Growing up, anyone with any mental issues was called "retarded." That was the only word I heard, though today, that word has a totally different meaning. Anything else I'd known about it came from one advertisement on Bangladeshi television that I saw when I was in college. It was an ad about depression in which a lady who was clearly very upset sat in a rocking chair, slowly moving back and forth with a blank look in her eyes. At the end, a voice-over talked about where you should go if you're experiencing these very sad emotions. This ad created much uproar and commotion in our community because many people claimed that after seeing it they actually felt depressed. As a result, the government banned it.

When I saw the advertisement on television myself I was confused. What are they talking about? I thought. Why would someone go to a doctor if they felt sad? How little I knew. I also remember a friend mentioning that people in the United States went to counselling. Are these people so busy they don't have time to talk to friends or family? I wondered. It was such a bizarre concept to me. Now that I think about it, I hadn't even heard the words 'mental health' before. Now I found myself fighting for mine.

The only thing I had to do in those days and weeks after the hospital was take medication daily, have my blood drawn weekly so they could manage my medication, and see a psychiatrist twice a week. Her name was Dr. Churchin.

One of her jobs was to monitor the various medications that I was on and adjust them when needed. I was also supposed to meet with her twice a week for talk therapy, there was never much talking. In order to ensure that I actually attended therapy, one of my parents would bring me to my appointments. We would sit together in silence during the 20-minute car ride from our apartment to the city, they would settle into the waiting room until I was finished. I hated these appointments. I didn't need a psychiatrist and each visit only reminded me that I was ill.

Dr. Churchin's office was in the same hospital I'd spent those horrible 28 days. The room had a single chair where she sat and a couch where I sat. There were a lot of books, a desk, and a window with a view of the Queens Boro Bridge. From the first appointment, I felt uncomfortable in her presence and the cold, formal aura that surrounded her. Unfortunately, things did not improve, even after months of our meetings. She seemed distant and rigid and I could not open up to her. The 45-minute sessions seemed to last too long and I had nothing to say.

Our common therapy routine would begin with me walking into her office and she giving her usual nod hello.

'How are you?' she would ask, more out of routine than of genuine interest or concern.

Oh, you know, great, life's wonderful. I'm stuck in a three-bedroom apartment in a strange city with my parents as bodyguards. I feel so depressed I could quite happily jump off of that pretty bridge outside your window. Oh, and did I mention I'm drugged to the eye balls and feel permanently sick? Apart from that everything is just bloody brilliant.

But I replied, 'Fine, I'm fine.'

'You're not fine,' she would briskly reply. *That explains all those framed degrees,* I thought.

'Why are you saying you're fine when your obviously not?'

Is it because I can barely think straight with all these tablets? Or could it be because my whole world has been blown apart? Maybe if I could explain how I felt I wouldn't need to be stuck in this room with you. I stayed quiet.

I dreaded those sessions and spent most of them staring at my watch, wishing its hands would move more quickly so I could leave. She inundated me with questions, which I hated because I had nothing to talk about. I didn't understand what I was feeling or what was wrong with me so how could I explain it or share it with someone else?

Often I didn't stay for the full 45 minutes. Rather, I'd forcefully insist I was fine, thank you, and get up and leave the room. I just wanted to go back to Bangladesh and start my life all over again. I wanted all this to end. Believing that this was temporary brought me some relief. I was under the illusion that the treatment received at the hospital and days spent as an outpatient, would be effective and consoled myself that I would be fine soon.

After about twelve sessions, I asked Dr. Churchin, 'How much longer will I have to do this? When can I stop my medication and these lame therapy sessions, too?

'You're not going to stop,' she said.

'What do you mean?' After all, my illness was a temporary thing. Wasn't it?

'Aalinna, you have to take this medication for the rest of your life,' she informed me casually.

'The rest of my life?' Wait? What?

Shit, I thought, *maybe she was saying this because I'd pissed her off.* I was all ready for making promises to talk more in sessions, of trying harder, of taking my meds without complaining. Anything but this.

Chapter 8
Frozen Tree Trunk

"God grant me the serenity to accept the things I cannot change, the courage to change the things I can, and the wisdom to know the difference."

'You have Bipolar Disorder, so your moods go up and down,' she said, using her hands to mimic an undulating motion, 'the medication keeps your moods in the middle.'

Dr. Churchin continued talking I think, because her lips may have been moving, but I heard no sound. In fact, I didn't hear anything that she said for the rest of the session. In the weeks of my hospitalisation I may have heard the phrase bipolar disorder once or twice but my mind was so hazy, I could barely grasp a hold of anything that made sense. I could barely put any two pieces of information together. I understood a little that I had been sedated at home and at the hospital because I was having a 'manic episode'. I heard bits and pieces about 'extreme mood swings', 'depression' and 'mania' but I couldn't connect them with my own life.

In that instant, my life had changed. Bipolar disorder. Mental illness. The phrases sounded ugly and shameful, wrought with personal failure. What is wrong with me? I was in shock. How can I live life with a mental illness? How could I possibly take medication for the rest of my life?

I had always been so healthy, never hospitalized for anything and the only medication I ever took was a rare Tylenol here and there. Even the few times I was prescribed an antibiotic, I never finished the course. Medication was not part of my world. To me, it was something you took if you were very old like my grandmother or if you had a serious illness like my uncle who had diabetes. But me? Take medicine forever? I could not fathom needing to do so for the rest of my life. I could not accept that I was never going to be the same girl that I used to be. I had thought the medication was a temporary thing, something I'd take for a few weeks or months. Then I'd be fine and go back to my normal life. I couldn't stop staring at the Queens boro Bridge. Dr. Churchin was talking, but I interrupted her.

'Why did this happen to me?' I asked.

'Genetics, 'she said, 'Bipolar disorder is a genetic thing.'

'What?' I shook my head. 'No one in my family has this. There must be another reason.'

Dr. Churchin just shrugged and raised her eyebrows. I left her office feeling furious and even more confused and unwilling to buy this genetic thing.

*

Weeks, months and even years after this pivotal moment in my life, I started connecting the dots. I looked back and did see this illness in my family — I'd just never had a name for it.

Growing up, my uncle was very moody, going in and out of dark periods at uneven intervals. Sometimes he was really up. Other times, he was so down that there was nothing any of us could do to pull him out. I even remembered a family joke we had about a time when my uncle lost a lot of money from a business deal. Apparently, he wouldn't talk to anyone for weeks. My father joked that he had a nervous breakdown. Although they laughed it off, I realise that it was a form of depression, probably bipolar disorder.

I also remembered how, during a certain time of the year, my father's mother used to get sick. We never had a name for it, but it seemed to be more related to her mind than her actually being physically sick. Sometimes my grandmother stayed in her bed for long periods of time. Or she would wear the same clothes and not shower for days. She'd become extremely talkative and laugh senselessly at anything. My aunts, too, had this kind of problem that had no name. One of my cousins used to joke that we had a pagol family – pagol being the Bangla word for crazy. It wasn't until my grandmother was very old that she was diagnosed with bipolar disorder.

I even began to look back and identify mental illness in people outside of our family. When I was eighteen years old, we had a neighbor whom my mother was extremely close to. She was an exceptionally warm, happy, confident person. I was naturally surprised, therefore, when she one day appeared at our door completely disoriented. She didn't know where she was, she did not recognize anyone, not even my mother. I was so confused and hardly knew how to react. My mother, however, just made her a cup of tea, sat her down on the sofa and reassuringly chatted away as if everything were normal. My neighbor finally stood up and absent-mindedly walked out the door.

'What's wrong with her?' I asked my mother. "I saw her last week and she was absolutely fine.'

My mother dismissed the whole event with a wave of her hand, but I was unwilling to let the matter drop. I pressed the issue with my neighbors until I finally received the simple explanation, 'Sometimes that happens to her, but then a few days later she's herself again.'

Unfortunately, all my dot connecting didn't come back to me until many years later. So at the time, in 1998, when I was sitting in that in that doctor's office staring at the Queensboro Bridge and in my parent's home in Long Island staring at the walls, I honestly thought I was the only one in the world who had this mental illness.

During that time, my mother pushed me to invite people over. Of course, her intentions were good. She eagerly wanted to help me and to see me laugh and smile again. She wanted to revive the old me, the girl who could socialise with everybody. . Now with my confidence gone, this was an enormous struggle.

I worried about what I would say to the people my mother was inviting to visit us. Small talk was stressful and social events taxing.

*

Maryam flew to Long Island to visit me whenever she had short breaks at school. Over time, many of my cousins, friends and other family members came from all different cities to stay with us for two to three day visits. Normally, that would have thrilled the old me but now it was horrible. I didn't know what to do with them or in front of them. I was convinced that I was making a fool of myself all the time. Fears and inhibitions were raw new emotions that were scary to me and I didn't know how to handle them.. I longed to be the carefree girl I was before, the one who felt at ease with people, with life, and her took her confidence for granted.

At times someone would say, 'why are you so quiet?' If it was someone I had known before my illness, I felt foolish like I wasn't living up to their expectations of me. At other times I would hear, 'What would you like to do?' and I'd fall to nervous pieces because I didn't know. How many of our friends and family knew about my illness? Did they believe I was really just on vacation? What would they think when they found out or did my nervous behavior betray all?

One of our visitors was my best friend Zoha whom I had called every day when I was in the hospital. We had known each other since we were in the sixth grade. About a week after I was discharged from the hospital, my mother was on the phone with her.

'Why don't you come to New York City for a long weekend?' I heard my mum ask her. 'We'll pay for your ticket.'

'Oh good!' my mother said moments later, so I knew that Zoha had said 'yes'. My parents were thrilled that she was coming, hoping that seeing an old, close friend would snap me back into the daughter they used to know. But I was nervous. I couldn't pretend to be someone I was not and I felt certain this unfeeling zombie was not who Zoha expected to see.

'I don't want her to come.' I told my mother.

'Don't worry,' she said. 'When Zoha comes, you'll be laughing all the time just like you used to.'

I wasn't so sure. I put a huge amount of pressure on myself to be the same exact person I was before my illness; the friend she'd known for years. Looking back now I realise that of course that's not what Zoha expected. She knew I was sick, very sick. She knew it was serious and that I wasn't going to just bounce back in a matter of days or even weeks. That's exactly why she was coming to visit. She expected nothing from me, but my own insecurity kept me from seeing that.

Because it was Zoha's first time in New York City, I wanted to show off things like the Empire State Building, the Twin Towers of the World Trade Centre, the Statue of Liberty, the Metropolitan Museum of Art and Central Park. Before my illness, giving her a tour of these famous landmarks would have been thrilling, but I did not have the energy to take her anywhere. On top of the stress of just being with another person, planning anything was an added pressure.

When she arrived, I could tell she was shocked, and can only assume it was because I had lost so much weight. Besides that, she didn't let on that she felt I was different. She was warm and supportive. Luckily, Nadera, a very close friend of mine who lived in New Jersey also came to visit. I'm not sure if my mother arranged this or not, but having this friend and her husband come with me to take Zoha sight-seeing was a huge relief. Gone was the pressure to be the sole entertainer, the dancing bear. I just went along and didn't plan anything. My tension was slightly relieved, although I still felt uncomfortable.

During Zoha's visit, we saw two popular, award-winning Broadway shows, *Rent* and *Phantom of the Opera*. As we watched these performances, sitting in these two different, ornate and beautiful old theaters, I saw how much my friends were enjoying them. After the show, they talked nonstop about what we saw, about the two shows messages, their sets, their stories. They couldn't get enough.

I, on the other hand, didn't understand anything. It was as if we had seen totally different shows. I'm so stupid. It was becoming my mantra.

Having my best friend visit should have been a comfort, but in some ways I was getting more stressed. She was my closest friend and yet I couldn't talk to her about what I was feeling. It wasn't that she would judge me or make me feel bad. No. I knew that she would have understood and been compassionate, but how could I talk about something that I was struggling to understand myself? I also felt that I wasn't living up to my friend's expectations and that I was a very different person than before, I was sick being so pathetic. When Zoha left, I felt exhausted. In the weeks after her visit, I was still like a zombie. Time felt like it was not moving. I had a gold Cartier watch with a maroon leather strap. It had a tiny second hand and for me, everything was still, except that second hand. The only thing that kept me moving was my watch. I would stare at it thinking to myself, it's moving. Time is passing. That watch was everything to me back then. I rarely turned on the television because I couldn't understand what they were talking about. I couldn't concentrate. I couldn't focus. Nothing made sense, so I spent a lot of time alone doing nothing.

The only thing I did want to do – besides sleep – was eat; I was still faintly haunted by the fact that I was 94 pounds. After I came back from the hospital, my goal was to gain weight, so I ate like crazy. This wasn't hard to do because my appetite was huge thanks to the antidepressant I was taking. I loved burgers and pizza, and pretty much anything because I was hungry all the time. Sometimes if I couldn't sleep, I would sneak quietly down to the kitchen and raid the fridge in the middle of the night. Not only was I happy to add weight to my skeletal figure, eating was one of the few sensations I could actually feel.

I could experience the enjoyment of hamburgers, but I could not feel my own emotions. Before I got ill, I was a very compassionate person. If someone was in pain, I was in pain. If a friend was sad, I was sad, too. But since having this illness I was totally numb. During that time, my maternal grandmother died. I had loved her very much and was very close to her. We had spent a lot of time with her and throughout my childhood we ate dinner at her house at least once a week.

But upon hearing about her death, I could not shed one single tear. I wanted to be sad, to feel something, but I didn't feel anything. Unfortunately, this sensation would last for a while, a horrible sensation that would put a distance between me and other people, sending me further and further into my own world. The only impressions I felt were the taste of food, and the only thing from which I could get some satisfaction was eating.

Just a month after getting out of the hospital, my weight had shot up to 125 pounds. My parents took the fact that I was eating and putting on weight as a sign that I was healthy but the frightening speed with which I had gained it made me even more depressed.

My father, after seeing me sit and stare at my watch all day for weeks on end, decided it was time to help me move toward a more normal life, to engage my mind in healthy activity. He had a thriving business in New York and soon invited me to his office to work for him. None of it was hard work, just simple tasks like filing and organising. Unfortunately, it proved to be too much. Upon arriving at his office, I was debilitated by feelings of being clueless and helpless. I couldn't understand what was going on or what I was supposed to do. Even the smallest task made me feel like an idiot. My confidence plummeted even more – as if that was even possible. My father never pressured me and clearly it was the pressure I had put on myself that made the situation so bad but either way, it didn't work out.

About two months after my hospitalisation, my parents and I went to a relative's house for dinner. They had known me my whole life and our two families had remained close. Just seven or eight months earlier, before my illness, I'd actually stayed with them for a few days. During that first visit, we passed the nights away with me telling animated stories that kept everyone laughing. What they didn't know was that this time they'd invited the new me to dinner. I didn't say anything except a mumbled hello. Having had no idea about my illness, they were utterly confused. My parents had not told anyone about my diagnosis. All they saw was the drastic contrast between the previously confident young woman, always smiling and chatty, and the new quiet, withdrawn little girl who couldn't crack the smallest smile.

'Aalinna, why are you so quiet?', I smiled and excused myself for the bathroom, once inside with the door locked I grabbed fistfuls of my hair and watched my face in the mirror as I opened my mouth and screamed silently at my reflection.

'What's wrong with her?' I'd heard them whisper to my mother, their concern was genuine enough and they didn't intend to make me uncomfortable, but they did. The more they asked, the more pressure I put on myself to be what they expected, and the more anxious I got.

When we returned home that night, I immediately rushed to the bathroom, eager to splash cold water on my face, and wash away the tension of the evening. I glanced in the mirror, then stared for a long time, mesmerised by the stranger's eyes staring back at me. I had always been told I had expressive eyes, but now they were blank. I saw it, and I knew my relatives had seen it, too. They weren't the only ones who couldn't relate to me. I couldn't relate to myself.

*

The weeks went by, and the cold winter months kept us locked away indoors most days. Whether we braved the winds and snows that rolled across the Great South Bay or not, I continued to remain enclosed within my own shell. I was unable to do the things I normally did. I was very nervous around people besides my parents and could barely carry on a normal conversation. Even small talk was excruciatingly painful. I thought everything I was saying was stupid. Nothing inspired me. I felt numb.

The months that followed would be the most terrible five months of my life. I was an outpatient, doing regular counselling only to hate every minute of it. Taking medication was embarrassing, living like a child under my parent's wing was humiliating and enduring lifeless counselling sessions wore away the little energy I now possessed. I still could not connect to my psychiatrist.

During one of my more lucid moments I had signed up for a six-week two days a week real estate course in an attempt to keep me busy and shift my focus, but I couldn't cope. I was immensely uncomfortable around so many people – there were about 50 in the class. Naturally I was required to interact and answer questions.

The mere sight of so many people left me sweating and shaky, so eventually I began skipping classes. Spending the time hiding from my parents and my failure I would pass the morning hours in Central Park, staring into space, giving my brain some rest. I could do nothing and feel nothing. The peaceful surroundings in the park and the lush green trees were soothing to my soul. I felt safer and happier there, in the company of ducks and birds, relishing together in the gentle breezes that rippled the water in the pond and rustled the leaves on the cherry blossom trees.

Often I would visit central library and sit looking at all the books, breathing in their smell, feeling the textures of their covers and longing to read them all. I loved books, I loved knowledge. I loved the opportunity books gave you to enter another world but even this pleasure was denied to me; my learning difficulties were another cross to bare and another stick to beat myself with. How stupid could one person be? I did not find the motivation or clarity of mind to continue with my studies. The course was a disaster and soon I dropped out.

My college convocation was coming up in December and the prospect managed to stir another feeling; the desire to go. I felt strongly that being back in Dhaka was the only way that things would be normal again. I was convinced that once I returned home, in a familiar place where the 'normal' me had once lived, I would put this strange experience behind me and start my life over again. My friends, family and especially my little sister and all that was familiar, awaited me in Dhaka. To me, they were like a rewind button that would take me back to the old me.

Another month went by and though nothing had changed in my condition, numb and scared I desperately searched for a way out. I made arrangements to leave New York and return to Dhaka, despite my parent's insistence that I stay put. Once they realised how serious I was, they arranged to come with me. I planned to stay for three weeks, I was convinced that a brief stay in Dhaka was all the medicine I needed to revive my soul again. Contrary to my expectations however, the emptiness within me grew. I could not connect to those around me. People I got along with in the past seemed estranged and distant again. I could not even open up with my best friends. I felt completely numb. I had nothing to say to anyone and was extremely anxious when anyone tried to converse with me. I could not understand what people were saying and did not know how to answer them. The pressure to be my old self and to perform like I used too was too much for me.

Instead, I would sit still for hours in one place without uttering a word. My friends started making fun of me and called me

Brikkho Manobi a Bangla phrase, which literally means a frozen tree trunk. To their credit, it was a fitting title for someone like me with such deeply empty eyes, who would stare into space for hours on end. I was stiff in mind and body and couldn't function.

I couldn't relate to the things that my peers were doing in their lives – attending graduate school, working and getting married. A few times, friends said things like, 'Aalinna, remember when we did ...' and the story they'd tell about me was shocking. Shocking, not because it was scandalous or dangerous, shocking because the girl they described was happy, confident and fun. I'd smile and nod at their stories but inside, I'd think, *I said that?* or, *I did those things?* The stark contrast between their lively stories, and the now frozen tree trunk that was previously their main character, only made me feel worse.

The actual convocation ceremony was tiresome. I had been looking forward to the event but my enthusiasm had completely disappeared. My confidence shattered when the day actually came. I wore my gown and held my degree and pretended to smile but my soul was not in my body. It was floating away, evaporating into another world. Nothing made me happy. I just wanted the ceremony to end as soon as possible.

The whole trip tortured me. I should have been reveling with pride over my hard work in college. Instead, I was devastated to discover that the new me still existed and couldn't thrive in surroundings the old me once had.

Even more disturbing, everywhere I looked, were the unwelcome images that flashed through my mind. Faraz. Course schedules. Samama. Each memory was like a horrendous thunderclap, catching me completely off guard. A crumpled car. A joint. Samama. Every time I remembered, I wanted to throw up, Go to hell, the answering machine. Samama.

I wanted to go back to New York so I didn't have to face the ghosts of my past. In fact, I never wanted to go back to Dhaka again.

I could not stuff my bags full of the basics quickly enough. I could care less if everything even made it into the bag. A few sets of clothes. A toothbrush. What else did I really need? I closed the lid of the suitcase on top of a haphazardly assembled pile of clothing, breathing heavily and attempting to steady my shaking hands. I barely knew the bag's contents. I could not even see them through the tears now filling my eyes. The memories now roaring through my body, and weakening my knees. Grades. Marriage. Samama! The memories would not stop.

Now, I was livid. My confidence was gone. My life was gone. My carefree spirit was gone. I flashed an angry eye at the framed photograph of Samama and me, once so happy and alive. How could life take so much? How could a grown woman like me be reduced to a fearful little girl? I snatched the photograph off the nightstand and drew back my arm to smash it into the wall.

When my mother finally found me, I was asleep on the floor, cradling to my chest the memory of Samama, photographed and framed. My mother knelt down next to me, silent. Tears streaming down her cheeks, she gently stroked my hair as I dreamed through a fitful sleep.

Chapter 9
Summer Thaw

"Your only obligation in any lifetime is to be true to yourself. Being true to anyone else or anything else is not only impossible, but that mark of a fake messiah."

Richard Bach

After my disastrous trip to Dhaka, I went back to New York for six months. My parents again took turns, one of them staying with me in New York, one staying with my sister in Dhaka. They periodically switched places and Maryam visited when she was able to take a break from school.

The following June I returned home to Dhaka. This time, I was coped much better. Before I'd left New York, my doctors had finally figured out the proper medications, the combination and dosage that I needed daily to level the waves that were my moods and emotions. I felt more balanced and was able to think clearly allowing me to mix with others without feeling overwhelmed or anxious. It also helped to keep my appetite in check, this left me feeling like I was more in control. When I was with friends or family, I could interact a little more, the frozen tree trunk now starting to thaw. Very slowly but gradually, I began to feel more like myself. I was more independent and my parents were letting go, trusting and hoping that I was getting back to being the Aalinna they knew.

Even though rationally, I knew the medication was helping,

at times I got scared that it made it difficult for me to concentrate and left my mind blank. The old me was back and tired of taking pills. *I'm completely in control now. So why am I taking medication?* A month went by and as far as I was concerned, I did not have any symptoms of my illness. I was fine. I decided that I was better. I was cured. Thinking that I knew better and without consulting my doctor or telling my parents, I made the detrimental decision to stop taking my medication.

In August, my mother, sister and I travelled to Thailand. It was to be a special trip as it had been so long since we had all been able to be together. Maryam was delighted and had been excitedly preparing for it for weeks. Anticipating that my mother would ask me where my medication was, I filled one of those pill boxes – the ones that have seven slots for each day of the week – with an array of multivitamins. When my mother asked, "Where's your medication?" I pulled the vitamin box from the drawer and showed it to her. She was satisfied.

Not surprisingly, before long my condition worsened and I soon had a relapse. I gradually became completely manic. I felt happy and was enjoying the fun of being in a manic state. Well, it was fun for me. Being manic only convinced me that I'd done the right thing by stopping the medication. Initially, my mother hoped my 'good mood' and 'socialising' was down to the benefits of my medication and Maryam was enjoying having her fun loving sister back. However, as I became increasingly euphoric, and once again began to talk ceaselessly and dominate every conversation, my mother's heart sank as was beginning to know the signs and behaviours that came with my bipolar.

Our holiday in Thailand was a disaster. My mother, sensing something was wrong with me, consulted with Dr. Imran. Dr. Imran was a new physiatrist who I had been referred to on my return to Dhaka. He was a sweet guy who I saw once a week monitored my medication and moods, though not very well as it turned out.

'I'm not sure what to do with her, I can't keep up with her. She is jumping from one subject to the next, flirting with anyone in sight and then trying to go off alone or dragging Maryam along with her on some crazy adventure or idea she comes up with,' my mother explained. 'I can't even sleep at night for fear she will go off!'

'I don't think you have much choice, she is obviously having a relapse, and you're going to have to get her back into hospital."

So after only five days our holiday ended and we had to fly to the States to get me treatment. Maryam was devastated, she had waited for this trip for such a long time. She had so wanted to spend quality time with me and our mother – fun-time where all the focus wasn't on me, and how well I was (or wasn't), but once again my bipolar dominated everyone's lives.

The journey to America was a nightmare for my mother, though I was perfectly happy, cocooned in my state of euphoria. I had been incredibly friendly, talking to anyone and everyone around me. I even made a visit to the cockpit where the pilots let me sit with them for half of the ride from Dhaka to Brussels! My poor mother sat anxiously in her seat trying to ignore or play down my behaviour whilst praying to God that I did not get it into my head that I wanted to be a pilot and decide I would need to take over the cockpit. I do remember a flight attendant going out and asking my mother if I was okay. I don't know my mother's response, but I was soon politely ushered back to my seat where I continued to introduce myself to everyone and anyone. Clearly, this flight was overwhelming and embarrassing for my mother and a little too reminiscent of a certain other flight where I was, without question, having a manic episode.

In the car on the way to our apartment on Long Island from the JFK airport, my mother and I began arguing about my behaviour on the plane.

'Aalinna I am not a fool. Are you going to tell me what is going on, that was quite a display you just gave?'

'You know what?' I yelled. 'I stopped taking my medication. I don't need it anymore!' I rolled down the car window and threw my box of pills onto the street. 'I'm not going to take it!'

This was another part of being manic, no scared little girl this time that was the depressive Aalinna.

'What? I knew it!' my mother raged. 'Oh! Aalinna, can't you see you need it? 'She said wearily. I didn't care, I was adamant I knew the truth of it and I was happy. I hadn't felt this good in so long, I didn't need the medication, and I was fine, I was better without it. The more my mother insisted that I needed it, the more angry and aggressive I became, before my parents had went along with anything I wanted, |I wasn't used to being challenged and they began to see a whole no side to my manic side. 'Leave me alone, give it a bloody rest mother, why can't you be happy for me' I screamed in her face, immediately backing down when I seen the hurt look on her face.

'Trust me,' I said. But my mother knew better than that. She had been down this road with me before. Once again, she brought me to the hospital but not before I vehemently protested against going. My mother had to call my doctor, who then somehow managed to cool me down enough over the phone to convince me to go willingly. When we got to the hospital, they admitted me immediately and once again I had to be sedated. Being hospitalized at Cornell was the only similarity between my first and second admission. It was a totally different experience and an incredible turning point in my illness. In many ways, I needed those twenty days to completely alter the course of my life.

Although I was in the same hospital, I was in a different wing. I also wasn't depressed. In fact, I was upbeat and fairly content with my surroundings. The first time I had felt so alone. I didn't talk to anyone and only interacted with others when I absolutely had to. This time, I was quite popular and made many friends. There were about six or seven of us who would eat our meals together and then hang out, talking for hours. The topics were not incredibly important nor were they memorable but I do recall how pleasant the time was. Rather than sitting alone in my room for endless hours, I interacted with the other patients, playing checkers and Ping-Pong, or sitting in the common area watching the US Open.

I would also talk to the patients who were completely alone. These were the people who never spoke to anybody – the people who were just like me the first time I'd been hospitalised. Since I had been through this whole process before, I possessed that slight edge of being somewhat of a veteran. I utilized all the confidence that it brought, to help others through the first-time anxiety I had once experienced. This confidence was assisted by my own natural tendency to always want other people to feel comfortable and included. Even during my school and college days, I made the effort to find the new, unpopular, or quiet ones, to be their first friend, and to help them make more of their time. Now, in the hospital, it was no different. In fact, seeking out the wallflowers and helping them to blossom and come alive again was a part of my own healing process.

Not only was I socialising and a little more familiar with the whole hospitalisation process, but this second time around, my overall mood was just a bit different. I had a sense of being very much in control. Clearly it showed, because a lot of the other patients would question me as to why I was even there at all. During the first hospitalisation, I was in a room by myself and would have been miserable if I had a roommate. This time, I shared one with Lisa, an American girl my age who had graduated from NYU. Lisa was married and worked for some large financial institution. She was smart and easy to talk with and we got along pretty well.

I also willingly attended the group therapy sessions this time, whereas before, I hated group therapy. I had considered it very childish, attending once and never returning. This time I actually enjoyed the sessions. I saw that people from all walks of life had mental issues, many very similar to my own and that was comforting. At night there was a group of about ten or twelve of us who would hang out after therapy and just talk for long hours.

It also helped when I saw other people taking their medication. Here were smart and functioning people taking pills, too. They were out in the world doing great things with full and busy days but they needed medication for the rest of their lives too. This, for me, was a monumental realisation. It almost completely lifted the enormous social stigma I had mounted on my own shoulders and freed me to begin moving forward with a new self-assurance. Although my second stay in the hospital was a relatively happy one, I was very angry with my mother for putting me there again. I made unrealistic plans of breaking free from them and making a life of my own as soon as I was out of the hospital. I began dreaming: I would move out of my parents' house, get a job in New York City and support myself.

The idea made me feel strong and in control, but in reality this dream wasn't feasible. I had no means of supporting myself outside the protected environment of the hospital. I did not have the mental stability to get a decent job nor was I trained to earn my own living. I had not grown up believing that I could and should have a career. I liked the idea of being on my own but was completely dependent on my family financially, and was in a mentally unsound and unstable condition. Though it was painful to finally accept the truth, I realised that I was in fact lucky that my parents were supporting me. I would otherwise have been in real trouble.

When I was released from the hospital twenty days later and went to our home in Long Island, that wretched sense of emptiness began, once again, to insidiously seep its way into my soul. Maybe that apartment reminded me of the first time I had been hospitalised or maybe it was just getting back to reality. In the hospital I had a group of friends to hang out with, people who were in a similar situation as I was and who understood. It was a safe, controlled environment. Facing real life was a stark contrast. I began attending an outpatient therapy group four days a week for several hours at a time. There, a group of us met with three facilitators. Sometimes we'd all talk together; other times we'd break up into smaller groups with just one of the instructors. We would discuss our lives and our struggles. This was the first time that I talked to other people – strangers, no less – about the deeply painful subject of my illness. I opened up to them as if they were old friends I'd known all my life.

Every time we got together, I'd look around the group amazed at the mix of people, both young and old from all walks of life. There was an NYU student who was clearly very bright and well-read. There was a professor from Columbia University who was probably in his early 50's, and a businessman who ran a huge, well-known corporation. There were other people too, some in college, graduates from top universities and others with prestigious careers. Not exactly the picture of hopelessness I was afraid I was becoming.

At one of the first meetings, the girl from NYU, a very pretty girl with thick, shiny hair and dark eyes, bravely looked up and said. 'I'm going to meet a few of my friends tomorrow and I'm really worried.' With eyes lowered, she nervously folded and re-folded a small square of paper. 'I don't know what to talk about, so I've been reading the newspaper so I have topics.'

I was stunned. I had seen this girl for several days around the hospital and every time I saw her I thought she was one of the most confident people I had ever met. Clearly, she was intelligent and yet she was worried about making small talk and sounding stupid. I knew exactly what she was talking about. I had been there.

Then another woman, probably in her mid-thirties, who had a high-powered position at an advertising agency, spoke up. 'My insurance covers this hospital stay, but if my employer finds out that I have this kind of depression, they may discriminate against me,' she said. 'They may think I'm not competent, not up to the job.'

Each session was just like this, with everyone revealing what they felt inside. The people were so different from me, and yet their emotions and fears mirrored mine. If I had seen any of them on the street, I'd never imagine that they were going through a mental illness. For lack of a better word they seemed so 'normal'.

Through them, I realised there were other people – successful, bright people – who suffered from the same illness that I did, and many others besides. Illness that pulled them away from their everyday lives. They showed me that having bipolar isn't something to be ashamed of. It wasn't something that I did wrong, it wasn't something I chose and it wasn't a reflection of me. It was part of me, yes, but it didn't define me. For the first time, I realised I was not alone. I was not the only person in the world who had this illness.

Some of us became friends and quite enjoyed going out for a coffee or making other plans outside of our group therapy sessions. Not everyone, though, was eager to be found in the same social scene as their therapy buddies. One girl in particular was surprised one day to find me in the same elevator as her as I was returning from a doctor's appointment. I was just about to say 'hello' to her and to the three friends she was with, when it became clear that she did not want to acknowledge me. It was peculiar enough but I understood completely. Aside from her, most of us were perfectly content to make plans together. We'd been through something together and we all wanted to keep in touch. A friendship had been born, through much struggle and was not to be easily broken.

One day, I found myself talking a little about my country to one of my therapy friends during an evening out. She was curious to know all about Bangladesh, knowing so little about the tiny country tucked into a little pocket under India. I began relating to her the endless, beautiful fields of rice paddies that cover the land outside of the bustling city of Dhaka, their long thin grasses flowing like bright green waves under the gentle breezes from the wide-open skies. It is a breath-taking picture and one would hardly realise how fragile the plant really is. Its cultivation process is specifically designed to nurture and strengthen it for the harsh, uncertain environmental conditions it will face. And in that moment, with my friend, I felt a connection with the earth like none I had ever experienced.

The tender rice seedlings are originally planted very close together, in a very small space, the individual seeds are able to flourish in an environment where they are supported and protected by one another. When they are tall enough and strong enough, helped by their neighbours, they are lifted up and planted in large, wide open fields. Far from one another so they have room to grow and are ready to thrive.

If they had not been kept originally in close quarters with another, feeding off of each other's strength and protection, they would never be prepared for the instability they would face: the sudden, fierce Bangladeshi storms, or the torrents of rain that will flood their roots or, the annual cyclones. Those tender rice seedlings, delicate and fragile that they are, when given the close support and strength of their neighbours, are meant to survive.

The nurture and protection we could offer one another, in those few hours each week, helped to develop in us the root systems and the fortitude we would need to be planted in the real world, the wide open spaces of life. In such a place there were many harsh, uncertain conditions we would face and though our daily lives and the demands of work took us to very different places, those tender hours together helped give us what we needed to grow.

The friendships I had formed in my therapy group were giving me the support I needed to face life outside of the hospital. Taking my medication regularly was bringing back stability to my mind. My gradual acceptance of my bipolar disorder was giving me the courage to move towards life. The frozen tree trunk had thawed and the blossoms were beginning to open.

Chapter 10
Help is on the Way

"I crawled back into bed and pulled the sheet over my head.
I had nothing to look forward to."

Sylvia Plath

If you're really lucky, you just might meet at least one person who truly changes your life. I met that person, she not only changed my life, she saved it.

I continued to attend my group therapy sessions throughout the week and gained an incredible amount of support and confidence, not to mention wonderful new friends, in doing so. I eagerly looked forward to each session and had become quite comfortable sharing my thoughts, emotions, fears and small successes with the group. Individual therapy, on the other hand, was the bane of my existence.

Every psychiatrist, therapist or counsellor I had spilled my guts to so far had been rather difficult to connect with. To be honest, it felt like I was talking to a brick wall. There was absolutely no reciprocity and I could never understand their body language; sitting stiffly at a distance I always felt like I was being interviewed and they were waiting to catch me out. There must be a handbook somewhere explaining the nature of this mechanical therapist-patient relationship but I have never seen it. How anyone is supposed to open up, talk, and begin a healing process, in an environment that is cold, while also expecting to avoid any sort of emotional connection, is beyond me.

Every doctor I had seen made it clear that I was not to ask them any personal questions about themselves, as this was breaching the doctor-patient boundary. To them, this was professional; to me, it was cold.

There was no connection, only distance and it didn't work. On the odd day or two when it did work, and I was brave enough to open up about my emotions, I ended up being shot down by the timing of it. I would sit through a forty-five-minute session and not feel comfortable enough to reveal my deepest thoughts and anxieties until minute forty. Five minutes later, regardless of emotion or state my time would be up and the conversation ended with a sardonic smile and a tapping of the watch. I would stand up to leave the office, while trying to pick my heart and guts off the floor. I would vow to never share anything again.

During one therapy session with Dr. Churchin, I began trying to re-address a topic very personal and important to me. She looked at me quizzically, brows furrowed and finger on chin, as if hearing it for the first time.

'I told you about this.' I said ashamed.

'I don't remember that,' she said, shaking her head and shrugging her shoulders. 'You can't expect me to remember everything, can you?'

I'd never connected with Dr. Churchin from day one and knew in that moment there would be no other opportunities to do so. As expected, this was exactly how yet another session was going.

One day, as she attempted in vain to get me to open up while I tried to tune her out, she announced to me that she would be going on vacation and would be referring me to another doctor in her absence.

Oh, great. What a fantastic idea. Subjecting me to yet another therapist. It's what I've always wanted. I was less than excited to say the least. However, I figured that I could easily tune-out my new psychiatrist, Dr. Anna, too.

For our first appointment Dr. Anna suggested we book a double session – almost two hours – so I could fill her in on my health history, my life, etc. I prepared to meet with yet another doctor. On the day of the appointment, I arrived at Dr. Anna's office only to find she wasn't there. I waited and waited, getting more annoyed as the minutes passed. I am a very punctual person so the longer I waited, the more restless I became, pacing up and down the corridor, wondering whether I had made the right decision to meet with her. After twenty minutes I was furious. I had just picked up my hand bag and began marching in the direction of the elevator when I looked up saw a woman rushing down the hallway towards me.

'I'm Dr. Anna, 'she said breathless but smiling. My first thought was that she was a little too casually dressed for a doctor, wearing beige slacks and a white shirt with her hair pulled back loosely into a ponytail. Something about her felt right and my anger dissolved. I felt instantly calmed… if still somewhat hesitant. I tentatively made a mental note that this might not so bad, and entered her office.

Dr. Anna did not have the air of a typical psychiatrist, as she rambled on about the reason for her delay and dragged a pair of chairs over for us to sit on, I was surprised by the amazing feeling of connection and comfort that washed over me. My instincts told me that I could trust her. She was very understanding of Bangladeshi culture because she had been to that side of the world. She wasn't 'stuck up' like the other psychiatrists I had met over the last five years and she didn't keep her distance.

There was an unconventional openness about her. She was warm and kind, so when she asked 'how are you?' I reciprocated with:

'What about you?' I was shocked and delighted when she casually responded, telling me about her hectic morning.

I know that not every patient asked Dr. Anna those kinds of questions or cared to. But for me it was different. I was revealing myself to her so I wanted to know about her life. Where did she grow up? Was she married? How many children did she have? The fact that she didn't mind these queries spoke volumes to me. Sitting in her office was as comfortable as sitting with an old friend and yet I also felt like she could take care of me, that she could really help me.

Dr. Anna was the first therapist who seemed to understand that every person has a different state of mind and varying emotions and needs—I wanted to see her. I looked forward to it. Dr. Anna not only listened but she understood what I was talking about. Initially, I was only to see her while Dr. Churchin was on vacation but after a very short time the differences between them had become too great.

After only a few sessions, I told Dr. Anna, 'I want you to be my regular doctor. I'm very comfortable with you.' She agreed, I never went back to Dr. Churchin and I didn't miss her for one single second.

When I returned to Bangladesh, Dr. Anna and Dr. Imran, my psychiatrist in Dhaka, regularly consulted with one another about my treatment. Dr. Anna even continued counselling me in Bangladesh via weekly telephone calls from New York.

Our meetings were not very regular but despite that, her help was immeasurable.

'When are you coming to Bangladesh?' I asked her at one of

our first phone meetings, 'I need you.' I could not see her, but I could almost hear her smile.

Over the years, Dr. Anna has seen me during very trying and difficult times, the worst moments of my life, and been there for the joys. She knows everything about me – truthfully, she knows more about me than my husband. She has seen everything and has patiently accompanied my personal growth to bring me to where I am today and I've told her a lot of things that I've never shared with anyone. She helped me achieve a balance, so that I could gain control of my illness.

One of those ways was helping me find the right medication. She understood and helped me see that when it came to bipolar disorder, there is no one-size-fits-all prescription and finding the right one that works for any one person can, sometimes, be the most difficult aspect of recovery. Fortunately for me she introduced me to a drug called Seroquel, now with time and armed with the right medication it felt as though the fog was lifting and my view of the world was becoming clearer. I felt more alert, energetic and calm. In turn, this feeling of being more like the old me, of seeing life more clearly, was just another little jolt of confidence on my road to recovery. Another one of those tiny steps that, when added to all the others, was getting me back to an even better version of my former self.

Today, after over a decade of on and off counselling, Dr. Anna has become more like a friend than my psychiatrist. I never imagined that there could be a doctor like her and actually I don't think there are many like her, but one thing I know for sure: I am convinced that Dr. Anna was sent to this world to rescue me when I was sinking, I know that I couldn't have stayed afloat without her.

Part 2

New Beginnings

Chapter 11
Zayef

"Your task is not to seek for love, but merely to seek and find all the barriers within yourself that you have built against it."

Rumi

One year went by without any dramatic incident and then another. We all returned to our home in Dhaka, not long after I found myself across a table from my father. He rested his hand on my own and in a deeper-than-usual voice began. 'Aalinna, you're 24 now.'

I knew exactly where this was going and gave him a warning look. Marriage was still not quite on my radar, though it had remained an erstwhile priority to my parents. He took the hint. My mother, who sat nearby pretending to read a novel, let out an almost imperceptible sigh before resigning herself to her paperback.

My parents knew it was no use forcing me into something I did not yet feel ready for. As much as they would have loved to see me married, more than anything they just wanted me to be and stay healthy, to have a smile on my face.

We had a mutual understanding on these grounds and it constituted an injection of independence. I had the freedom to learn to live again, to find stability again – maybe, possibly, kind of – and to do so without the pressure of matrimonial commitments.

My moods remained, but by now I had accepted my bipolar

disorder and the medication and the sleeping patterns. I even began to work with my father. It was ideal for me, my father understood the importance of my sleep pattern to my well-being. Whilst I was treated like any other employee and got no special treatment, he understood what other employers would have seen as laziness. If I hadn't had enough sleep the night before because of a restless night or was battered by my medication half way through the day, I could adjust my hours to suit, though I would still have to make my hours up like everyone else.

I enjoyed the work and found I was good at it; I don't deny the link between the two things. Nonetheless, it was something in which we both took great pride. I realised that the many procedures and routines of the office were acutely tuned to soothing anxiety, more so than simply not having the time to let it take hold, as it did in New York. At first I dared to spend time hanging out with some old friends, but it proved to be difficult. They'd known me in the past; I still felt that I could not live up to their expectations to be the old me again.

Rebounding from these cut ties, I became a regular at the Gulshan Club where my cousin Maher hung out. Social as ever, I began to become good friends with his crowd. They were regular patrons of this upper class establishment though it wasn't them that made it famously highbrow, nor the Club part, more the Gulshan part. This area of central Dhaka was a bustling business metropolis with offices of major Western, European and local companies, as well as famous hotels and Embassies.

Maher was now engaged to a beautiful girl called Ema. We were the same age and soon became friends. One afternoon when I arrived I was greeted by an excited Maher.

'Come, Aalinna look who is here,' he said, dragging me across the room to a window table. A guy around my age stood up as we approached. Tall, fair hair, *hmm… pretty cute!* If I recall my assessment.

'Hi, Aalinna. It's good to see you again.'

Zayef. He had, for almost as long as any of us could remember, been best friends with Maher.

'Oh! Zayef,' I said, embracing him in a sisterly hug. 'I'm sorry, I didn't recognise you at first, and it's been so long.' In fact, the last time we had met was at Aunt Sabera's house when Samama died. Zayef had flown to Dhaka and then to Canada to support Maher and the family and to bring her body home.

He laughed at my surprise and before long we were chatting like old friends. Zayef told me how he had finished his undergrad at Rutgers in New Jersey and had begun working for a well-known firm. He had now been back in Dhaka for the last six months.

'As you have probably heard my father has been… unwell. I've had to come back here to run the family business.' His shoulders slumped, 'I really wanted to settle in America – my girlfriend is still over there.' He went silent for the first time since starting the conversation, the club stirred around us.

'But hey, maybe it won't be so bad here,' he laughed, a little embarrassed. 'Sorry, I've just spent the last hour talking about me, tell me what's been happening with you,' he said, slapping the table, 'I'm all ears!'

Thankful for the brief window granted by his summoning of a waiter, I fumbled around with my reply. *Oh you know, I've had a few psychotic breaks, in counselling, and on some serious medication but apart from that life's just dandy.*

'Come on,' I said, standing up, 'don't worry about another drink in here, let's go sit outside with the others – I've kept you to myself long enough.'

I skipped off with him following me, laughing. I was relieved when we got outside to find that the others kept him busy in conversation and that my answer to his question had been avoided.

The next time I saw Zayef at the club, he asked me to play doubles with him in the upcoming badminton tournament. Badminton was played everywhere in Bangladesh . Lines would be drawn in the street and nets put up across narrow streets and car-parks. Young, old, male and female could be seen playing in the late evening after work, with only the light from the balconies of the looming apartments or the headlights of the flowing traffic. There were no street lights in Dhaka then.

The Gulshan club was also a sight to be seen at this time of year, when it would be draped in fairy lights, outside and in. The walls around the pool and badminton courts twinkling blue and white, mirroring the stars shinning in the night sky. I loved badminton and I was actually pretty good at it, having been the singles champion three times in a row when I was at school. Still, I didn't feel very confident about playing as I hadn't played any sport since my diagnosis.

'Come on, Aalinna. We've got two weeks to practice, it will be fun,' Zayef yelled over the music. 'Plus, everyone else has a regular partner they pair up with each year and being the newbie I have no one to play with.' I felt a sense of excitement, and competitiveness get the better of me … I happily agreed.

We were becoming good friends. I found Zayef to be a really sweet guy in a way I had never noticed when we were younger. I was amazed at his intelligence – he was very well read and his down-to-earth nature never betrayed any sort of haughtiness. Becoming friends with him was easy and comfortable. The more we got to know each other, the greater the comfort.

One day, when we were talking after badminton practice, I confided in him about my bipolar. It wasn't an intentional thing;

it was just as comfortable as every other topic. He had been telling me that he and his girlfriend had broken up because of the sheer distance between them. The conversation segued into the difficult relationship he had with his father.

To my astonishment, Zayef didn't appear phased at all about my bipolar. Instead he was more sympathetic and curious. He came to know all about my bipolar disorder and my two hospitalisations in New York. As I very openly and honestly confided in him about the details of my life in the past couple of years, I was struck by how much I was able to share with him and still feel so normal. This was what it meant to have a best friend.

The two weeks that we practiced for the tournament were great fun and I enjoyed sitting together, drinking, chatting and enjoying the cool night air after a practice session. It was on one of those nights that Zayef revealed to me that he liked Raeesa, who was a friend of Ema's. I could understand why, she was very pretty and always good fun when we were out, but what I couldn't understand was why my heart sank when he told me. I lay in bed that night replaying his words and trying to re-feel my reaction, was I jealous? Was I falling for Zayef?

The following day, when we were practicing on the court, the two players next to us commented that we made a nice couple and looked cute together. I was beginning to harbour hopes that Zayef liked me and found myself quite excited by the prospect, but a few days later when we were once again being teased about what a nice couple we would make, Zayef put me and everyone else straight.

'Right,' he said, putting down his racket and turning to the culprits, 'let's get this straight. Aalinna and I are nothing but good friends, OK? I don't want her being made to feel uncomfortable.'

On the way back to the car to go home Zayef caught me by

the hand and took me aside. I was surprised to find my heart pump faster at his touch.

'Look, Aalinna I'm sorry about all that teasing. I've been getting it for a while now, so I felt it was time I put a stop to it. You're so special to me and our friendship means so much that I don't want to lose it because of silly teasing.'

I managed to laugh it off, to tell him not to worry, and that I had taken no notice. Now at least I knew he saw me as no more than a friend. The day of the tournament arrived and we played pretty well, reaching the semi-final. Afterwards, all the participants went out for dinner including myself, Zayef, Maher, Ema and Raeesa. We had all begun to hang out together a lot normally at one of our houses, depending on whose house was free. Zayef and I were still seeing each other often and talking on the phone every day. Things got a little more complicated when Zayef began dating Raeesa. When he talked to me about her, I would listen and give him advice as a dutiful friend. I would smile and return eye contact.

One day, a friend, Izan, invited us all for dinner. It was a great evening with a lot of laughs and flowing wine. As the evening went on I noticed Zayef and Raeesa more and more, each flirtatious comment, each instance of whispering in each other's ear and shuffling closer together. I took a drink for every time they did this and before long I was completely wasted.

'Shit, we can't let her go home in that state her parents will freak out, 'said Maher, noticing me in the chair in the corner gulping another glass of Merlot. It was swiftly organized that while they tried to sober me up with coffee, Maryam – who had received a hasty call from Maher – would encourage my parents to go out for dinner, allowing them to get me home to my room unseen.

*

When I awoke in my room the next morning, I promptly hid back under the covers. I scoured my thumping head for any bad behaviour from the night before. *What is wrong with me? Why did I react like that? Making a fool of myself.* For the first time ever I realised I was interested in someone who simply wasn't interested in me back. Zayef liked Raeesa. I vowed to accept it and move on. The last thing I wanted was to lose Zayef as a friend. In a moment of telepathy, the phone rang.

'Hey, how's the head?' He teased.

'Not too bad,' I lied. 'Sorry about last night, I obviously didn't realise how much I'd had to drink.'

'No worries, as long as you're OK. You are OK, aren't you, Aalinna?'

'Just one too many.' I forced a casual laugh.

'OK, well, great. I'll catch you soon, bye for now.'

I put the phone down, vowing to pull myself together.

We all continued to hang out. I got more used to seeing Zayef and Raeesa together. Zayef and I remained friends, socialising within the group and talking on the phone regularly. Still, the whole situation had set me thinking. I was 24 years old now, hanging out with all these couples. I realised I might be open to a relationship myself.

I told my parents that I was open to the idea of meeting a man and I can still see my mother's face. It was like all her prayers had been answered. It gave me a thrill to be finally making a choice that made her so happy, after all I had put her through. As for my father he simply smiled and gave me a wink, he didn't need to say anymore.

It didn't take long for my mother to start the wheels turning and pretty soon she had arranged for me to meet with a guy at his parents' house. This was common practice in Bangladesh at the time and still is now, to an extent, though the rules of dating are a bit more relaxed. Now young people can meet up in public, at a restaurant or even a party to date, whereas my friends and I were not allowed to be seen alone together publicly and could be arrested if caught. This resulted in us often doing our dating by driving around in the car and maybe trying to find a quiet place to stop to talk, or even risk a kiss. Dating back then was also hindered by the fact that whilst living at home, a girl would be curfewed to 9.00 pm and male visitors to the house were taboo, regardless of age.

The guy I was meeting was called Abeed. This was the first time I was actually meeting someone when we would both know why we were there, as opposed to one of my mother's ambushes. Whilst it was initially awkward, Abeed was a nice guy and we soon relaxed. He lived in California and worked for an I.T. company, he also came from a 'good' family and was classed as a 'good' catch. After the first meeting I called Zayef for moral support.

'Hi,' I said when he answered.

'Hey, how's you?'

'Actually I'm not sure, good, I think.'

'Sounds ominous. Tell me more.'

'Well,' I began, 'I have just come back from a date with Abeed. You know, the guy my parents had set a meeting up with. He seemed really nice and I think I'd like to see him again, which surprises even me,' I added a nervous giggle. There was a long silence.

'Hey, you still there?'

'Yeah, look Aalinna, I'm going to have to run I was just on my way out.'

'Oh, OK.' I replied, a little crestfallen. *He'll probably call me back tonight.*

'*OK*, catch you soon.' I said cheerily.

I didn't hear from Zayef that night or the next.

In the meantime, a friend of mine had given Abeed my number. He called and we spoke for an hour. It was fun to be so normal and relaxed. Now on a high, I called Zayef again to share my excitement and get some advice. I was in the midst of telling him all about Abeed and how we had talked for so long, when Zayef finally piped up.

'Give it a rest, Aalinna! I've better things to do than listen to you gushing on. I need to call Raeesa.' He roared down the phone.

'Hey! What the hell's wrong with you? Why are you being so rude?' I screamed back.

'Aalinna I don't have time for this bullshit.'

I was astonished. I put down the phone. I catalogued his unfairness, the hours I had spent listening to his problems on the phone – to his bullshit. I vowed not to speak to him until he called back and apologised.

Abeed invited me out to dinner – this was acceptable as we had been introduced by our parents and they had agreed to our meeting. My parents really liked Abeed, he was everything they would have wanted for me, perfect husband material. I trusted my parent's judgement and was happy to continue seeing him.

As always though, my bipolar was never far from my mind. The weekly counselling and daily medication was there to remind me, but I was happy. I felt really settled and – dare I say – normal for the first in a long time, but my old doctor's words kept coming back to haunt me.

Never get into any relationship, that includes any sort of emotional attachment, this will only aggravate the situation. About 90% of marriages, where one partner suffers from bipolar disorder, fail.

*

With dating Abeed becoming a regular occurrence, the alliance between myself and my parents prospered. As we were getting on so well I decided to invite him to the Gulshan Club, where Abeed could become one of our number. Though first, the inevitable had to happen, I would have to introduce him to Zayef. We still hadn't spoken since *that* last phone call. Whilst Abeed and I sat waiting at the club in the cool night air, I looked up and saw my friends tripping and lolloping between the tables, smiling and waving as they approached and filtering into the half a dozen remaining seats with greetings and glasses.

'Zayef,' an outstretched hand appeared before Abeed, Zayef remained standing, ignoring the vacant seat.

'Hi,' said Abeed, shaking his hand, smiling.

Suddenly Zayef immediately turned on his heels and left the Gulshan Club, shoving through the door in a burst of light and roaring traffic. Fortunately, the others didn't notice but Maher and I had.

Seething, I called Zayef a few days later to have it out. I began by telling him I never would have expected this kind of behaviour from him.

Silence came back through the receiver.

'I wanted to share things with you, Zayef. Very personal things.'

Nothing.

'I wanted to be there for you when you shared very personal things.'

I could hear him breathing and little else.

'What is wrong with you?' I asked him. Still no reply. I gave up and hovered the receiver over the phone. I was just about to end the call when I heard his voice.

'You're my best friend,' he said. 'My best friend, who I didn't want to see close to another man. I couldn't stand it.'

Now it was my turn to be silent.

'What do you see in Abeed?'

'He's nice, he's smart and my parents happen to quite like him.'

'You were flirting with him, Aalinna'

'Yes and?'

'The man is a nerd.'

'No, he is not' I squeezed the receiver and kneaded the cord between my fingers. 'At least the man knows how to talk to me, how to be sweet to me.'

'Bullshit. I hate him.'

I slumped on the counter, propping my chin on my forearm. I turned to kneading my fingers through my hair instead. 'Why?'

'I don't know, I know he is not good for you.'

'And who are you to decide this?'

'Your best friend,' he began 'I want my best friend back, my close friend back.'

Sinking myself lower into the counter did nothing to help me imagine a reply.

'I want you to stop ignoring me, to stop shutting me out,' Zayef went on, 'I wanted to share something very important with you.'

I took the bait.

'Go on, share something'

'We are friends. But you, you are so special to me.'

'OK, so does that mean I can't like anyone else?'

'You can't like Abeed. I can't stand the man.'

'You said that.' About twenty minutes ago, according to the clock. 'Zayef, you met him once. For five minutes.'

Silence once more.

'What is it you want from me?'

'I don't know,' he admitted.

'Well then, find out and call me back in the morning. I'm falling asleep here.' I lied, I wouldn't be sleeping tonight. 'I'm sick and tired, Zayef. And you're not helping.' I flipped the receiver over once more and lay it down on the hook. No sooner had I put it down when it rang again. On snatching it up I was initially disappointed to hear Maher's voice. I immediately began telling him about the conversation I had just had with Zayef and how fed up I was getting with it all.

'You saw his behaviour towards Abeed the other night at the club, what is his problem?!'

'Come on, Aalinna. Don't you get it? He has feelings for you, deep feelings – he never shuts up about you.'

I realised that this was secretly what I had been hoping for. I wasn't used to being the one with the feelings. The one who had to do the chasing. I decided to play it cool and wait it out.

*

For a period, it was quite literally the case that my evening telephone conversations with Abeed blocked any further calls from coming through and inadvertently spared me from another awkward back and forth with Zayef. After one of these calls with Abeed I brought the receiver down on the phone with a smile on my face and my bed beckoning. Immediately, it rang again, giving me a start. Zayef. My stomach flipped over.

'I've been trying to call you for two hours.'

'I've been on the phone to Abeed.'

'I'm coming to your house. I need to see you.'

'And what should I tell my parents?' I snapped back?

'That you are going out with Maher and Ema.'

'And?'

'And really you'll join me, for a short drive.'

So I had got the attention and the high drama I wanted, I was scared, excited and thrilled, but I still had to ensure my cover wasn't blown.

I needn't have worried. Maher had put a plan in place that gave Zayef and me a few hours. We drove with only the low radio breaking the silence, I sneaked a look at Zayef, watching as his face lit up by the headlights of the oncoming traffic. God, he was handsome. I couldn't believe how excited and happy he made me feel just being around him, I'd never felt like this around a man before, I had been out with plenty of boys but it was normally me who was nonchalant. I had enjoyed the thrill of being admired and having fun, seeing what the new experience would bring with no real care or commitment to whether it lasted or not. But now with Zayef it all mattered and I was doing the admiring, I realised I really cared.

The harsh totting of the horns and persistent ringing of the rickshaw driver's bells began to fade into the distance as we left the bustle of the city behind and turned off the bypass on to a quiet country road. Here only the sound of the bullfrogs and the occasional cattle's mooing could be heard. Zayef brought the car to a stop in the middle of three towering husks which were soon to be condominiums, currently cocooned in scaffolding and breezeblocks. The building site looked alien in the lush countryside. Deserted and silent until the workers returned with first light. Once stopped we sat a few moments in silence. Now that the moment had come and we were finally alone neither of us seemed to know where to begin.

'Hey,' I said quietly, causing Zayef to finally turn and look at me, I smiled reassuringly, realising he was as nervous as me. His hand slid over and took mine from my lap.

'Aalinna I need you to be mine, I can't take it, I can't bear the thought of you with anyone but me. I have tried, really tried, to not feel this way.' He bowed his head now appearing relieved to have finally said it out loud.

Now it had been said out loud and all the shouting and game playing had stopped, I could see that I truly felt the same way and had done so for a long time. I felt a flood of relief rush through my body and let out a long breath that I felt I'd been holding for months.

I lifted Zayef's face to look at mine, putting a hand on each cheek.

'Me too,' I said.

His eyes widened and we both began to laugh with relief, giggling like two teenage sweethearts. As our laughter and nervousness eased we slipped into a soft long hug. All the previous arguing and rights and wrongs of what we were getting into put aside, at least for that moment.

We continued to meet in secret, needing to be with each other. We would talk for hours, sharing our secrets, hopes and fears. Slowly however, our guilt at our deception of Raeesa and Abeed began to raise its head. We knew what we were doing was wrong and we weren't being fair to them. Many times we vowed to stop meeting, taking it in turns to let our guilt rightfully overwhelm us.

'This has to stop, Zayef. Last night when we were all having dinner together I felt so bad. Raeesa was being so sweet to me and telling me how much she cared about you, I felt sick.' But our feelings for each other were stronger than any other emotion and we continued until one night, when fate took over.

*

Ironically, as we sat in the car one night discussing our guilt at our deception, things were taken out of our hands.

'I know, sweetheart, 'said Zayef.

'I just don't know where we should go from here.'

As he pulled me into a hug we looked into each other's eyes and leaned in to kiss, suddenly our faces were illuminated by a harsh light shining in through the rear window. Initially thinking it was simply another car with another young couple seeking privacy, we moved apart waiting for them to pass but once we saw the pulse of the blue lights we knew we were in trouble.

We were escorted to the police station. After questioning as to what we had been doing and why we were out alone so late, a policeman proceeded to give me a lecture on my virtue, and Zayef a stern warning about taking, and having a young lady out alone, especially without the permission of her parents.

This went on for a hours. It was eventually decided that as Zayef's parents were out of the country, he could leave once some friends came and vouched for him. I was not to be so lucky given that I was a woman and the late hour I would not be allowed to leave without my parents coming to collect me. I was sick with fear and nerves. My parents were called and I awaited their arrival. My thoughts jumped continuously between fear of my parent's reaction, worrying about Zayef and the shame we would bring on poor Abeed and Raeesa if this got out. Each time I looked down at my watch I had frayed more and more of my jumper sleeve by kneading my fingers through the weave in an anxious fit. I rocked the bench I sat on into a squeak jumping at every croak of the bullfrog.

Zayef's friends arrived and were just giving some details when the door opened and my father entered. I froze in shock. Zayef stopped talking and turned on hearing the door, only to be caught in my father's glare which then swung to me. I was rooted to the seat.

'Get in the car. Now.' I had never heard my father so angry. As I headed for the door I watched my father compose himself as he approached the desk.

I got in and sat in the rear passenger seat of my father's car. My mother occupied the seat next to me but she hadn't turned away from the window when I entered the car. We sat in silence until my father got behind the wheel. Through the sting of air conditioning, I could feel my father's anger radiate from the driver's seat – I wondered if he had deliberately dismissed his driver, not wanting him to see his shame.

So I sat, calculating my explanation. The car rumbled underneath me and the engine started. My mother and father continued staring out of the car windows, seemingly at nothing. The car chugged into reverse gear and rolled away from the hedgerow lining the perimeter of the police station. My father began speaking as he wheeled around:

'It's a good thing,' he began, breaking my mother's trance. 'It's a good thing that you like Abeed, but these things, this behaviour… it is a step backwards for you, Aalinna. Abeed is a decent man, we thought you were happy,' he continued, turning to me and rolling the car forward, 'But such acts will harm his reputation and yours.'

Oh God. He obviously thought this was a one-off thing, one of my crazy bipolar moments. Whilst I found it annoying that anything I did, out of the norm was put down to my bipolar, this was not the time to argue the point nor inform him that Abeed was no longer for me. I stayed quiet, my parents had had enough excitement for one night.

We drove in silence. I played a game of glimpsing the sky past the tall buildings lining the streets. With each one that passed the sky grew paler and dawn rose up. I closed my eyes and counted the rights and the lefts, two of each were left until we arrived home but my eyelids wouldn't reopen and my hands relaxed for the first time that night.

I awoke in the car to birdsong and a blanket of new heat. I was alone in the car with my door and the front door to the house wide open. I dragged myself to the front steps and looked back at the morning and, at our closed gates where the occasional rickshaw zoomed past. I entered the house and made my way to the living room. My father occupied one of the chairs in front of the garden facing window and my mother the other.

'Aalinna?' we stared at each other, him waiting for an explanation, me not having one. 'Why were you with Zayef last night?'

'We just went to hang out. To talk.'

'You were alone with him?'

'I was.'

My father looked at my mother who had such a look of disappointment on her face I wanted to cry. Yet again had I disappointed her, to be fair she was the one who would have to face Abeed's mother and the shame of my behaviour if this got out? Finally, my father exploded.

'What is going on with you? What about Abeed?! God Aalinna how dare you shame us like this. Have we not been through enough? We thought you were happy. Settled.'

He was right of course.

'Just get out, leave us, go.'

As I softly closed the lounge door and turned to go upstairs

I was surprised to see Maryam sitting on the stairs listening. She gave me a look of disgust and shaking her head said, 'God, Aalinna it never ends with you does it?' She marched past me, head up and nose high. She walked out through the front door, slamming it behind her.

This day is just getting better and better. I went to my room. Once I had sat down on the bed, finally alone, I realised I was shaking. What had we done? I had to call Zayef. On lifting the phone, I found the line was busy and when I listened closer I could hear my fathers raised voice coming from his study.

'Did you know about this? She is your cousin I trusted you to look out for her.' Silence, I could only assume Maher was trying to respond – he obviously didn't get much chance as my father started up again. 'What kind of man is this Zayef? I thought he had a girlfriend and anyway, what kind of man takes a young woman out alone without her parent's permission, especially at that time of night?!'

Another short pause then my father's voice again. 'Well I am disappointed in you, Maher. I will go now, but I trust I have made myself clear.' I then heard the phone slammed down.

I put my hands on my head, how many more people were we going to hurt with our deception? This could not continue. Once I heard my father descend the stairs I reached for the phone, the line now clear, I dialled Maher. It rang out for a long time before he finally answered.

'Hi,' I said sheepishly.

'Shit, Aalinna. I've just had your father on and he is not a happy man.'

'I know, I heard, I'm so sorry.'

'He was going crazy about it all, thankfully Zayef called me as soon as he got out of the police station so I knew what was going on, and what was coming. I tried to explain to your father that Zayef does care about you deeply and is a good guy but I think he was too angry to hear it.'

'God, Maher I'm so sorry you have been dragged into this as well, I will sort it, I promise.' The first thing I had to do was talk to Zayef.

He answered with his voice croaky.

'Hello.'

'Hi.'

'Oh, thank God it's you, Aalinna. I have been so worried but too scared to call in case I got you in even more trouble.'

'I don't think that would be possible. What have we done?' I was now crying and shaking, finally letting go on hearing his voice.

'Oh, please do not distress yourself we will sort this out, my friends that picked me up last night have sworn not to tell anyone and I'm sure your parents won't. So at least Abeed and Raeesa won't get to know about it.'

'That's not the point.' I sniffled.

'I know, I know, I am just trying to limit the damage as much as possible.'

'I think we're a bit late to be doing that, even poor Maher has been dragged into it. My father has just got off of the phone telling him how disappointed he was in him, they are very close you know.'

'Oh shit, poor Maher. I must call him and apologise.'

I felt drained and exhausted and all I wanted to do now was lie on my bed and think this whole mess through.

'Zayef, I need to go now, I think we both have a lot of thinking to do and should lie low for a while until we see what comes out of this, and things quiet down.'

'OK,' he said, the disappointment evident in his voice. 'You will call me soon though, won't you, Aalinna?'

'Yeah, soon,' I said as I put down the phone, too drained and exhausted to think straight.

A few weeks passed and my parents slowly let the incident pass without further comment, seeming satisfied that I had no further contact with Zayef and was on my best behaviour. Being home on time, hanging out at family dinners and spending time with my girlfriends, were my small ways of trying to make it up to them. But I missed Zayef, Maher told me he had been keeping his head down as well, his parents or Raeesa had never got to hear about that night, and I was glad.

'He does keep asking about you, Aalinna? He wants you to call him.'

I finally gave in, calling him when I knew my parents were out to dinner. I was heartbroken but determined to end it.

'Please, Aalinna, meet me just once more. I've been thinking about this a lot and we need to talk.'

I gave in and agreed, secretly delighted and excited just for having heard his voice. I hastily dressed and redressed, wanting to look my best. Once ready I went to where I agreed to meet him.

As soon as we saw each other, we embraced. With our arms still around each other and him slowly stroking my hair he stunned me by whispering in my ear.

'Marry me, Aalinna, I love you.' I knew exactly what to say. 'Yes.' I said laughing and squeezing him back.

*

After much discussion it was agreed that Maher would speak to my father and ask him to meet with Zayef at our home, Zayef would then tell my father how much we meant to each other and express his wish to marry me. As I sat in the lounge that evening, nails almost chewed to stubs, I felt like my whole life was hanging in the balance. My mother, who sat on the chair opposite, had surprised me earlier that day encouraging my father to let go of the past and give Zayef a chance and to be open to what he had to say.

As the office door opened, my father exited first. I could tell nothing from the look on his face. I looked pleadingly at my mother who appeared just as nervous as me. Zayef came out grinning and shook my father's hand, in that moment I knew it was all going to be OK. Rooted to the spot my mother gently squeezed my hand, looking up I saw the tears in her eyes. I ran to my father embracing him in a hug. 'Thank you, Baba.'

I was looking forward to my happy ever after.

Chapter 12
For Better or Worse

"Every person, all the events of your life are there because you have drawn them there. What you choose to do with them is up to you."

Richard Bach

Zayef, our families and I began making wedding preparations. My mother and Maryam were in their element. I too was happy and excited. I was in the best state of mind I had ever been since my illness began.

I wouldn't say the "old" me was back 100%, but I was getting there. I was able to function normally, simple acts that I had taken for granted in the past that had previously been impossible, were easy once again. I could chat and socialise without my heart racing, palms sweating and the constant fear of making a fool of myself. Coffee with friends or a trip to the mall was no longer a challenging, head spinning, experience where I yearned to make it through the encounter and just make it home. The many wedding plans and decisions were not a chore or a dread. I enjoyed the decision making and was amazed at how good it felt to confidently express my opinions and ideas.

This was the me I missed, the happy, confident, fun and outgoing girl who loved life. Our wedding was an enormous event with at least a thousand people joining us to celebrate. Zayef and I were going to begin our new life together.

Our honeymoon was a dazzling stream of halcyon days and

courtship dating by night. We enjoyed spending time meeting other couples, socializing long into the night, dancing and chatting. Mingling was once again fun. It was nice to feel like – and be treated like – adults. No longer simply 'the children of that rich family.' We were a couple in our own right and one day, we would be a family.

*

I returned from my honeymoon relaxed and happy, looking forward to and planning the future. We visited and had lunch with my family before going to Zayef's family home. Initially, as was tradition we would be living with my in-laws for around the first six months. Maryam rushed to greet us even before we got in the front door,

'Hii!' she screeched, pulling open the back door of our car before our driver even had a chance to open it. She looked beautiful as always, dressed lavishly but modestly, her long dark hair shimmering in the sun. I took in a deep breath of coconut shampoo as she embraced me. She immediately disposed of me and ran to do the same to Zayef, who embraced her, laughing. Her sense of excitement was contagious. I loved the relationship they had, Zayef was now like the big brother, constantly teasing but very protective and she adored him for it.

As they walked up the path towards my parents, I stopped for a moment to take in the scene. My parents stood side by side at the front entrance, framed by the huge glass doors leading to the hallway. They had their backs to the stairway behind them, which had been the scene of many fraught encounters, now it sat ignored. My mother was so relaxed, grinning from ear to ear. She laughed as Maryam and Zayef approached, she looked years younger. It felt good to be responsible for giving my mother such happiness; not being the focus of hardship was a wonderful feeling. I caught my father looking over at me when he had finished embracing Zayef. He put a hand on his back to welcome him and steer him inside to the cool of the air conditioning – and the food that awaited. My father then extended his hand and beckoned me to him, winking, I knew we were thinking the same thing. I ran to him, taking his hand, squeezing it as we joined the others inside.

The meal was wonderful. The table was, as always, laden with food. We all chatted over each other, excited to be in the same room and share our news. I was delighted when Aunt Sabera joined us. I glowed upon hearing her compliments.

'Aalinna, you look amazing, married life suits you and your wedding – well, people have been talking about it ever since.'

I excused myself once or twice to take calls from Yushra and Nadera who wanted to hear all about my adventures.

'Was it amazing? Did you visit all the sites? And what were your hotel rooms like?' They giggled. I laughed childishly with them and ended the call, ensuring them we would get together soon and that no detail of the honeymoon would be left untold.

Things at Zayef's home were not quite so casual when we arrived. I stood by the car door and waited for Zayef to join me, we approached hand in hand. I was a little nervous, but my new confidence assured me that it would all work out. Zayef's mum, dad and brother greeted us, a little formally for my taste but in fairness it was a new experience and an anxious time for everyone. I could tell they had made a huge effort to ensure everything that we needed was there and to make us feel as welcome as possible.

Initially I was content, enjoying the independence. I'd walk through the mall chatting with my new friends, selecting items I thought would go great in my eventual new home, simply enjoying the feeling of being relaxed and able to experience the moment.

Evenings were spent mainly with Zayef. Like typical newlyweds we were either out at dinner with Maher and Ema or in our room, always sitting within reach of a held hand. I'd sit in wonder, watching Zayef's animated face and gestures so full of excitement and happiness, wrapped in my own cloak of contentment, savoring the ease with which I could now sit and plan my future.

Yes, I missed the comfort of my close knit family but I endeavored to bond just as closely with my new in-laws. Initially, this notion played out well. Until one morning, when I entered the lounge and caught Zayef and his mother in a hushed discussion.

'But we have brought you both into our house, our home,' she pleaded.

'But it's ours too, no I will not put these restrictions on her.'

Creak, went the door handle.

'Oh. You're awake.' Silence.

I felt the first stirrings of worry as I looked at their faces and their attempts to look occupied. Zayef's mother busily read the back of a cereal box. I waited until we were alone in our room that evening.

'What's going on?'

'What do you mean?'

'Come on. This morning in the kitchen and it's not the first time either.' Zayef told me how his mother was becoming upset that we did not eat our meals with them and how it had been expected that I would spend the majority of my time with them and not be "out all the time". Apparently I was to tell them ahead of time if I wished to go out. I was dumbfounded. 'Seriously? Is she crazy? No way.'

'Come on, she's my mother, she's just old fashioned. I will talk to her, she'll come round.'

Zayef was now caught in the middle of me and his mother, not wanting to upset either of us. This led to a lot of tension for all the family and an awkward environment for all to live in.

Whereas previously, Zayef and I had sat over dinner laughing and sharing our plans for the future, we now sat iron-backed at the family dinner table, chatting about the latest news or the local gossip. Eventually, my mother-in-law and I became uncomfortable in each other's company, one silently blaming the other for causing such awkwardness and both refusing to back down. Zayef was the eldest son and the first one in the family to get married, making me the first wife and the first outsider to come live with the family. It was a new experience for them too. Still, I resented it, I had fought hard and struggled in life for my independence I wasn't prepared to give it up.

As a new bride a felt I did not have any personal space and as a couple, no privacy. Inevitably, we began arguing. Where once we would sneak off too our rooms to whisper endearments to each other and plan our futures we now exchanged hissed accusations.

'I thought we were out to dinner tonight, with Maher and Ema.'

'We were out the night before last with them, so when my mother asked me this morning if we would be dinning with the family I said, yes.'

I spun round, throwing my brush down on the dressing table. 'I was really looking forward to getting out of here!'

'Shh, Aalinna. They will hear you!'

'Bloody hell, Zayef. We can't even argue in private,' I screeched. All around me, the household was beginning to experience my requisite mood swings first hand.

Three months in, I reeled over the difficulty of adjusting to married life, a new setting, new people and new rules to live by. I found myself stressing over the small things and constantly looking out for any hint of accusation or slight when interacting with Zayef and his family. I felt like I was suffocating. Then unexpectedly, something small came along that would not stay small for long. I was pregnant. Zayef and our families were beside themselves with joy. I was stunned, the unexpected news of a baby so soon, frightened me.

My mind was a jumble of thoughts and questions. Whilst everyone around me excitedly made plans and shared the news, I bowed under the weight of my fears and concerns.

'Congratulations, you two,' Maher said, pumping Zayef's hand and beaming at me.

The jubilations that were common to so many were a cluster of blows to me. It was difficult for me to feel the pleasure that was expected from their congratulations.

I would often sit rubbing my bump, loving the feel of my baby moving but confused at how I could feel nothing myself. Cravings for strange foods, crying at the drop of a hat, forgetting things, these, I would later find out, were normal parts of pregnancy and hormones. For me though, this was not something I could sit with my girlfriends over dinner and laugh at. Nor could I whisper about them in my husband's ear as I cried softly, enjoying his reassurances. No, for me I would sit quietly whilst all round me fussed and congratulated, analyzing every odd emotion, notion or twinge. If I was too happy I worried, if I was sad I worried. I did not know which emotions were normal and natural and which might be the beginning of another manic episode. *What is wrong with me? Why can't I feel? How the hell could I look after a baby?*

I retreated into myself, becoming quiet and subdued. I could not share my fears and concerns with anyone; and everyone I met was so excited and happy. *What would they think of me? I didn't even know what to think of myself?*

'I can't wait to be an auntie!' Maryam would giggle. It stayed in this vein.

'There you are! Look. At. That. Bump!'

'Ten weeks.'

'You must be so excited.' They would nod and smile.

'Yes I am.' I would lie.

On and on it went, doing nothing to abate the numbness and fear I felt or to stop the swell of my belly.

As my pregnancy continued I was monitored regularly, my medication was changed to Lithium which was better for the baby. I had no ill effects from the change physically or mentally. My moods and mental health remained more or less stable, but my fear at my lack of emotion and enthusiasm remained. Hiding it was a lonely place to be.

I simply sat, quiet and withdrawn, among the hive of activity, feeling like I was slowly suffocating. I was to be continually questioned on my moods and behaviors, I became my own physiatrist, surrounded by people whose kind questions and friendly advice only making me feel churlish at my own lack of enthusiasm.

The rounder my belly grew, the more ubiquitous the joy and excitement of my family and friends became. I, on the other hand, continued to silently stew. I longed for the day my baby would be born but my persistent worries made me scared to death of her arrival. No matter how we hope or plan, a baby comes when it is ready to come and mine, surprisingly, came quite early. At only 33 weeks of pregnancy. My beautiful daughter decided it was time. She weighed five pounds, five ounces and I named her Nadja, *hope*. She would change my life and mark the biggest turning point in my recovery from mental illness, truly living up to her name.

Nadja was born at Lake View Clinic in Dhaka. She was delivered by caesarean-section leaving me too weak to even hold her. She was a tiny 'premie' and was immediately transferred to the neonatal intensive care unit, where she remained in an incubator. Although I was naturally exhausted, with high blood pressure and my body racked with pain, I felt better than I thought possible. As I sat in a wheelchair next to her incubator I felt the anxieties of the past few months assuage and the quiet dark room, with only the sound of the beeping monitors, was surprisingly soothing. I felt safe there and seeing the look of love and devotion Zayef bestowed on both of us filled my heart with hope – with Nadja. In this calm environment where only the three of us existed, my anxiety all but disappeared.

Alas, it was not to last. Although initially only I and Zayef could visit our daughter, people *could* visit me. For two long weeks I stayed confined to the hospital, with no way of escaping the continual stream of visitors coming and going. My feelings of stress and anxiety not only returned but increased ten-fold.

When Nadja was released from the hospital, Zayef and I brought her to my parents' house and we stayed with them, a tradition that is common in Bangla culture. Our families were beside themselves with excitement, grandparents, aunts, uncles and cousins made sure to meet us as soon as we arrived. My parents' home was a revolving door to friends and family who all wanted their chance to hold Nadja, congratulate the new parents and give their advice about child-rearing. And I was stressed out of my mind. One day, as I sat perched on a high-back chair in my mother's living room. I heard yet another ring on the door bell and my heart sank. The room was already full of people cooing over the baby and drinking copious amounts of tea.

I felt like I was on display, I sat with a smile pasted on my face as I listened to exclamations of how beautiful and tiny she was, how lucky I was to have her.

And, of course 'What you really should do with her is...' or 'Oh really we didn't do that in my day.' Or 'Maybe it would be best if you try this.' Or 'Oh you must adore her and never want to put her down.'

Inside my mind I was screaming, *shut up, shut up, leave, and go home.* How could I make people understand, it was not that I did not care about my child or did not love her, I just couldn't feel the emotions that were meant to accompany it. And I felt wretched about it. Petrified that I would never feel them. Of course I said nothing, they would think I was some kind of freak and who could blame them. So I sat with my pretend smile trying to keep it together, my stomach in knots and my head pounding. The ringing at the door bell I heard had been my Uncle Abraham, my mother's only brother. He was considered eccentric and wild, had not married, not really believing in it, and he did not conform to most people's way of thinking on most things, much to my mother chagrin. He wasn't afraid to express his opinions either. I loved him dearly and as a child, always loved to listen to his stories. As he entered the living room greeting people politely, he spotted me sitting quietly among the throng. I smiled my first genuine smile in weeks, but by my whole demeanor he must have guessed something was wrong.

'My Lord!' He said, rolling his eyes,'they're like a swarm of bees around a honey pot.' He nodded to the crowd of women that encircled me and the baby in the crib nearby. I felt like they were stealing my air and wanted to run from the room.

'A large can of insect spray is what's needed here, that will get rid of them all don't you think, Aalinna?' He winked and waved his hand, pretending to waft them away. I burst out laughing, the sound of my own voice surprised me. Uncle Abraham sat next to me while my mother, red faced, made apologies for him to the ladies.

'Well Aalinna,' he said looking directly at me 'how are you?' His kind words were nearly my undoing. I didn't say a word I simply lay my head on his shoulder and enjoyed the strength of his arms as he gave me a lingering fatherly hug. The screaming in my head stopped for a moment and my breathing slowed.

'Give it time, you're going to be fine,' he whispered before quietly walking off to greet my father. I don't think he will ever know how much his words meant to me.

On top of everything, I was overwhelmed with the lingering feeling that I just didn't know what I was doing. Throughout my life, I had never spent much time with little babies, other than my little sister Maryam, and I never had to take care of her. Now I was fully responsible for another human being, a very tiny and dependent one with basic but constant needs.

I reeled at the amount of work that a baby required. Help from family members was always on hand, whether I wanted it or not. It was a difficult period for my mother as often I found her attempts to be helpful and supportive overbearing.

'Where are you off to? 'She said as I made my way upstairs.

'I'm just going to have a nice relaxing bath'

'Where is Nadja, have you fed her?'

I stopped mid step and turned to stare at her. 'She is safely wrapped up, fed and sleeping, 'I growled.

'OK, alright,' she said, hands raised, 'I was only going to offer to fed her so you wouldn't have to rush.' She walked away with her head bowed and I had one more reason to feel bad. I took her words of advice as criticism and her constant presence only deepened my own sense of ineptitude.

What's more, Zayef's work required him to travel out of country quite a bit leaving me feeling alone and frazzled and when he returned, his attention and concern would be all about the baby. I'd be left disappointed and angry when I made a concerted effort to look good for his return only for him to come through the door and immediately ask how the baby was. 'How's she doing, is she feeding ok?' he'd say as he lifted her from her crib.

'Yes, she is doing great. I've missed you.'

'I've missed you both too.'

'I've had a lovely meal prepared shall we have it in the dining room together?'

'Lovely, thank you, I'm starving, let's bring the crib with us, it will be great to have her with us.'

Yeah! Great.

If I'd realised it at the time, it would have been a comfort to know that the feeling of being a little jealous, was natural for a new mother. Whilst I loved the fact Zayef loved Nadja so much and was a wonderful father, I felt lonely and wanted my husband back.

*

For an entire year, I struggled quietly on. Appearing for all intents and purposes to be the typical, doting, new mother. I washed, fed and cared for Nadja. I greeted visitors and family dutifully. I chatted about my day and what I'd been doing. I sat quietly, interacting, pretending all was fine. For a year.

'Hi, I've just popped in to see you both. How's she doing?'

'Yeah, thanks, Ema, we're great. She's getting bigger by the day. Can I get you a drink?'

'Oh darling do you think maybe she is a little hot in that outfit? Here come to baba darling, have a cuddle,' my mother would say, not wanting or waiting for an answer.

'Yes, mother, she's fine but change her if you'd like to.'

'Look at her! She's starting to look so like her father, I remember him at that age, is she feeding ok? You look well also.'

On and on it went through each day into the evenings when Zayef would return home from work and it would start all over again.

No one knew of the fear and anxiety I coped with daily. Visits to the doctor or a simple call to make an appointment meant another sleepless night. Worrying about what I would say, how I would appear. Would they know? Would they be able to tell? Would they see what a useless mother I was? I would get dressed, sweating profusely, and physically shaking, feeling like I was walking headlong into battle. I was certain I'd be transparent and vulnerable under their glare and knowledge. Afraid I would be exposed, friends and family visits, bath times and shopping trips were all momentous battles that had to be fought and overcome, occasions to get through and survive. I had a growing sense of fear and was still haunted by the feelings of emptiness.

Instead of floating on a cloud of love and excitement, like everyone told me I should be, I was like a robot mechanically going through the motions, getting the job done. The irony of my life was not lost on me, I had every reason to be happy but I wasn't. I had a husband, a child, a beautiful home, and loving parents, extended family and financial security – and still I wasn't happy. Not surprisingly, I had a depressive episode.

Though short lived, it had a huge impact on us all. This was the first time that Zayef had witnessed me in a totally depressive state. Yes, I'd been quiet and subdued but this was a whole new realm. He knew about my bipolar before we had married but there's a huge difference between *knowing* it and actually *seeing* it. I would lie in bed at night tossing and turning, my mind and heart racing, dreading facing another day of battles. Zayef's attempts to comfort or talk to me were useless. 'Come darling try and sleep. Can I get you some water? Here let me get you a cooler blanket maybe that will help?'

'Oh, for God's sake just be quiet will you?' I'd screech pulling at my own hair. 'I'm sick of the sound of your voice.'

My moodiness was even showing in front of my in laws, I was losing control. 'Please can you just put the baby down, I'm trying to get her to sleep, that's twice I've asked you,' I'd snap as I slammed the living room door and marched out with Nadja in my arms. The combination of a lack of sleep and being permanently anxious and stressed, caused me to burn out within a few short weeks of feeling the initial descent towards depression.

All attempts to even pretend to be coping or care were replaced by a deep darkness; I couldn't even muster the energy to look after the baby. *What's the point? She is better off without me.*

My mother visited one day to find the baby with the nanny, and the staff told her that I had not got out of bed yet. On coming to my room and opening the door she saw me cast across the bed, eyes blank and room darkened. She knew. As she closed the bedroom door and headed downstairs she met Zayef on his way in. He stood stock still on seeing my mother.

'What happened?' he said, as he rushed towards the stairs.

She's in her room and the baby is with the nanny. How long has she been like this, Zayef?'

'A week, maybe, a fortnight? I don't know.' He sat on the

stairs running his hands through his hair. 'That's why I've come home from work, I've been so worried, I just don't know what to do anymore.'

Not only was this the first time Zayef experienced the effects of my mood disorder first-hand, it was the first time my in-laws even heard that I had bipolar. Later that same day, on arriving to visit, Zayef's mother was stunned to find me still in bed at noon. Zayef greeted her with the baby as she entered the living room.

'Where is Aalinna? Why aren't you at work at this time of the day? Zayef what is going on? The staff just told me that Aalinna is still sleeping in her room and I was told the same thing last night when I called to see how she and the baby were doing. I can't even get her to speak to me without her getting upset.' Zayef had no choice but to sit her down and tell her.

'Mother, Aalinna has bi-polar disorder.' He told her the extent of my hospitalizations, to communicate the severity of the matter.

'Why haven't we heard of all this before? And what exactly is this Bi-polar?' Zayef held his breathe and waited for the tirade to continue.

'Well I can learn more about this in time. For now, we just have to look after her and the baby and get her well again.'

Zayef embraced her in a strong hug. 'Thank you.'

Zayef's family also visited mine, reassuring my parents and asking for advice on how they could help. They accepted my illness with grace, being kind and respectful, giving just what I needed: a lot of support and privacy. They went out of their way to be sensitive to my needs and patiently waited for me to get healthier. Their love and support was not lost on me and proved to be a great turning point in our relationship.

Things began to slowly change and improve. No longer having to hide my illness or my fears, lifted a huge burden off of my shoulders, I began to slowly feel able to re-enter normal life and settle back in my daily routine. It was in the midst of a very ordinary, run-of-the-mill trip to the grocery store where the sparks of a lovely new relationship with my little girl began to fly. Nadja was tucked away safely into the shopping cart's baby carrier, it entered my head that she had fallen asleep without eating. As I looked down at her beautiful little face snuggled up so peacefully and looking so vulnerable, all I wanted to do was take her in my arms and protect her forever. I started crying.

In that moment, I felt it, the bond, the connection, they'd all been talking about. I knew I could never possibly love anybody in the world like I loved her and would happily die protecting her. She was everything to me. I realised I not only wanted to be happy I needed to be healthy for her. I wanted the "well me" back. It wasn't just me anymore, I had someone else relying on me, someone else who was intricately connected to me.

I couldn't lead my life with all this anxiety, these negative feelings and fear. I knew it would be difficult and gradual but it was a change I was determined to make. I fought my mood swings. The more I took care of her, the more we bonded. Now with every trip to the doctor, every diaper change and every bath, I gained confidence. Motherhood was growing on me, it was becoming a more natural fit and my precious daughter was the motivation I needed to strive for a healthy mind.

*

I realized that I not only needed a healthy mind, I also needed to pursue being healthy in every way possible now. I had to take care of myself. I didn't know exactly what that meant but I began the gradual process of learning. I took my medication every day, even if I felt that my moods were fine. I tried to get as much sleep as possible and I carved out times in the week to just enjoy myself, either going out with Ema or Zayef. I gradually became more comfortable asking others for help, much to the delight of both sets of grand-parents, who now had the opportunity to bond with, and enjoy, their first born grandchild. The more I took care of myself, the more my self-assurance grew as I cared for my daughter. With every passing day, I felt more able to simply enjoy my daughter. It was my love for her and our ever-deepening bond that motivated me to do what I did next.

When Nadja was learning to walk, I was so proud to hold her and help her take those first momentous steps. I thought of the days to come and hoped she would always be able to lean on me when she needed the strength to move forward. I realised years later that this was exactly what my little girl had done for me. She helped me to stand and move forward, when I didn't think I had the strength.

I made a decision.

'Zayef, we need to talk.'

He had just come in the door from work and was making his way to sit with Nadja who was happily perched on the rug, playing with her toys, her little face now all smiles at the sight of her father.

'What's wrong?'

'Nothing, that's the point.'

'Aalinna, you're not making sense,' he said as he now sat on the sofa beside me. 'Are you feeling ok?'

I knew by the look of panic on his face that he thought I was becoming unwell again. I took his hand to reassure him, 'this might sound a little crazy.'

'OK, go on.'

'You know how recently I have been trying so hard to get myself well, both mentally and physically? Well, I think it is having a huge effect on my relationship with Nadja.'

'Yes,' he interrupted, 'I'm so proud of you and all the strategies you've put in place. I'm always watching and I can see how close you two are for your efforts.'

'Yes, well, that's my point. I want to take it further; I want to go away for a while. Now that I can see clearer I realise how important it is for me to keep being well. I need to deal with some things from the past, things I don't want to come back to weigh me down. I need to explore new ways of staying well. I love her so much, Zayef. I need to stay well for her and us. This way, as she is so young she will not even know.'

He wrapped his arms around me. 'You do what you need to do and we will be waiting right here when you get back.'

Telling my parents was not quite so easy. I had decided I would go alone, leaving Zayef to bathe Nadja. As I left through the front door I could hear their squeals of delight and a lot of splashing.

My mother was already tense when I arrived. I had called her the day before saying I wanted to talk. No matter how much she probed, I refused to give her any details; this was not something I was prepared to get into over the phone. As soon as I entered the living room she pounced:

'What's the matter? Tell us.'

'Let her get in the door,' said my Father.

'Is it Nadja? Zayef? Are you unwell again? She asked, concern in her voice, not pausing for breath.

'No, mother. We are all fine.'

She slumped back in the chair, her relief was evident but it wasn't to last long. I took a deep breath and told her what I'd explained to Zayef. She sat stunned, her head swinging between my face and my father's, willing him to say something as I rushed to get the words out. There was only silence when I stopped speaking. I waited. 'But why? You are doing so well, and you and Nadja are so close, why now?'

Had she heard or even tried to understand a word I said? I decided to ignore her question. 'It will only be for a few months and she will have Zayef and all of you of course'

'It's her mother she needs, a child needs her mother, if you must do this can you take her with you?!'

I looked at my father for support, I got the feeling he understood a bit better but he obviously was not going to defy my mother by saying so. My mother shot off the sofa.

'Oh no, don't look at him. What is it with you? Every time we think you're settled you do this, are you sure you're not becoming unwell again?'

'NO!'I shouted, my frustration getting the better of me, I tried to calm myself. 'That's the point I want to stay well; I'm doing this for her.'

'I just don't understand you, Aalinna. I never know what you're going to do next and can't read your moods. Now even when I think you're happy you're not.'

Now I was pissed, 'Welcome to my world, mother. You don't understand me; do you know how frightening it is to be me? Being afraid when I'm happy that maybe I'm a little too happy. Then the same when I'm sad or down – is it just I'm fed up or am I heading for a relapse? Have you ever tried living like that? Knowing that everyone is thinking the same thing, wondering, waiting to see what I will do next. Mother I couldn't even connect with my own child. You can never imagine the hell of that and I'm not going back there. I'm well, I'm going to stay well, and this is how I'm going to do it.'

The room fell silent again, my mum sat and stared at me with her mouth agape. 'I'm going now but I will call you tomorrow, I won't be leaving for a week or two, I have some things to organize first.' I kissed them both and left. It was only after I left that I realized my father had not said a word.

Zayef's parents were none too happy either, they immediately went to see my parents to see if they could coax me to stay but they were told that such an attempt had been made, and they couldn't change my mind. I put things in place and booked my tickets, I was nervous but excited; my only real dread was leaving my daughter. The night before I left I went to her room and watched her sleeping. I'd done this many times before, breathing in the smell of her baby powder and creams, listening to the soft sighs and grunts she made. I marveled at her small pink lips and long sweeping eye lashes. And this time I talked. 'I love you so much my precious girl, I'm going to get better, so we can be this close always. I want to be strong for you, support you and guide you through life. I will think of you every day and call to hear your voice, I may not be next to you but know I will never leave you.' I put my fingers to my lips, which I hadn't even noticed were wet with my tears, and pressed them to her head.

'Night, night beautiful.'

Chapter 13
For The Love of My Daughter

"In my daughter's eyes, I am a hero, I am strong and wise, and I know no fear, but the truth is plain to see she was sent to rescue me, I see who I want to be in my daughter's eyes."

Martina McBride

I travelled to the airport alone. Apart from leaving my daughter and husband, I now felt quite excited. I was nervous but determined to see this through. My parents and I had sorted things between us a few days before and it was a huge weight off my shoulders. They'd actually surprised me by calling and inviting me to come to their house to talk. I agreed, I wasn't looking forward to it but if there was a chance we could clear the air before I left, then I wanted to take it.

To my surprise, it was my mother who offered the Olive branch. On entering the living room, I was ready to eat humble pie to smooth things over. I was going now, regardless of what they said, so I was happy to try and smooth the way for Zayef, who would be the one left to contend with both sets of parents. My mother and father rose from their seats as I entered the room, I surmised this was not good, I stood looking from one to the other, vowing to keep my cool. Zayef had been so supportive and understanding, the least I could do was make sure his life was as easy as possible whilst I was away. Having two pissed-off in-laws did not make for an easy life.. My mother spoke:

'Aalinna, your dad and I have been talking. Whilst we don't quite understand why you want to go away to do this, we understand it is something you need to do, so we would like to do all we can to support Zayef with the baby – and you too of course. I was stunned but grateful.

'Thank you, Mum. You too, Dad. This really is the best thing for me, well, all of us. Having your support means so much to me.' I embraced them both.

The room was charged with emotion and even my father looked tearful. My mother took charge, telling us all to sit, ordering tea and sandwiches as a diversion to calm the atmosphere.

We spent the next hour chatting and making plans of how and what they could do to help.

Saying goodbye to Zayef was heart wrenching, I didn't want Nadja there, I didn't want her to become distressed, seeing us emotional; I'd said all I needed to say to her the night before as she slept. She was playing happily in the house with my in-laws, who were only too pleased to spend time with her.

'Right,' Zayef said finally, that's the last of your bags. I can't believe how much you're taking.' Zayef laughed, pulling me close to him. 'You are coming back, aren't you?'

It was said in jest but I realised that as strong as he was, he needed some reassurance too.

Embracing him I held on to him tightly whispering into his neck, 'You and Nadja are my world now, my home, I will always come back. Thank you for helping me do this for us all. I love you Zayef.'

'I love you too.'

Sitting on the plane I went through the list I had made, consisting of what I wanted to accomplish and what I needed to put in place to make it all achievable. One of the first things I had done was to let Dr. Anna know I was coming to New York. Whilst I had spoken to her on occasion over the last few years, she had not formally counselled me. Our conversations were more like chats and family updates; my regular counselling was now with a local therapist. Dr Anna had seemed genuinely pleased to hear from me and was totally on-board with what I wanted. For me there was no one else I would even consider. Not only did she know me but the bond and connection we had made in the past, was still paramount for me to feel able to, honestly and comfortably, work through things with her.

I drew a line through the writing in my notebook, *Contact Dr. Anna,* I smiled. This was exactly how I'd intended to approach this whole thing: acknowledge it, deal with it and draw a line through it. If only it could all be this simple.

I enjoyed the flight, it was nice being alone and having time to think. I couldn't actually remember the last time I'd 'done' something that was just for me and by me. It was great to have some independence and solitude, without the accompanied anxiety, euphoria, or even a hospital room for that matter (I allowed myself a giggle at my own expense). I naturally began to think about my 'other' plane journeys when I was manic: America with my parents for my initial treatment, the return trip to Thailand with Maryam and my mother all those years ago. I hadn't even know I was sick, never mind with bipolar disorder. I'd been living life on the edge, enjoying the highs and the buzz, just thinking about it now made me realise how vulnerable I was. The drinking until I was wasted, the late night parties ending up with strangers either coming on to me or me them, taking lifts from anyone or worse walking home alone. I felt physically shaken at the thought of it all. I ordered a tall glass of wine from the stewardess, the irony was not lost on me. As I resumed my thoughts I cringed at my own behaviour: loud, brash and talkative, pestering friends, lecturing shop owners and inviting myself into the company of strangers. Was this why in the recent past I'd avoided all my old friends? Was I nervous in company in case I made a fool of myself? But I am talkative, I love mixing and chatting with new people, so what was me and what was the bipolar?

I didn't know myself anymore, I needed to find myself. I knew how cliché this sounded, especially for someone who, when younger and full of confidence, couldn't even grasp the concept of someone needing counselling. But now, finally letting myself think about it all while I was well, I knew that taking control of this illness, once and for all, was the right choice, both for myself and for my daughter.

My mind grew weary at the barrage of thoughts that were now being allowed to break free, this was not the time or place to overthink all this. I refused to let my worry and anxiety overwhelm me, so decided I would think no more about it, and simply get some sleep. As the cabin lights dimmed I watched the sunset through the small window and drifted off into a comfortable slumber full of dreams of my little girl. I was, for the first time, taking things at my pace and on my terms.

Upon arriving at my parent's apartment I was exhausted, jet lag at its worst. This was another one of those things that people didn't understand – even I had to think about the effects, a long plane journey would have on my wellbeing. Sleep is paramount when you have bipolar and sleep does not come naturally or consistently on a 22 hour flight. On top of this, trying to keep medication balanced in the changing time zones is hard work. Try it – when you don't even know what day it is, never mind what time it is. I needed to rest and set an alarm to take my meds but first I needed to call Zayef and see how he and Nadja were doing. The phone barely rang twice before I heard Zayef's voice.

'Hello?'

'Hi, it's me.'

'Hey, how's you?'

'Tired but I just wanted to check in and speak to you guys. How's Nadja? Let me talk to her.'

'She went to bed a little earlier,' he laughed it's 2am, remember?'

I glanced at the clock above the kitchen sink, I'd forgotten the 10 hour time difference.

'Oh no, sorry, now I've woken you up as well.'

'Don't be silly, I've been waiting to hear from you. I'm glad you've arrived there safely.'

I was quiet disappointed at not being able to talk to Nadja, even if her only response would have been heavy breathing. 'Hey!'Zayef was responding to my silent disappointment. 'She's fine, we talked about you at bedtime, and how you were on a big plane in the sky.'

'Hug her for me.'

'I will.'

'I'm going to let you get back to sleep. I've got to get some sleep to.'

'Ok, honey. I love you.'

'Love you too.'

It was quite strange getting ready for bed, it was so quiet with no one else in the household, normally there would be the comings and goings of staff, friends and family as well as the usual bustle of looking after a small child.

The apartment had been stocked with the basics before I arrived, so I made myself a quick sandwich and coffee. Sitting down at the kitchen breakfast bar I watched the city lights outside.

I only got half way through it before my two eyes began to close together. I quickly brushed my teeth, took my meds and crawled under the bed covers.

I began to think, memories embedded in my mind of the previous times I'd spent here. The despair and confusion, the feelings of loneliness and isolation I'd felt when last laying in this bed, when actually this was the first time I'd ever been alone here.

*

I felt surprisingly refreshed when I woke and decided to go for a run through Central Park. I had a day to myself before I had to meet with Dr. Anna. It was strange deciding what I wanted for breakfast or if I would have breakfast at all, what time would I leave, should I shower first, or after, or both. Simple decisions that people take for granted everyday were a little overwhelming, but now all mine to make. There were no more concerns as to whether I was doing the right thing, and no one to comment or criticise my decision – no matter how well meaning.

The run felt fantastic, it was a beautiful morning and as always the park was busy with other people getting their daily exercise. I watched as joggers, dog walkers, roller bladders and pram pushers all started their day, I was just another one of them and it felt great. After an hour I sat on a bench, breathless but invigorated. Sipping on my water, I thought about the days where I would come here and walk or sit aimlessly for hours trying to either hide from my thoughts, or fight my way through them to ease my pounding head; trying to find a way out of my minding-numbing depression. Then there were the walks to the library where I would stare longingly at all the books, running my hand over their smooth covers, desperate to hear what they had to say to me, wanting them to bring me to another world and another time, anywhere other than where I was. I was about to give myself a stern talking to about self-pity and not letting my thoughts bring me down when it hit me: it was ok, that was the point, *this is what I was here for.* It was okay to think about my feelings, okay to get sad, okay to acknowledge them, to analyze them and to find ways to deal with them, for now and in the future. Hiding and running away from them is what had started all this. For a few years after meeting Zayef things had gone smoother, but at the first sign of a hurdle this had all come back to haunt me. Well, no more, I'd tried to convince myself it had never happened, never allowing myself to dwell on it for fear of what? Seeming self-pitiful? Being ungrateful for every time I felt better? Fear of cracking up again? Probably all of the above. No more, I was allowed to feel happy or to be sad or to make mistakes and wrong decisions. It was not bipolar or its tendencies, it was being human. Yes, I needed time to grieve the Aalinna I'd lost, I was entitled to it, but I was sure as hell going to enjoy the Aalinna I was becoming, this was the person I wanted my daughter to see and look up to; it's true what they say, you can't love anyone else properly until you truly love yourself. Well I was beginning to like myself.

*

My reunion and subsequent counselling session with Dr. Anna was an eye opener. Initially the pair of us chatted like old friends before we inevitably got on to my depression during my pregnancy and subsequent break down after having Nadja. She listened without interruption as I talked.

'I was so scared of having this baby,' I told her. 'I didn't really know why, which frightened me more than anything. How could I fix it if I didn't know what the problem was? I felt completely out of control. I would just sit and think for hours about how I was going to be responsible for this tiny human being. Was I capable of being a good mum? Everyone around me seemed so matter of fact about it, assuming I would be fine. I think for the first time ever I've realised that I had less confidence in myself, and put more pressure on myself, than anyone else ever really did. Their advice and information was just that, not the criticism and nagging I took it for. They were just doing what all parents, aunties and in-laws do: trying to get involved. They would share their wisdom and make me feel like part of the club. But it was my own fears of my illness that frightened me, making me judge myself too harshly. Come on, Anna, let's be fair, I was a newlywed who'd just had a surprise pregnancy while still living with my in-laws and I was expected to live with my parents after the birth. Who wouldn't be ready for cracking up?' I laughed nervously. 'I couldn't even be intimate with my husband for fear we'd be caught. Everywhere I turned during the pregnancy there would be a queue of people watching and ready to give me advice, shit, I was a new mother, what do we know? I was so jealous of Nadja and Zayef, you know? I've never really admitted that before. But he was just so damn good with her, so loving, so normal, I felt left out, I missed him rushing home to scoop me up in his arms, then it was only the baby he seemed to want to rush home for.

Dr. Anna simply smiled at me from where she sat, with one leg tucked under the other, sipping her decaf.

'Ok. Are you listening to me? Aren't you meant to be counselling me?' I teased.

'Aalinna, I think you're doing a pretty good job of that yourself', she smiled, putting her cup on the glass table next to her.

'Yeah, I am, aren't I?' I smirked. 'Not bad for a drop-out and someone who's never even read a book, eh?'

She thumped me on the arm none-to-playfully, 'Just when you were doing so well, 'she winked. 'Look, Aalinna you're perfectly right. You're starting to get it. So what if you take longer to process things or process them in a different way or need to do it five or ten times for it to feel right, or if you need to tweak it, or if you feel things differently from other people? It doesn't matter. What matters is that know you can do it; just maybe differently sometimes. That doesn't make it wrong and it doesn't make you weird. You're just you and you're starting to accept that's a pretty cool person to be. It's pretty exciting really.'

I sat for a moment lost in my thoughts, she could just be right.

'I want to talk to you about something else you just mentioned and I've been thinking about it since you called me again.'

My heart stopped, this wasn't good. So much for progress. Anna laughed, having read my thoughts. 'Still the same old Aalinna, wanting to be perfect wanting to sort it all out immediately.' I smiled back at her sheepishly. 'Baby steps.'

Her words immediately made me think of Nadja – she was learning to walk and I was going to learn to take my steps along with her. Once we were both up and running there would be no stopping us – nor parting us, for that matter.

'So this idea of mine,' Dr. Anna's words brought me back into the room. 'We've talked before about your struggles in school. How you couldn't follow what was happening in class and the same when you went on to college, I know this has left you feeling stupid and less educated than your peers. Have you ever thought that you might have dyslexia?'

'What? Great.' I protested, sitting upright on the couch. 'I thought you were meant to make me feel better, not worse. Haven't I got enough to contend with without another illness?'

Anna did not reply.

'Sorry.' I said, feeling embarrassed at my childish outburst.

'That's OK. Look, it's not an illness, it's a type of learning difficulty. It just means you see words – written text and such – in a different way from others.'

'Oh,' I said, huffing, 'that's all right then.'

Anna smirked. 'If it is dyslexia, it can be fixed and it means you could learn to read.'

Now she had my interest. I could smell the pages already. 'So what would I have to do?'

'It's simple, I can refer you. They do the test and if you are dyslexic they give you methods to learn and, hey presto, you're cured.'

I raised my eyebrows and gave her my best *seriously* look.

'Well OK. That's the jist of it, they will be able to tell you in a few hours if that's what the problem has been.'

I couldn't even imagine it, all those years Samama had sat taking notes for me, lovingly copying away, spending her time after school patiently tutoring me.

'What are you thinking?' Anna asked.

'Nothing really.'

We both knew who I was thinking of but we both knew it was just too soon to go there yet.

Baby steps.

*

It was after 6pm when I returned to the apartment through the Manhattan rush hour traffic. I ordered a pizza and opened a bottle of wine for dinner. Once showered, I sat comfortable in my PJs mulling over the session with Anna. The phone by my side rang.

'Hello.'

'Hello big sister.'

'Hey, Maryam, how's it going?' Maryam had left Dhaka just after the birth of Nadja, and was now studying for a degree here in the States.

'I'm good. How's that beautiful niece of mine, I don't know how you can be parted from her.'

Did I hear accusation in her tone? No I was obviously being paranoid.

'She is doing great, I'm actually just trying to keep my eyes open long enough to call her and Zayef – this time difference is a pain….

'So when are you coming to see me?'

'Well actually that's why I called. I've got a free weekend on the 21st, if you want, I can come see you then?'

'That would be great, Maryam!'

That gives me a few weeks to deal with this lot, then we could have a really chilled girly weekend. I couldn't wait, I missed her so much and was so proud of her.

'Ok, I will look forward to it! Love you, look after yourself.'

To my surprise when I called home a few hours later it was my mother-in-law who answered the phone.

'Oh hi! How are you? Is all okay there? I just wanted to say hello to Zayef and check in on Nadja.'

'Just a minute, I will get him, he is just getting ready for work.' I heard her call to him and we exchanged pleasantries.

'How are you? How was the journey?' Then I heard a few clicks as Zayef picked up the phone in our bedroom and his mother replaced the receiver.

'Hello you, how's the Big Apple? He asked. I could hear the smile in his voice.

Well it's 9pm here and I'm exhausted. Actually that makes it 7am your time. Why's your mum there so early? Hasn't the nanny turned up? And what's that constant tapping? It sounds like a construction site there.'

'That, my dearest wife, is your daughter using a spoon to play the drums on the bath taps,' he joked. 'We escaped up here to get away from my mother who has been here since 6am to check we're okay,' he said with an aggravated sigh.

'Oh! Let me talk to her.' I heard Zayef's feet pat across the bedroom floor towards our bathroom.

'Come on you! Come and talk to your mama.' The tapping stopped and was replaced by Nadja's giggles as Zayef swooped her into his arms and carried her on to the bed. I heard her childish breathing and listened as she tried to hold the large receiver to her head. 'Come on, let papa hold it for you, say "hello".'

I could just imagine him sitting cross legged on the bed with Nadja between his legs, him resting his chin on her shiny black hair that would inevitably smell of the jasmine shampoo I used on her.

'Mama, mama.'

'Hello, beautiful.'

'Mama Mama, plane.'

'Told you we've been talking about you, Mummy, 'shouted Zayef in the direction of the receiver. 'We miss you.' I heard a bunch of crackling as Nadja munched on the phone I could imagine her four new teeth reflecting of the bright red phone.

'Come on, down you get' said Zayef as he put her back on the floor to crawl around. 'Ugh it's soggy,' he laughed as he put the chewed receiver to his ear.

'So you guys are doing okay?'

'Yeah we're okay, she is so amazing, just like her mother.'

'I miss her so much.'

'I know but it will all be worth it.'

Things went quiet.

'Hey,' I said, trying to make things more upbeat, 'I spoke to Maryam today, she is going to come on the weekend of the 21st to stay with me, I can't wait to see her.'

'Great. She's a good kid, she's been calling to check on me and Nadja, I think she's a little home sick so it might be good for her to catch up with family.'

'How's Maher and Ema doing? You heard from them?'

'Yes, actually, I wanted to talk to you about that. We were out for dinner last night and Maher told me Rabab isn't doing so well; well actually he is in a pretty bad way. He is in Bangkok and he's lost his job, his friends and basically spends all his time drinking and taking drugs. Aunt Sabera is distraught, apparently it's been going on for a long time. She's tried to help him but she can't get through to him. It seems no one can anymore, Maher has even flown over there to try and talk to him but he says Rabab is either drunk, high or in bed.'

'Do you think this is about Samama?'

'Yeah definitely. Maher says he has never been the same since, and has just gotten progressively worse.'

I knew that feeling. 'God, I knew he wasn't doing so well but I didn't realise he was in such a state, I should have kept in touch more often.'

'Hey, you've had a lot going on yourself, so don't go there.'

'Yeah, I know but if anybody can understand him, it's me.'

'Look, just get well first and then maybe you can reach out to him.'

'Ok, Ok.' I ended the conversation promising to call soon; I didn't mention Dr. Anna's suggestion about being assessed for dyslexia, it didn't seem appropriate now. Plus, if, I'm honest, I didn't really think I had a problem other than being stupid. So I didn't want to build myself up for disappointment.

Chapter 14
Rabab

"Your desire to change must be greater than your desire for things to stay the same."

All thought of sleep was gone as I thought of Rabab. I reminisced about when I first brought Nadja home from the hospital to my parent's house. I remember Aunt Sabera being there often, I wrecked my brain to remember if she'd said anything or given any clue to what was going on but I had been barely functional myself. Maher must have known too and said nothing, not wanting to stress me. *My God I really had been out of it*, it shocked me to realise I hadn't really thought of anything or anyone other than me for the past year.

After many hours of tossing and turning I sat up and turned on the bedside lamp, I'd tried to convince myself earlier that I was tired and went to bed. 'Who am I kidding.' I said to the empty room as I threw the covers back. I checked the bedside clock, 2am.

I lifted the phone and dialed.

'Hi Aunt Sabera, it's me.' I had contemplated calling Rabab but for one thing I didn't really think I would get the truth from him – or much sense for that matter – and for another I honestly wasn't ready to go there yet.

'Hi, Aalinna. It's so great to hear from you, how's it going over there? Are you okay? Are you eating well?'

I smiled, one word from me and she would have her pans out cooking something for me that would have me feeling better in no time. 'I'm fine, it's going well,' I reassured her. 'How are you?'

'Oh I'm well. I've been busy keeping up with that uncle of yours 'she laughed. I had dinner with your parents last night, they were telling me all about Nadja, she is so sweet and clever.'

I smiled and thanked her.

'How's Maher doing? I haven't had the chance to speak to him since I've been out here,' I tested the water.

'Yes, he is fine, you need to speak to him though. When is he going to get married and give me some grandchildren? I will be too old, or in my grave, to enjoy them if he doesn't hurry up! Can't you have a word with him?' An age old story, not so long ago my parents were the same about me.

'I will put Maher straight on it,' I teased. 'So how's Rhabab? Have you heard from him lately?' Now I was jumping in with both feet, I didn't want to be cruel but I wanted to catch her off guard so I could get an honest reaction. No response.

'I'd heard he's in Bangkok.'

Silence.

'Oh Aunt Sabera, please talk to me.'

Through a series of sobs and hiccups, she attempted to tell me what had been going on. Rabab had naturally been quiet for the first few months after the accident, which was only to be expected, given what he had been through emotionally – and physically.

'I thought he was starting to get a bit better.' Aunt Sabera sobbed. 'He still wouldn't talk about it, but at least he was getting out of bed, going out with friends. To be honest there were late nights and drinking was involved,' she confided. 'His father was not very happy about this and there were some awful arguments but, God forgive me, I didn't care. I was just glad to see him up and moving, talking, doing something other than sitting in a chair staring. This is the way with men sometimes, they need to get it out of their system.' I resisted interrupting her. 'He then started talking about going back to study or going travelling, secretly I was glad, I thought it meant he was looking ahead and making plans. You know it's not that I wanted him to go, I'd already lost one child.'

'Yes I understand.' I really did, I was a mother now.

'Rabab and his Father began constantly arguing, often I wasn't sure what it was about. I'd find them at times glaring at each other, snarling like two rabid dogs. Aalinna, it was a nightmare. Of course, as soon as I entered the room it stopped, I'd demand to know what had been said but Rabab would either walk past me with his head bowed or storm back to his room. I even caught him sobbing once. Naturally I didn't enter his room because I did not want him to feel ashamed but he's my baby, Aalinna, no matter how big he is, I just wanted to wrap him in my arms until he felt better.' We both took a moment to dwell on this image. 'So, you see, that's why I was glad when he said he was going. I thought some distance between them might help and Rabab could start to live again, I don't know.' The sobbing came back. My heart ached for her, I could feel her pain. I got it; the thought of losing my baby made me feel physically sick and now it appeared she might lose another. This is how my mother and father must have felt all these years.

'Oh, I shouldn't be putting all this on you,' Aunt Sabera continued, 'you've had enough to contend with and I promised them all and myself I would not distress you with this. Now look what I've done.' It went quiet, she knew she had said the wrong thing. I imagined who the term 'them all' was to encompass. My husband, parents and even Maher, presumably. I was hurt and angry, did they think I was that incapable? I was pissed and I would be telling them so.

'Oh, now what have I said? Aalinna, please don't be cross.'

'Look, its okay don't worry about that now it's not important.'

It seemed the situation was basically as Maher had said: Rabab had never gone back to study; he had lied to his mum, wanting to save her feelings. He couldn't go back there; he couldn't face it. He had gone straight to Bangkok, trying to make a new start but he had been kidding himself. Before long he was hiding behind alcohol and had moved on to drugs to try to numb his pain.

I thought it all sounded pretty familiar.

After reassuring her that I would keep her confidence and she could call me anytime, I returned to bed. I was more emotionally drained than tired. But knew I did not have the luxury of being able to stay up all night, my sleep was as important as any medication. I took a sleeping tablet and lay down, replaying the conversation in my head. Whilst it was all very sad and distressing one thing kept going around in my mind: why the volatile arguing between my uncle and Rabab? He had always been such a placid man, a family man, it's not as if at this time Rabab was doing anything wrong. Yes, ok, there were the late nights and getting drunk at times but as aunt Sabera said he was a man – and my uncle would be of the same opinion. He even saw it as a somewhat natural outlet, so why such anger? Something else was going on here.

*

Sitting on the balcony sipping a juice after my run, I still had the same thoughts going through my head. I checked my watch and realised I needed to get a move on; I had an appointment with Dr. Anna in an hour.

Whilst showering, I caught myself whistling, it startled me. Was I really in a good mood? Yes, there was no doubt, I was happier, I'd worked through a lot and things were going really well. I'd surprised myself with how quickly I became self-sufficient, not just cooking, cleaning and organising my own day but also in dealing with the ever-changing events that came into the average day of most people.. This was no small feat for me. I even went out to dinner alone and went to see a show, casually chatting with people the whole time. All this I was really pleased with but something was different this morning.

I quickly dressed and rushed to the car, then it dawned on me. My mood started to sink.

As I entered her waiting room, I could see Anna through the glass windows to her office. She sat behind her desk, her hair scraped back in a ponytail. She cradled a phone receiver in her neck whilst one hand held the pencil she had between her teeth. The other waved around whilst she made some point or other to whoever she was speaking to. On spotting me through the glass she quickly looked at the clock, her face saying she didn't realise how late it was. She put a warning hand up to stop me entering and mouthed her apologies, signaling she'd be two minutes. I wasn't inconvenienced. Knowing her she was probably on a call from a distressed client who she couldn't simply ignore. She had done it often enough for me, so I wasn't going to complain. I smiled and gave a small wave and turned my back to the window, pretending to look at the art work on the walls. I felt I was somehow giving the caller some privacy.

Within five minutes I heard a rapping on the window and turned to see her beckoning me in.

'Sorry, sorry, I really had to take that call' she said, as she wound the cord to close the blinds in the office.

I stopped her mid-explanation, 'Please don't worry about it, I remember when I use to need you like that. It's no problem.'

'Used to need me?' She smiled.

'Yeah, check me out!' I laughed. Actually I was secretly pleased and I know she was proud of me, another step forward.

'So what's happening? What has you so reasonable this morning?' She teased, knowing my intolerance for being kept waiting.

'Funny you should ask,' I said as I sat down on the seat facing her and dropping my handbag at her feet.

'Sounds ominous, tell me more.'

I explained about my call with Zayef telling me about his and Maher's conversation about Rabab and my subsequent call to my aunt.

'Rabab was the one Samama was in the accident with,' said Anna, refreshing her memory. 'You guys were all pretty close up until then.'

'Yeah, we were,' I said quietly. 'He is as much my brother as Maher. I felt so bad not knowing what he's been going through. Well, all of them, actually. It killed me to hear Aunt Sabera so upset, well… devastated. She's always been there for me.' I put my hand up before she interrupted. 'But I know I was in a bad place myself so I couldn't really be expected to do much, I just still feel bad.'

'You are getting good at this,' she smiled.

We were both quiet.

'Aalinna, there's something you're not saying.' She shuffled in her seat as she wrestled with her phrasing. These were the snippets of body language that I had learned to interpret from her. 'Is it that Zayef, Maher and your parents had kept this from you? I know it probably hurt to hear it but they were doing what they thought what was best at the time, surely you understand that.'

'Yes, I was pretty hurt at first but when I thought it through I understood. Zayef had to keep me well. He was doing it for Nadja, so that gets him a pass.' I smiled.

'So what is it?'

I'd regretted starting this but she wasn't going to give up. 'This morning before I came here I was on such a high. I was happy and excited more than I'd been in a long time.'

'So?' she asked, raising her eyebrows.

'So, I was happy because of Rabab, well not because of Rabab, I felt invigorated at having a purpose I suppose – having the chance to be the one who helps the problem instead of being the cause. It's a chance to be me. Not the sad, pathetic, scared Aalinna, or the irrational one The Aalinna that was always there for her friends, the one people turned to in crisis or asked for advice from. I know it's weird, right?' I didn't give her a chance to answer 'I mean, who gets off on someone else's misery?'

'Aalinna, you're coming back into the real world. This is great, not weird. That's what makes us human, that's what we are: social creatures. We need to love, to lose, to feel, to help, to bitch about people even. It's all just part of the crazy interaction that makes us human, that's why it's so hard to put a definition on what's normal behaviour. We're kind of complex as a species, you know.'

Still I said nothing but her words were really making sense.

'Look, go now, think about what we've talked about, and think about this too, after all this time Zayef tells you about Rabab. Why now? Maybe he's seeing the change in you, maybe you're further along than you think.'

I walked for almost two hours wandering aimlessly, I wasn't sad, just thoughtful, but slowly Dr. Anna's words sank in and I could feel a bounce in my step and a smile on my face. I think I just might be okay.

I needed to get back to my car, I wanted to call Zayef, then Maher and then Rabab. As I turned, trying to get my bearings, I looked up and noticed the building I was standing outside.

Oh don't you worry I will be back, see you soon. I gave its tall red breaks and countless windows a mock salute. I laughed as a few bystanders gave me a strange look.

*

The call to Zayef went a lot more smoothly than I thought, I wanted to let him know that I'd be getting in touch with Maher to get Rabab's number. I needed to talk to Rabab for myself. I braced myself for Zayef to answer the phone, expecting him to be totally against it and try to persuade me out of it but Dr. Anna had been right.

'I was expecting you to get in touch with him, I did feel bad keeping the extent of it all from you Aalinna but there didn't seem a good time before.' He had a plea in his voice.

'It's OK. I understand, really, I do. But I can handle this'

'I know, I'm so proud of you. I miss you,' he said longingly.

'Me too. I will be home soon, a few more weeks. OK?'

'OK, give Maryam my love when you see her next week.'

I got the number from Maher, reassuring him that Zayef was aware of what was going on.

'Look, Aalinna he's in a pretty bad way I think there is a few things I should tell you.'

'Thanks,' I interrupted, 'but I'd really rather just hear it from him. He might tell me nothing for the minute, I just want to reach out to him.'

I took the number, playfully reminding Maher of his need to

produce some grandchildren for his mother.

'Don't you start; she's driving me crazy.'

Once I had the number I lost a degree of conviction, what would I say? It was practically years since we spoke. I needn't have worried, though. As soon as I heard his voice the bond came flooding back.

'Hey.'

'Who's this?'

'Well that's not very nice, not remembering your favourite cousin.'

'Oh my god, Aalinna, is that you? It's good to hear your voice.' I laughed through the tears that had welled up on hearing his voice.

I hadn't really spoken to him since my wedding. Whilst I hadn't seen him much on the day, given how many people I had to meet and greet, he had seemed really happy, chatting with everyone, dancing, in fact he had been at the center of the festivities. We had emailed often but I had never really worried about how he was. Initially I was busy living my new life, then trying to sort my own head out, his replies to my emails had always been upbeat and when I asked the family about him I was told he was fine, a conditioned response that was part of their anti-manic propaganda.

'Where are you? Are you in Bangkok? Where's Zayef? And Nadja? Are Mum and Maher okay?' There was a creeping fear with each question. 'Wow, too many questions. Everyone's fine.' I noted the list of those to be concerned about didn't include his father. 'I just wanted to speak to you, it's been too long. I'm in New York.'

'Cool, are you on holiday?'

'No. I'm surprised they haven't told you, I've been here a few months getting some counselling, sorting my head out. I went back downhill for a while after the baby but I'm doing better now, what about you?'

'Yeah, I'm great.'

'Bullshit,' I laughed.

'Ah, so you have been informed of my behaviour,' he probed.

'Bits and pieces. Your mum and Maher are flipping out; they are really worried about you but I'd rather hear from you what's going on.'

'Look, they exaggerated, okay? I have a few beers and maybe the odd puff of something but I'm fine, I'm just having a little fun.'

'Really? You do realise who you're talking to, you don't have to pretend with me, Rabab. Jesus I've done things that would make your head spin, plenty of which I'm none too proud of. I wouldn't be judging or easily shocked for that matter.'

'Aalinna, you wouldn't understand. Shit, I don't know how I got here, so how can I explain it to you? It's all just got so out of control.' I could hear the stress and agitation.

'I don't want you to explain anything to me or make you talk through it or to lecture you? So anytime you feel like picking up the phone I'm here day or night.'

He sighed, 'I've missed you and didn't even know it.'

I smiled at the receiver, 'me too.'

'I miss her so much as well.'

God, please don't do this, not now.

'I know. Me too.'

Rabab broke the silence. 'So you have a kid now, is she as bratty as I remember you being?'

'Hey!' I screeched, 'She's perfect and anyway you were the brat.'

We made idle chit chat for a while, both avoiding anything painful.

'Listen,' I said, 'I've got to go. I've an important appointment to get to.' I reminded the both of us.

'Oh yes, very sinister.'

'Well. I haven't told anyone yet but you will be the first to know how it goes. I'll call and let you know.'

He didn't push for details 'Good luck with whatever it is. Call me soon.'

'I will, you're not getting away so easy again.'

'Damn, I knew I shouldn't have answered the phone this morning,' he teased. 'Aalinna,' he continued, as I moved to put the receiver down.

'Yeah?'

'Thank you.'

So nothing had been resolved, it was never going to be in a single phone conversation. But I'd let him know I was there for him, I hadn't wanted to pressure him and scare him off, but he knew he had a friend and I had a feeling we would be talking a lot more.

I couldn't believe how nervous I was; I'd been early but I had sat in the car so long I was on the verge of being late. I got out and locked the door, running up the steps of the building. The reception gave me directions to the waiting room.

'Hi,' I said to yet another receptionist. 'I'm Aalinna, I'm here for an assessment for dyslexia.' I could hardly pronounce it never mind spell it.

'Hi, have a seat please. Sorry we're running a bit behind so there are still one or two people in front of you.'

'Great.'

'OK, thanks.'

I looked at the others who were waiting, when I had the same thought I had at the hospital counselling sessions sometimes: they looked normal. As I waited I distracted myself by thinking about

Maryam, she was arriving at the weekend. I was excited about her visit, I'd made plans to take her to one of my favourite restaurants, and I'd had got tickets to the *'Cats'* at the Minskoff, but most of all I was just looking forward to seeing her and spending some time catching up. Deep in thought, I didn't hear the receptionist call me, only realising when I looked up to see everyone looking at each other. 'Sorry, sorry. Yes, that's me.'

The receptionist smiled, 'they're ready for you.'

'Thanks.' I recall a vain hope that I was ready for the experience before I stood up and made my way to the door she had pointed at. I took a deep breath and turned the door knob

*

Even recalling it now I don't believe it. That was it, all these years and that was it. It had taken no more than 90 minutes. I was dyslexic and within 15 minutes of this news I was given some strategies.

'This is just to get you started,' beamed the assessor, 'to let you see that this is a manageable situation.' I didn't know whether to be happy or furious. Years of struggling in school and university, being punished and ridiculed my teachers and parents, assuming I was stupid all this time.

'Try reading it this way, 'the assistant encouraged after giving me a few pointers.

I read it, it made sense, *oh my god! I just read a whole chapter and it made sense*, the words weren't jumping out of the page at me, swirling round and coming back down in a heap of letters.

The smiling assistant reached out and squeezed my hand. 'It's alright, we often get this reaction, it's just the relief.'

I looked at her confused, then heard a splat as a huge tear fell onto the page I had been reading.

I sat on a bench outside the building. I went for my emergency pack of cigarettes, shaking as I tried to get one from the box. If this was how it felt to be so happy, euphoric, then no wonder I enjoyed my manic states. I was excited yet nervous, my stomach was doing somersaults: I wasn't stupid, I could teach my little girl, the people I secretly looked up to who sat in offices or in cafes reading the paper, I could do that. I would be able to keep up with all the current affairs, travel, history – all the information I longed to know about the world and I longed to be part of. Not bothering to light the cigarette I threw it in a nearby bin and headed for the car. I knew exactly where I needed to go.

'Sorry, can you spell that please?' For the second time that day I was giving my name.

'Here you are madam.' I felt like I had just been handed the winning lottery ticket. My library membership card. 'Feel free to use the facilities now,' said the receptionist cheerfully. I turned to look at the vast room with the rows of long tall book shelves parading in oak.

I sat for hours, initially not touching a book, sitting at one of the long rows of benches and chairs each with its own reading lamp, breathing in the smell of the polished wood, watching as people entered, some casually nodding at me. I nodded back, I belonged. I walked up and down the long aisles enjoying the feel and smell of the perfectly ordered books and the quiet calm of the room. Eventually, I made a few selections, not pontificating on the subject. I checked them out and carried them to the car wrapped in my arms like an expensive antique. I set about placing each of them reverently on the passenger's seat. I closed the door and turned to the building. *Told you I'd be back.*

On the way home I picked up some food, I was drained; the initial euphoria was beginning to wear off, l was still delighted but I now realise how tense and nervous I'd truly been about going. I hadn't slept well, either, I promised myself a long bath and an early night with my books. I lay on top of the bed, my music playing quietly in the background, enjoying the feel of the crisp sheets. My body light and relaxed from the long soak I'd had, the smell of the bath oil permeated the room. Still my mind would not switch off. I wanted to talk to Rabab but didn't want to call him again too soon. I decided instead I would call Aunt Sabera, it might reassure her to know I'd been in touch with Rabab and would be keeping an eye on him, so to speak.

After our initial hellos, I told her about my call to Rabab and my intention to keep in touch with him.

'How is he? How did he sound?'

'Ok. He was quite up-beat actually.'

'Did he talk to you and tell you what's going on in that head of his?'

'Not really, Aunt Sabera. I just wanted to let him know I was around.' Truthfully, I wouldn't be sharing it with her even if he did open up to me. There are some things you just don't want other people to know, especially your mother.

'I am just so grateful you have reached out to him – and that you have thought to call me. I've been so worried, I don't know what he is up to half the time and his friends here say he doesn't get in touch anymore, or if he does he is normally drunk or spouting rubbish. I only know this because I overheard Maher telling Ema. But I knew there was something wrong: the last time he was home, while you were on honeymoon, he showed up to a family dinner and spent most of the evening challenging and insulting everyone at the table. His father eventually had enough and told him to get out. I was so ashamed. He didn't turn up for two days, I was worried sick.' Rabab had a lot he wasn't telling me.

'I can barely sleep anymore, Aalinna. I keep waiting for that call in the night again, I can't go through it again,' she sobbed. This must be how my parents felt when they were going through this with me. I was beginning to realise the fear, stress and shame they must have gone through for years now. Being a mother myself I could appreciate what a nightmare it must have been. At least my parents had each other though, and had managed to survive it together., No wonder they were so frightened about me wanting to come to America. They must have thought it was starting all over again, but by the sounds of it poor Aunt Sabera and Uncle's marriage was being battered. They'd already survived losing a daughter, I hoped they could survive this..

The sound of her sniffling brought me out of my contemplation. I hushed and reassured her.

'Thank you, Aalinna it's so good to have someone to talk to, someone who understands and will not judge. But please look after yourself first you have a little girl to think of.' I knew she wouldn't understand but this was part of the whole journey to be able to look after my daughter: fighting my anxieties, controlling my emotions and fears, taking one situation at a time not allowing life's ups and downs to overwhelm me or be drowned under the weight of other people's problems and expectations. I was finding my strengths but just as importantly accepting my limitations. Staying well had to be my first priority I was no use to myself or anyone else otherwise.

'I will be fine, Aunt Sabera. Please try not to worry. Get some sleep now as it's very late.' She laughed, I could hear her rub at her nose with a tissue.

'It might be late where you are but it's early here, so you should be the one getting some sleep,' she said gently. I didn't.

*

I turned up for the next morning for my appointment with Anna, ten minutes late and yawning. She was sat at her desk facing the door as I tapped and entered, giving many apologies.

'You're late,' she laughed, rising from the chair to greet me. She stopped to look at me closely.

'Aalinna, have you had any sleep? You look rough, come sit down' she said, concerned. 'Tell me what's been going on.'

'I'm fine, I just stayed up too late last night reading.' I watched as the confusion on her face changed to realisation when it dawned on her what I had said.

'Oh, wow, I'm so pleased!' She exclaimed, grabbing me in a big hug. This is one of the reasons I loved her, she genuinely cared and wasn't afraid to show it.

'Well,' I began 'I'm exaggerating a little, but I am reading. It's just going to take some time and practice.' I told her that I wouldn't be telling Zayef yet, I wanted to surprise him – ever the perfectionist, I want to get better at it first.

I sighed and stretched out on her coach, 'Any chance of a coffee?'

We sat sipping on our coffees in a comfortable silence.

'I think I might go home soon.' I looked up and tried to judge her reaction. She looked at me over the rim of her latte. 'Do you think I'm ready?' I asked.

'What did you come here to accomplish?'

'Peace, closure, acceptance, confidence. Resolution.'

'Oh, just a few things, then.' She smiled as she put her drink on the table, stretching her arms and coming to sit on the sofa next to me.

'When I first came I was so clear about why I was coming. I had it all planned in my head. I'd wanted to figure out why I was jealous of my own husband and daughter's relationship. Just watching the ease with which they interacted made me feel so incompetent, even though I'd made that breakthrough and found that bond with her, I'd still felt incapable. Not good enough.'

'And now?' Asked Dr. Anna.

'Now, I've realised I'm normal. All mothers feel that way, those that admit it anyway, and as for not knowing enough as a mother, who does? It's got nothing to do with my illness, my past or the fact we didn't bond immediately, it was about me accepting who I am, accepting my own limitations. Yes, of course, my bipolar is an influence on my life but it's not the cause or blame for everything. For the first time in my life I've been looking after myself, making my own choices and decisions, deciding how much I can take on without feeling overwhelmed and not feeling guilty or useless when I have to step back. I've put strategies in place for when I feel I'm getting overwhelmed: take things step by step and accept that there might be things I have to do differently from others or maybe never be able to do, but that's okay.' I paused for breath.

'And your moods?' Dr. Anna asked.

'There are still some days which are not as strong as others, but I acknowledge them now. I try to manage them; I try not to let them frighten or overwhelm me. Since I have been here I've been taking my medication religiously, I've started exercising regularity and watching my sleep pattern, it's had a hugely positive effect. I feel in control of it, Anna. For the first time in years I feel in control and it feels great.'

'Well, you sound ready to me, but look, let's have a few more one-on-one session before you leave. I know you've got Maryam coming in a few days, so take a break from it all chill out, relax a little.'

'Yes, you're right it has been a pretty eventful few weeks.'

I left promising to call her and confirm an appointment after my weekend with Maryam.

The drive back to the apartment was long and tedious, I listened to a guy who must have been ten cars ahead of me call up the 10-10 bulletin and tell them that Broadway up to 53rd was a parking lot. I switched channels on the radio trying to keep myself awake As I listened to the words of the song playing, I realised their significance to me. I sang the words, having heard them before but never really having listened. I felt excitement for the future swirl in my mind. As soon as I arrived back at the apartment I changed into some slacks and a t-shirt, I set my alarm for 2 hours later and lay down to read. Within seconds I was fast asleep.

The beeping of the alarm was not a welcome sound, I was so comfortable and still felt tired but I knew I had to get up otherwise I wouldn't sleep tonight. I'd end up in the same situation tomorrow again. I coaxed myself up with the promise of a pizza – and time with my books. I'd gotten used to being alone, and on the whole enjoyed it but I desperately missed Nadja and Zayef. I was just about to pour myself another glass of wine, the pizza having been long devoured, when the phone rang. I almost jumped out of my skin, what was it about the shrill ring of a phone that did this to everyone these days? It was like a primal fear.

'Hello?'

'Hey, how'd your appointment go?'

'Hi Rabab!' I was a little surprised to hear from him but delighted. I told him all about my assessment, the diagnosis and my trip to the library.

'Aalinna, I'm so pleased for you. I never knew. I remember the days when you and 'she' would sit in her room, and she would go through all the notes she had taken for you. I just thought you were lazy.' He still couldn't say her name.

'Oh thanks,' I laughed. 'She was a good friend to me, Rabab.'

'He blames me you know.'

'Blames you? Who? For what?'

'For killing her.'

'Who?'

'My father.'

'Oh, Rabab. What would make you think that?'

'He told me. I think his words were: "Why couldn't you just leave her to study? Why did you have to pester her to go to that damn party? She would still be here if it wasn't for you." Don't think there is any way I could have heard that wrong.' Now it was all starting to make sense.

He talked and I listened without interruption, I could hear him slurp from his glass and his voice slurred as he went further into his story. I made myself comfortable on the sofa and listened. Sometimes that's all you can do.

He told me how initially, after Samama's death, he had gone to a bad place. 'I just didn't want to think. I was numb. I was in physical pain and glad to be, I deserved it, I was alive. I fought everyone's attempts to bring me into the real world, I kidded myself. I was punishing myself by not allowing myself to live because I didn't deserve to, but really it was because I was too frightened to face the pain and heartache that would come if I did. I was a coward.'

There was as silence which had me wondering if he had hung up. But we weren't done here.

'Every time I looked at my parents, I felt guilty for the pain they were going through. I knew I was only making it worse, especially for my mother. I could see the fear on her face as time passed and I fell deeper into my own world. As for my father he could barely look at me, his resentment bright in his eyes every time he tried to reach out to me. I wanted to scream at him, "say it, just say it!" I know what you're thinking. Instead, we both silently stewed. And for my mother's sake we said nothing.'

I waited as I heard him pour himself another drink, the glug of the liquid as it flowed into the glass told me as much about his mood as his words.

'Do you know, Aalinna,' he said as he placed the bottle back on the glass table next to him,

'He has never once asked how I am. Anyway, for my mother's sake I tried to myself. I began to go out with friends, go places with Maher. My mother seemed happier for seeing me happy, she would comfort me, not by talking or questioning, just cooking for me, smiling at me, loving me. Soothing my pain with her presence all through her own heartache and loss. She had suffered, but him? He couldn't take it. I knew my presence made his skin crawl, he would make snide comments like "well at least you have a chance to make choices." At first I tried to say nothing not wanting my mother to hear. He thought I was happy getting on with my life, that I'd forgotten, but I hadn't. Aalinna, I never could or would want to. I'd trapped myself. I couldn't let my mother see how I really felt; the least I could do was bring her a charade of happiness, letting her think I was getting better. So I pretended – drink's good for that.

'Eventually though my father and I could hide it no more, we couldn't be in the same room without arguing. I think my mother overheard us sometimes. One day it ended up in a huge argument where he finally admitted he blamed me.'

This was obviously the argument aunt Sabera had told me about. I stood up and walked to the window, looking out at the neon on the front of the hotels on 53rd as he continued.

'That night I went to my room and thought for hours. I decided the best thing I could do was leave. I was only staying to give my mother some comfort but now it was all only causing her more worry. So I came up with the idea of going back to study, but going back to Canada was not an option, I couldn't face it, I could barely even think about my time there, never mind revisit it. The more I thought about it, the more I actually realised I wanted to do it, try and start again but with new friends, new people who didn't know what happened. My mother, I think, was upset initially but eventually she came round, seeing it as a good thing that I was moving on.

'And I did try; I got my own place, made new friends, went to my studies. But before long, in the small hours when I was alone, it would all come back. I was able to control it, hide it, keeping it between me and the darkness of my bedroom. Eventually I began to drink more and more. And then I found the *coke*. My nightly habits began to creep into my days where I'd be late for classes or just not turn up. The more classes I missed, the further I fell behind and the more reason I had not to go – using the excuse to party instead.'

I felt a chill at the familiarity of what I was listening to.

'Oh, Rabab, would you not consider counselling?' I heard his sharp intake of breath at the suggestion. 'No, please listen. I know exactly what you're thinking. I was the same when it was first suggested to me but it really can help.' He dragged on his cigarette for a moment, I could have done with one myself. 'Just think about it, please. For me.'

'OK, but what do I need a counsellor for? I've got you,' he laughed.

'Now that really would be the blind leading the blind,' I joked back. 'I meant a professional.'

'I know, I know, look, I will think about it, Aalinna.'

'Thank you.' I didn't want to push it. 'Can you do me one more favour? Please try to lay off the drugs, even just a little.' I begged in my best bratty voice.

'OK, for you,' he said.

I didn't hold out much hope. At least if it made him think. It might go a small way to make him consider quitting. Enough had been said for one night, I could tell even though we were lightening the mood now, he was emotionally drained and so was I.

*

The day had finally arrived, I was having my morning run in the park before picking Maryam up from the airport. She wasn't getting in till 6pm so I had plenty of time but I was restless to see her. I had just planned for us to have a quiet meal out together, then back to my place for a catch up. The following day was the busy day, breakfast on the docks, shopping and then a Broadway show that evening, and a meal. She would love it.

I filled the rest of my day shopping for snacks and drinks I knew she liked, wanting to have supplies ready for the regulation long chat into the night. I whistled as I worked, airing the spare room and putting a set of Dolce and Gabanna bath oils in her bathroom for her to enjoy.

Once finished, I surveyed my handy work. I contemplated how at ease I felt, normally the thought of entertaining and having to host a visitor, even a family member or friend, would have put me in a flat spin. It brought me back to when my mother had tried to "help me" by inviting friends to stay. My stomach would churn, my brain pulsed at every decision or choice I had to make, fearing it would be the wrong thing. By now my palms would have been sweaty and I would have accomplished nothing other than a raging headache. Not today. I could control it, facing it head on, questioning it, acknowledging it and eventually overcoming it and managing it.

Now the only feeling I had in my stomach were butterflies of excitement and my brain was pulsing with ideas. We were like two teenagers, come to think of it she wasn't far off. As soon as I saw her, I jumped up and down, waving to her over the sea of people all here to greet their loved ones. As she raised her hand in greeting, her pace quickened to a run. She had spotted me amongst the throng.

We were both pushing our way through the crowd, Maryam dropped her bag at my feet and we both hugged, jumping up and down with delight.

I reluctantly let go of her, picking up her bag and taking her by the hand. Come on let's get out of here, I said. I couldn't wait to get her all to myself. Once at the car park we hugged again.

'Ah! I'm so pleased to see you, Aalinna! I have missed you.'

'Me too. Come on, let's get home.'

The car journey back was only a 30-minute drive. . 'Check you out, driving around Manhattan. Has someone let the local police know you've been let loose in the city?' We were back at the apartment a few quips later.

'Right, your room is in there,' I said, plonking her case on the bed. 'You have a nice bath and I will make us a bite to eat, then you can tell me *everything*,' I said with an exaggerated span of my hands.

'OK, bossy,' she winked. 'That sounds good.'

We sat at the breakfast bar with our meal eaten. 'Come on. I said. 'Let's sit on the sofa, it's comfier.' I put on some music and poured us both a drink.

I looked her over as she stood at the window looking out, waiting for me to join her. It was a funny notion. She was a grown woman now but I still saw her as my little sister, especially as she stood in her comfy pajamas with her shiny black hair tied back in a plait, smelling sweet from her bath. As she turned to join me on the sofa she caught me looking at her and smiling.

'Don't do that' she laughed. 'You make me feel about ten years old.'

I laughed, patting the seat next to me. 'Come on then, woman of the world, tell me all about it.' We chatted about her course and the friends she'd met, I was so happy to hear that she was coping with her classes with ease and making lots of friends.

'So what's been happening with you?' she asked. 'You seem to be doing okay here all by yourself.'

'Yeah, I'm doing pretty well actually. Did I tell you I've been back in touch with Rabab? He's in a pretty bad way over there in Bangkok, I do feel for him, but he's putting the rest of the family through hell. I've been keeping in regular contact with Aunt Sabera and Maher, poor Aunt Sabera doesn't know what else to do for him, he and Uncle are barely speaking. He's upsetting the whole family, Maher has to take on everything as the only other child, and it's so unfair on him.' She slammed her glass on the table, I jumped out of my seat as the glass rang to a near-shatter.

'Are you okay? 'I asked.. I looked to where she stood, with her back to me at the breakfast counter. No response.

'Maryam?'

'Are you for fucking real, Aalinna?'

I don't know what shocked me more, the venom in her voice

or the foul language coming from her mouth. 'What? What have I said? What's going on?' What could have made my sweet sister act like this? 'Maryam, what is the matter with you?' I said, approaching her with my hand outstretched. I moved to rub her back that was turned to me. The force with which she swung around to face me made me step back, her words hit me like a blast.

'Surely even *you* aren't that stupid. Selfish maybe.' I stood and gawped like a fish, I did not get a chance to respond before she continued. 'How can you sit there all compassion and sympathy for others with not a thought for your own family.'

'No, Maryam, you're wrong, I've done lots of thinking about what I put Mum and Dad through, I swear I just haven't had the chance to see them yet, to apologise and make it up to them.

She simply stared at me, suddenly looking deflated and disgusted. 'You really don't get it do you?'. I wracked my brain, trying to come up with the right answer. 'What about me? What about what I went through?'

'But you were happy, you were the good one, the clever one, the quiet one.'

'Exactly, I was afraid to breathe, Aalinna. Most of the time, I tried to make myself invisible or at least comply and agree with all that was going on or being asked of me. No one had time, for me they were always too busy either dealing with you or worrying about you to even notice me.'

'No, that's not true. Mum and Dad adored you, they are so proud of you.'

'Proud of me?!' Maryam spat. 'They barely knew me, they were either on the other side of the world seeing to you and if they were back in Dhaka they were too busy worrying about you to notice I was there! I lost my whole family, Aalinna. I was 13 years old, a teenager for God sake. One day my life went from a house of fun with lots of family and friends calling and a beautiful wacky sister, to screaming, shouting, accusations, doctors then hush whispers and finally, silence. The door was closed on me.' She paused for a moment and regulated her breathing. 'Do you remember the days after Dr. Chowdhury first came?' I could not.

'While you were in your own little world, I was in the real world. I watched you for days, you were lying on that bed like a zombie, waxy white and so thin I was sure you were going to die. I would sit by you, begging you to open your eyes, promising to be a better sister if you would only get better. The doctor coming and going, mother crying, father trying to be stoic.'

'Oh, Maryam.' I tried to reach out and touch her but she pulled away, tears streaming down her face, her cheeks red and flushed.

She wiped her dripping nose with the heel of her hand, sniffing loudly. It reminded me of when she was little, my arms ached to comfort her as I would have done then. She continued:

'Then when Mum and Dad said they were taking you America I was so confused. You seemed okay to me. From what I'd heard through whispers and listening at doors that were always closed to me they were going to hospitalise you, get you treatment, I was so scared for you, I wanted to warn you but I didn't and when they took you I waved you off, watching you, smiling. You thought you were going off on an adventure. Do you know how guilty I felt? How responsible I felt that I hadn't warned you?'

'No, Maryam, you weren't to know, it wasn't your fault.'

'How was I to bloody know that?' she roared. 'Weeks turned into months I didn't know what was happening or if you were ever coming back even, I missed you, I missed Mum and Dad. Then Dad comes back alone telling me you're fine, you just needed rest but I knew he was lying, I'd over-hear him talking to Dr Chowdhury, saying how much worse it was than they'd initially thought. Did you know I confronted dad? We had a huge argument.'

I opened my mouth to answer but I didn't get a chance – she was off again.

'No, I don't expect you do. I told him I'm sick of this, that someone should tell me what's going on. Then, and only then, they finally allowed me to call you but I was warned on what to say and what not to say. No one was allowed to upset you. I was just to stay here all on my own and defend the family, from the whispering, the snide remarks, the questioning. But that was okay, as long as you weren't upset.'

By now I'd sat on a stool, my legs none the less shook underneath me.

'I worked so hard in school, Aalinna. I was so afraid of failing, bringing anymore burden on our parents. Struggles with coursework or teachers, fallouts with friends, periods, crushes on boys, who do you think I talked to? Who was there?' She was gasping for breath through huge sobs, I put my hands in my head and joined her. She wasn't finished yet.

'Oh no, you don't get to do this, you are not going to make me feel bad, no way, Aalinna. You look at me.'

I did.

'Then finally I thought that it was all going to be okay, you all came home and then you, Mum and I were all going and have a great time in Thailand – what happens? What do you do? You go all crazy again! Showing us up in front of the airline staff, the hotel staff, the guests – and who gets punished? Me! After three miserable days I'm shoved on a plane back home to Dad who looks like he's heading for a heart attack and friends who are bombarding me with questions, and others who are only too happy to have more reason to gossip about us. And you, you're whisked away in Mother's arms to get help, well fuck you! Where was my help, where was my comfort?'

'I'm sorry, I'm sorry, I'm sorry.' I repeated, trying to calm her. She was practically hyperventilating, pacing the kitchen in furious strides. I wouldn't have been surprised if she had of hit me. 'Please, please calm down.' But she was too far gone.

'And now, now that you have everything, a wonderful husband, a supportive family, a beautiful daughter, what do you do? You piss off and leave her.'

My chair hit the floor with a scrape of metal and my hand coiled around Maryam's neck, she choked on my lunge.

'Don't you dare? Everything else I will take but don't you dare bring my daughter into this. You do not know what you're talking about.' I released my sister.

We both stood face to face, breathing heavily, our faces were streaked with tears. Her whole body seemed to deflate, her head bowed forward as her body shook with sobs, the rage had left her, and she was my little sister again.

I wrapped her in my arms and rocked her. 'I'm so sorry, so, so sorry, Maryam. I never knew.'

I led her to the bedroom, tucked her in and stroked her hair till her sobs softened and I heard her steady breathing as she fell into a sleep. I kissed her lightly on the head as I tiptoed from the room.

I went to the kitchen and picked up the stool. I sat on it, I put my hands on my head and I cried for her.

I woke late the next morning, I had taken a pill to help me sleep. *She was right about one thing my illness always had to come first and that meant sleep otherwise I would be no use to her or myself.* I lay, listening to her as she moved about the kitchen, I actually felt ashamed to face her. Where to start? Or more to the point where would she start? I chided myself: lying in here hiding wasn't going to help, reluctantly I got up from the bed and went to the kitchen.

'Hi, sorry I slept so late it's just-'

'I know.' She said with a weak smile. 'You need your sleep.'

'Me, me, me.' I replied.

'Aalinna, look, I'm sorry, I meant what I said, well not the part about Nadja, but I didn't mean it to come out the way it did, actually I didn't mean it to come out at all,' she said, biting her lip.

'Oh no, sweetheart, I'm so glad you told me, you must of been hurting so much. It's not healthy keeping all that anger and pain locked away. I should know.' I smirked.

We instinctively moved together and hugged. 'I'm always here for you.' I added, squeezing her. 'Don't ever keep things like that to yourself again, promise me.'

'I promise.'

I smiled at my sister. 'You told me, didn't you? Not so little anymore.' I laughed. 'But seriously, do you promise me you will talk to me about this when you're ready?' I swept a stray hair off of her face and tucked it behind her ear. 'Don't hold back thinking you're going to upset me, ok?'

She nodded..

It lead the way for her to feel at ease asking me about my illness and experiences and for me in turn to ask and acknowledge how she felt during that time. We both knew we still had a lot more talking to do, but it was a start.

Chapter 15
The Dream

"Maybe You Are Searching In the Branches For What Only Happens In the Roots?"

Rumi

I sat alone. I'd dropped Maryam at the airport a little over an hour ago. I was trying to coax myself to go for a run; it was a beautiful day outside with the air crisp and chilled but the sun was shining. I couldn't muster the energy. I felt the familiar vertigo of my mood plummeting. I was trying to fight it but I felt wretched. I looked up the meaning of the word in my newly acquired dictionary.

Personal Adj.

In a very unhappy state.

Synonyms: miserable, unhappy, sad, broken, sorrowful, sorrowing, mourning, anguished, distressed.

Yep, that just about sums it up. Jesus, how could I have been so blind to it all, Anna?. Whilst I hadn't managed the morning run, I made it to Dr. Anna's office and entered with knitted eyebrows.

'I just feel so bloody bad, I had no clue what she'd gone through. I didn't even think about it. What kind of sister does that make me?' I said as I paced the floor of the office.

'Come on, Aalinna, give yourself a break here. You weren't exactly off sunning yourself on a beach. Like she said herself, you were out of it most of the time, I'm sure she understands that now.'

I flopped down on the chair. 'Yeah we had a long talk the night before she left and she does. But that almost makes me feel worse. This whole thing with Rabab has made me realise what I've put my parents and her through. They must have been petrified. Jesus some of the ways I've behaved. Anna, I'm embarrassed even thinking about it – they must have been mortified!' I ran my hands through my hair, the frustration of what I'd done tormenting me. 'Fuck. I hate what this illness brings me to. They've really stuck by me through all this, I never realised just how much they've done and been through for me. I'm so lucky to have them.' I felt shaken, the thought of just where I might have ended up if it wasn't for them, I'd probably never have gotten Zayef and Nadja. I never would have had them. This was big.

I vowed not to let my fight with Maryam or my guilt over my parent's drag me down that was the selfish way out again. For them I would fight this and come out of it stronger. I wanted to be strong for them, pay them back for all the hard work they had put in with me. It was my turn now to put the work in for them. I felt my mood lift a little with the thought of it; it could be enjoyable, this quest for reconciliation. I felt like crawling into bed and hiding under the covers from the relative trauma of the session but I made my way to my class. I had been learning strategies for my dyslexia; I wanted to learn, I wanted to read, every class and every small achievement helping me to reach my goal of being able to read for myself. Once I became a confident reader, I'd have another way of bonding with Nadja.

I'd spoken to Maryam about my learning difficulties the night before she left. We revisited the argument, as we referred to it now. I was talking to her about my first hospitalisation in America, trying to fill in the gaps of time for her – whereupon she did the reverse for me. I told her about when I was an outpatient and how

I tried to lift myself and get out of the confines of the apartment.

'Of course, I dropped out of the real estate course.' I told her, as we sat cross legged on the floor picking snacks off of the coffee table. 'I was still too nervous and anxious around other people and of course I couldn't understand a word the lecturer was saying, so before long I was gone.' I said with a shrug of my shoulders.

'Was he a foreigner?' Maryam asked, her eye brows wrinkled.

'Uh no. What makes you say that? How much wine have you had?' I laughed.

'You said you couldn't understand what he was saying?

'Oh!' I laughed. 'No I mean cause of my learning difficulty.'

'Whoa. Go back a bit, you have a learning difficulty?' She sat up now on her knees to stare at me open mouthed. 'Wait this doesn't make sense. I remember when I was little you and Samama studied everyday straight after school. You guys would hide out together, I was so impressed, that's why I always studied so hard; I looked up to you both, especially when you went off to university. I thought that's why you were so smart.'

The familiar lump in my throat. 'You thought I was smart?' I broke eye contact, I played with a spring roll until I was confident that my voice could reflect the requisite amount of shame.

'Maryam, we weren't studying. Samama was teaching me. She would take notes for me every day.' I threw another slug of wine back. 'I was too stupid to understand what the teacher was teaching. She would explain it to me, Maryam; help me to understand it.' I hung my head. 'I needed to be honest with you.' I whispered.

'Aalinna, you need to give yourself a break is more like it. Come on, you finished university with all that going on! Damn you're clever. I'm impressed.'

She raised her glass. 'To you!' she exclaimed. The cold rolled glass clinked. Maybe she was right. The shame of my inability to read ran deep. .

Our disagreement had started me thinking about Samama, how she must have felt after the time I'd put the phone down on her, rejecting her attempts at making up – twice. I hadn't even stopped to think about it before. She may have needed me for all I knew. I didn't give her much chance to tell me so. God, she must have been so hurt, did she hate me for it? *God, I was such an asshole. I will do this for you my friend, I won't let all your hard work on me go to waste.*

The lessons were hard but were a revelation. I was amazed at how such small changes could make such a difference to my ability to understand and comprehend. I knew with determination and practice I could simply pick up a book without anxiety and read, the sheer joy of it! I comforted myself with the image of Samama encouraging me all the way.

*

As always, after class I was exhilarated but exhausted. My brain was frazzled and eyes strained to stay open. This particular evening though, I was glad of the weariness I hoped it might go some way to helping me sleep and some way to stopping my guilty brain from going over the argument with Maryam verbatim.

I lay on the sofa, the lights low and the Vivaldi soft to ease my racing thoughts. The pulse of the strings in rhythm with my headache spoiled any comfort I tried to take from the music. It reminded me of the time I was trying to get my medication right. Even now, if I didn't take it regularly or get enough sleep, my head would pound, and my anxiety would begin to stir at the thought of the world beyond my front door. The anxiety made my stomach churn and muscles contract and spasm. It was a vicious circle; the headache would worsen until it became a one-man band leaving me incapable of focusing on any task or anyone. My stomach, which had started as a small flutter, would eventually be like a launderette washing machine on spin, the vibrations spreading out and causing my body to shake and teeter on loss of function. I'd described it this way when Maryam had asked me how I felt during my low times.

'I know what you're like when you're having a manic episode,' she laughed, recounting some of my funnier moments. She'd obviously been reading up on the subject but I didn't comment. It started me thinking though – how did I actually *feel* when I was becoming manic? Yes, I could use the normal words you would find in any text book but how did it feel for me? How could I ever describe it? If I could express it, maybe I could own it, shape it, and cull it at the first signs.

I turned away from these images of Maryam and back to an image of myself lying my eyes now closing.

*

I'm standing outside my mother's house. My parents are standing by the gate as if waiting for someone to arrive, they look tense and nervous, they keep looking back to where I now sit on a bench, happy and oblivious to their concern.

I hear the *put-put-put* of an engine as it comes up the drive. A small battered motorbike comes through the gates. I do not take any notice. My parents however are trying to push it out of the gate. It has no driver.

The *putting* of the engine becomes hypnotic; I start towards the bike. My parents look even more anxious now. I run my hand along the length of the fuel tank, my heart now beating to the steady rhythm of the engine. It feels good, excitement and happiness stir inside me. *I'll just sit on it for a moment* I tell my parents. I put my leg over and sat on the hot leather of the seat. *No, Aalinna* someone screams. My father puts his hands on his head but it was too late, I feel compelled to ride it. I slowly move out of the gate. *We will be here for you when you get back.* My father stands shoulder to shoulder with my mother. He has tools in his hand. I drive slowly at first, enjoying the breeze through my hair. I pull back on the accelerator, the motorbike, small, shiny and new, the seat encompasses me and holds me safely in place. I feel my excitement rising, I am getting faster and happier at the greater pull of the engine.

I ride confidently through the narrow streets. I weave between rickshaw wallah's and overladen pickups carrying building supplies and workers. Their horns toot and blast at my getting in their way. *Go to hell* someone says. I notice my Aunt Sabera, Maher and Zayef standing on the high lipped curb, its height never really serving its purpose when the floods come. They wave at me to slow down. I smile and wave at them breezily; how silly, they don't realise I am an expert at this. I resent their interference. *They're trying to spoil my fun!* I pull back harder on the accelerator. I'm going so fast the trees and people are a blur of colour. The bike is a huge roaring confluence of steel and oil at once shiny and black. The speedometer is gone. There was no need for one. There are no limits. I know people are staring now. I pity them and their lack of understanding. Their inability to feel what I could feel. I barrel along enjoying the fun and excitement. The roar of the engine is so loud I feel my ears vibrate.

As I swerve and turn I realise I am lost. I want to slow down a little but my brain can't figure out how to. On instinct it forces my foot towards the brake pedal but by now it has disappeared. I hang on, the bike was now in full control. I'm scared, unable to keep my seating as I take corners at high speed, the seat is nothing more than a small piece of wood wobbling on shaky bolts. I want to slow down, get off but I don't know how.

Over the roar of the engine I hear voices, they desperately try to reach me – trying to help me find my way safely back. *Aalinna come this way, come child follow me, I have my tools just slow down, I can fix it.* I desperately steer towards their voices. I hear Zayef too, *Aalinna come home now we need you*, the bike tries desperately to drown out their directions with the roar of its engines, but now I can hear them I must fight it. The engines begin to slow and the rev die down. I'm able to limp the bike back to my parent's gate where I'd started. They are all there waiting for me, arms open. My mother, my father, Aunt Sabera – even Maher and Ema. I'm glad to be stopped but I still cling to the bike. Instinct tells me not to get off. They all move forward towards me. I become anxious, breathing heavily and looking around for a way out. But the motor bike is done now, nothing but a rusty old machine. They try to prise my hands off of the handle bars. I grip on tight, fighting them. I can't make them understand, I know what is waiting for me. The harder they try, the harder I fight until over the din of our scuffle I hear a quiet sob. I look over to the kerb, there is Samama a small tear running down her face. *Please Aalinna. Get off. Let go now.* I immediately release my hold.

*

As soon as I got to Dr. Anna I told her about the dream.

'I think I get it,' I said excitedly. I think she was pleased to see me so animated and excited, she knew it had been a rough few days for me given my realisations, an guilt over my parents and Maryam. 'It's a pretty powerful dream. So tell me, what do you think its meaning is?'

'I've thought about it all morning. I'd been so deep in thought I'd run an extra two miles before I realised it. My body kicked in and reminded me of my thirst and that I had to take in some fluids otherwise I think I would still be running now.' I paced as I spoke. 'Well, to me, the motorbike was the manic side of my bipolar; initially I didn't realise it was coming but my parents did, that's why they were worried. They saw something in my behaviour that I had not been aware of.'

'I get where you're going with this, ' said Anna, now sitting forward in her seat, caught up in my excitement. 'You said your father had tools in his hands, do you think these represent him being ready? Preparing himself with the tools he will need to support you. Not physically though, more... emotionally. Strength. Parents understand that kind of thing.'

Shit, I hadn't thought of that. 'Yeah that's exactly it. When my parents see me show an interest in the bike and then get on it my mother screams at me, because she knows where I'm headed – for another manic episode. I'm oblivious, compelled to get on the bike, it draws me to it. I like it, I want it, and it feels good. I enjoy it at first. It makes me feel free, liberated without boundaries. But as it goes on, I need more – to keep the good feelings going. Like in the dream, where I push the bike to go faster, I feel safe at this stage, I still think I'm in control. My bipolar – it makes the rush appeal to me, it tricks my mind. That's why the bike gets bigger, sleeker and the seat is so comfortable, why it holds me fast. It's lulling me into a false sense of security. It has me. That's why in the dream when my family waves to try and slow me down I'm resentful, angry with them, I feel superior. I'm on fire. I'm better than them, than anyone. Why do they have to spoil my fun?

'Aalinna, this is great. Wow – I need a drink. I wish we had something stronger but coffee will have to do. Sit down,' she said waving her hand at me. 'You're making me anxious now. I'll get us some water as well.'

As she called through to the receptionist to ask for the drinks, I took her advice and sat down. Only then did I realise that I was sweating and red faced with excitement, the room felt hot and stuffy and I had some context for the offer of water now! As soon as Anna got off the phone I stood again.

'No sit, take a breath, let's get some water in you first. And some air in this room,' she said as she opened a small window above the larger one with the view of the bridge. She turned around and came to sit by me on the sofa. She took both my hands and we looked into each other's eyes. She squeezed my hands hard, we both laughed with excitement shaking our hands up and down like two excited school girls. The look on the receptionist face as she entered and wordlessly put the coffee on the table had us laughing tears.

'Right, back to work,' said Anna once we had finally stopped laughing. She was right I had needed a break, and sure enough I felt a little calmer.

'So, where were we?'

'I'd just got to the part where I was being a bitch to my family.' Anna gave me a warning raised eye brow. 'Sorry,' I said, shame faced. 'Well, in the dream, I'd gotten faster and faster, deeper and deeper into my delusional state my mania. Hence why the bike lost its speedometer. No limits.

'But soon it all started going too fast. I was losing control but desperately clinging on at first trying to find a way to regain control. I was frightened, I knew I was going to crash and burn, so to speak.' I paused while I played it over in my head. 'So this is your mania coming to its peak, the voices calling you, they were your family, trying to help to bring you back safely to the real world.'

'Yeah,' I said quietly. 'I was crying. I was scared. The delusions were going. Reality was coming back. Just like the bike, I could see it for what it really was, a rundown shabby hulk of metal. But I still didn't want to let it go.'

'Why, Aalinna?'

'I was too scared.'

'Why?'

'Because it was something! At least I still had a grip on something! I knew what would happen.'

'What would happen, Aalinna?'

I ignored her question. 'Maybe the bike was me. It was, beautiful, new, safe but really it was tired, run down, useless.'

'But I thought you said the bike was your bipolar side.'

'I didn't know which was which anymore,' I sobbed. 'That's why I couldn't let it go. I was afraid of the dark pit.'

'What's in the pit, Aalinna?'

'It's so hard to get out of it once you're in it.' I ignored her question again, thoroughly in my own world. 'I know I have to let go of the bike and go down there for a while. To get back to the real world. But it's so scary and lonely, I want to stay on my bike even if it's not real.'

'Aalinna what is in the darkness?'

'Depression,' I finally sobbed.

Chapter 16
Revelations

"Promise me you'll always remember: You're braver than you believe, and stronger than you seem, and smarter than you think."

A.A. Milne

I was shocked by my own revelations, but felt empowered by the understanding it gave me into my own condition. After all, this is what this trip had been about. My evenings where now spent mainly attending classes to help me overcome my dyslexia and my days were with Dr. Anna. I had upped my sessions and with some trepidation, had determined to continue to gain more understanding and explore things further.

Now that I'd revealed to myself my fear of facing a depressive state I wanted to explore more, to see what else I could interpret from not only the dream but the revelations that came through it. I was ready to rip off the Band-Aid and let air at the festering wound in the hope that if it could ooze out, allowing the wound to heal. Yes, it would be painful but I knew just the person who would push me to pick at it and peel away the layers.

'So, that was quite a session yesterday.' Dr Anna said, studying me from her chair. 'I thought about it all night, I think you were very brave, Aalinna.' Her voice softened, I picked at my fingers. 'Yeah, it was.' I said quietly. Once I was in her office, the determination I'd felt dwindled. I felt fear of the raw pain I'd experienced in the last session begin to grip me. All of my instincts were telling me to run, not put myself through this anymore – hell, hadn't I been through enough? Hadn't I done enough?

'I'm scared,' I admitted.

'I know, let's get started.'

I took my fear out on her.

'Oh thanks, is a drink too much to ask for first!' I snapped.

'Yeah, Aalinna, no problem. Coffee or water?' she asked breezily, not allowing my rudeness to divert the conversation.

I began. 'I feel quite liberated. I feel that now if I'm headed for a manic episode I may be able to recognise the signs and if I can't, I think I will recognise it through my parents behaviour, I feel it gives me a chance of controlling it. Owning it. Whereas before I could never judge where I ended and it began.' Dr. Anna just smiled.

'That's great, Aalinna. There was a lot more going on in that dream though, lots more to explore, don't you think?'

I said nothing. I felt nervous.

'What say we discuss some of the things you said, some of the people you saw and why they were there?' She Continued.

Still I said nothing, I began to fidget in my chair, crossing and uncrossing my legs. I avoided eye contact but Dr. Anna's eyes never left me.

'What made the bike go so fast that you began to lose control? Or should I say, why did you make the bike go so fast?' She kept her eyes fixed on me.

Pick pick pick.

'Aalinna.' She tried to speak but I put my hand up, stopping her. 'Please.' I beseeched.

'Ok.' She said.

I felt my stomach settle and let out a huge breath I didn't realise I'd been holding.

'Tell you what I thought about.'

Thank God I thought, grasping on to her words. *She's letting it go. But if I know her it won't be for long.* 'Go on then.' I teased. 'Stun me with your insight.' I was relived she was changing the subject.

'Well.' She said, throwing me a glare and a wink. 'In the dream when you were sitting on the bench, think for a minute, how were you feeling?'

'Well I…'

'No please, just sit for a minute and think. Put yourself back there.'

I thought back, I could almost feel the heat on my face and smell my mother's flowers as I sat on the garden bench.

'It's warm. I'm looking at the flowers.'

'Why are you on the bench though?'

'I'm resting.'

'Are you tired?'

'No, not tired. There is nothing else to do. I feel calm but not content, I'm bored, yeah, that's it. I feel bored, Anna.' I looked at her. 'Do you think it's relevant, Anna?'

'I think what you were doing before the bike got your attention is; you weren't waiting on it or looking for it, it found you.'

'Because I was bored.' I said, now getting her point. 'I had nothing else to distract me or occupy my mind, I'd try to distract myself, go outside, find something to look at, something to do but everything seemed… pointless. I wasn't depressed just disinterested. Bored. I realised I'd felt like this since being diagnosed and hospitalised, but not before. Before I'd always been occupied I suppose, things to do, people to see and places to go, especially when I was manic. But now I feel stable. Don't get me wrong, it's not that I want to be manic or depressed but now that I've experienced that rush I find it hard to be content with normal. After a while everything feels dull, feeling balanced starts to be mundane and sometimes even stifling. I feel I've lost my edge, invigoration I used to have for life.'

Dr Anna rested her glasses on her hand. 'Aalinna that's probably because on the lead up to and during a manic episode you experience increased energy levels. That's the high you get, initially you will have an intense ability to concentrate, so when you get well and you're stable on your medication after the initial relief, people can feel like their senses have been dulled. Hence why historically, people when first diagnosed will try and come of their medication.' She said pointing her finger at me. 'Like in your case when you returned to Dhaka and had to return from your holiday in Thailand.'

I immediately had a fleeting image of Maryam and feelings of guilt but now I could also smile. The night after our argument when we had talked she had done an impression of me during a manic episode, we had both laughed long and hard. I decided I'd hold on to that memory instead, maybe talking was working.

I returned to the conversation in hand.

'So do you think I need to keep occupied? Keep myself stimulated? Do you think that's why when I'd made up my mind to support Rhabab and his problem and Aunt Sabera I felt excited? I didn't feel overwhelmed, I felt involved.

'Yes probably.' She said simply.

'So how do I figure out what's healthy interest and excitement and what's the beginnings of becoming manic?' I asked, exasperated. 'How do I know what's being bored and what's getting depressed?'

'That's what we're learning here. It's all about balance, reading the signs, listening to yourself and others. Your family, your friends and your doctors, she grinned. It's about accepting that sometimes others can see what's coming even if you can't or don't want to see it.'

'Like when my parents knew before me, they knew the motorbike was going to show up they knew it was on its way, they tried to stop it and stop me but I didn't want to hear it.'

'Yes. Hey don't look so sad.' She said, squeezing my hand.

'I'm not I'm overwhelmed, God I really don't have to do this alone, I've wasted so much time trying to hide, trying to act continually in control in front of people, but I didn't have to – don't have to, they know anyway, they don't care. They are there for me, looking out for me not trying to trip me up and get at me, I was assuming they judged me like I judged myself, but they love me. I just need to love myself.'

I drove back to the apartment, stopping at the local grocery store to pick up something for dinner. I felt strangely calm wrapped in a blanket of warmth of the love emanating from the network of family and friends I had around me.

I was eager to get home, I wanted to call as many of them as possible and hear their voices with my new ears but most of all, I needed to hear my little girl's voice. The rain was coming down hard and the traffic heavy. Whilst I waited at the red light listening to the whoosh of the wipers, I put the heater on low to take the chill out of the night air. As I felt the soft warm breeze from the vent blow gently in my face, I thought of her soft breath in my ear when I would lull her to sleep on my shoulder. I just wanted to bury my head in the nape of her neck and breathe her in and feel her soft curls against my cheek. The blast of the horn behind me shattered the image but not my mood.

*

My meal, if not restaurant quality, was good and all the more satisfying cause I'd shopped for it and cooked it without incident. Though as I looked around the kitchen I felt the familiar dread of having to clear up the mess I'd made and was not looking forward to washing the many dishes now strewn all over the work surface. That job would take no satisfaction in having to complete. I was bipolar not crazy.

After a call to my parents, I called Zayef 'Maher is getting married.'

'What? No way. Finally, Oh I'm so pleased for them, hang on, I just spoke to my mother why didn't she tell me?'

'Ahh she doesn't know yet. Zayef only asked her last night so he is going over to see Uncle and Aunt Sabera this morning.

'I wish I could be a fly on the wall for that. Aunt Sabera is going to be ecstatic.'

'Yeah and your mother is going to be right in the middle of organising it, no doubt. At least it will get them off my back for a while.' We both laughed.

Talked out but relaxed, I could ignore the dishes no longer. I cleared up in the kitchen and made my way to bed. I had class tomorrow and the day after a double session with Dr Anna and I had a horrible feeling that she was going to start digging deeper at that scab. But for the time being I put it all out of my head and filled my mind with happy thoughts, granting myself a peaceful sleep.

*

I arrived at Dr Anna's with two coffees and a box of doughnuts. The receptionist glared at me, *well your coffee stinks*. I got the distinct feeling she didn't like me and I rather enjoyed the fact I didn't care. Even a small thing like this was progress, as before I would of worried that I'd upset her, rambled on making excuses for bringing the coffee and probably feeling bad most of the day about it. But now I gave her my best smile and went into the office.

'Ah. You're a saviour said Anna, jumping up to grab the coffees from my hand whilst I tried to steady the box of doughnuts under my arm. 'Rough morning.'

I laughed, the clock said it was 12pm but she looked tired already.

'We can do this another day.' I said hopefully.

'Ah no, sit down.' She said, smirking.

We chatted about my class whilst we drank and gorged on doughnuts.

I'm loving it, I can't believe I'm doing it really. It's just giving me so much confidence, Anna. Just knowing I'm not dumb, not feeling I've something to hide from the world, I can fit in, buy a morning paper, pick up a magazine to read over lunch, look up and get information by myself. It's so empowering. I can't wait to see Zayef's reaction. I'm like a big child I keep going over different scenarios of how I will tell him, like just picking up his morning paper and reading an article to him, seeing the sunrise and pride on his face.'

'Aalinna this gives me so much pleasure to hear you talk like this, I've watched you progress so much over the last weeks especially the last few sessions.'

'I know.' I replied. 'I'm delighted it's been a breakthrough. I'm using it every day, implementing what we've discovered and it's making such a difference.' I smiled.

'So.' Anna said. 'What do you think we need to address next?'

I felt the coffee sour in my stomach and the doughnut no longer tasted so sweet. 'I know where you're going with this.' I said, eyeing her.

'Samama.' She said.

She wasn't picking at the scab today she was ripping it off.

'Aalinna, we need to talk about this.'

'I know; I have been thinking about it.'

'You have?!' I'd caught her by surprise.

'She was my friend, my best friend, my sister, she looked out for me she was always there for me, but where was I when she called me? Not once but twice. She could have needed me. I miss her. So much.'

'I know.'

'I feel so bad.'

'I know.'

'You don't know, some of the things I said to her. I didn't mean it; I was just angry. I didn't know...'

'Didn't know what, Aalinna?'

'I told her to go to hell. That's what I shouted at the people in the dream, that's why I went faster trying to get away from what I'd said what I'd done. I've been running all this time. I realise that now.' I took another breath. 'I didn't know though. If I'd only have known.'

'Know what.'

'That she was going to die, that I was never going to see her again, that I would never get to tell her how sorry I am.' My body started to shake with sobs.

'You can tell her, Aalinna. She knows she loves you. She wouldn't want you to hurt like this.'

'I know all that!' I snapped. 'I figured that out but.'

'But what?'

'Ooh I don't know.'

'Yes you do.'

'I don't want to.' I was quieter now.

'You don't want to tell me?' Anna asked.

'No that's not what I mean.'

'Then what don't you want to do, Aalinna?'

'She said to let go, in the dream when I'd stopped and was clinging to the motorbike she was crying on the kerb.'

'She said let go Aalinna, let it go now.'

'I don't want to.'

'Why?!' Dr Anna sounded confused now.

'I don't want to let her go. I don't want to forget her. I'm so sorry Samama.' I buried my head in Anna's shoulder and cried the tears I'd swallowed down at her death bed all those years ago.

I didn't go to class the next day or to see Anna the day after that for our scheduled session. I'd called and cancelled our appointment but she called me anyway.

'Hey, Aalinna.'

'Hey, Anna.'

'How you doing?'

'I'm ok, tired.'

'Didn't you feel up to it today?'

'No, I didn't go to my class yesterday either. I just needed some space. I have been taking my meds though and making myself go for a run each day.'

'You eating?'

'A bit. I'm trying. I'm sad Anna.'

You're grieving,' she began. 'You never did properly before. But hang in there, you're doing all the right things, do you want me to come to you?'

'No thanks, I need this time alone. But don't panic, I'm not depressed.'

'I know.' She said. 'You're sad. Grieving, it is a very personal thing.'

'Thank you.'

'Ok, I will give you another day, then I want you at my office – comprende?'

'Yes.' I said simply.

'Look after yourself, I'm proud of you.'

'Thanks.' I put down the phone.

*

I spent the next few days alone and quietly managing my day. This did hurt but it was a different pain from the guilt. I cried for all the times we would never have together again, remembering the great times we shared and for the pain of missing her. Dr Anna was right; I was grieving but this time I felt like I was honouring her memory rather than trying to forget it.

I think it was the quietest I'd ever been on a plane, I felt subdued, I was happy and excited to be going home but nonetheless thoughtful. My last visit with Anna had been an emotional one, she initially hadn't been too keen when I announced I had decided I was ready to go home.

'Aalinna, are you sure? Do you think you're ready?'

'Yes.' I said. 'I need to start putting all I've learnt in practice, plus I'm sad, so I want my family around me – I need their comfort.'

She smiled. 'I guess you are ready then.'

She reminded me I could call her anytime and I promised to continue our sessions regularly over the phone.

'Thank you, thank you for everything.' I said as I hugged her.

'You did all the hard work, Aalinna.' She said, squeezing me back.

I realised I had revisited many places that had blurred or unhappy memories for me, the hospital where I'd first been hospitalised, the apartment where I took my first tentative steps into recovery, Central Park where I'd wandered lonely and frightened and Central Library that I had longed to be part of. Even trips out to the theatre and restaurants that had once caused me so much anxiety, I'd either made new memories or learnt from the old ones. I knew I couldn't rewrite the past but I could use it to better the future. There was however one more place I needed to go now to complete this journey, one I could never go before but now I needed to and wanted to.

I was met by the car and driver at the airport, telling Zayef I'd rather he met me back at home with Nadja. I wanted our reunion to be private he understood, even our parents were going to stay away, well for the first few hours at least.

I was taken aback by the heat. I'd forgotten just how warm Dhaka could be in these months; I welcomed the cool of the air conditioning as I sat in the back of the car whilst the driver loaded the bags in the boot. I told him when I first met him where I want to stop off before we headed home.

When the car pulled to a stop I got out, my eyes stinging in the bright sunshine. As I made my way along the paths through the rows of tidy cared for graves, I realised I wasn't quite sure where she was – I'd never went to the burial. Strangely, I wasn't concerned I knew I'd find her, I weaved in and out of the stones stopping to read some of the inscriptions, admiring the beautiful flowers and trinkets that had been placed so lovingly by friends and family members. I turned and looked behind me at another row of decorations and there it was, replete with Samama's birth date.

'Hello my friend.' I could almost hear her reply see her laughing face, *well you took your time.* I crouched down and felt the cool of the marble slab. 'I'm sorry, sorry for everything sorry for what I said what I didn't say, I'm sorry you're dead.' I cried. 'But I can't do this anymore, you're right.'

Of course I am.

'I need to let it go.'

I'm glad Aalinna

'I will never let you go though. I will never forget you, I will live this life for us both. I closed my eyes and saw her smile.

I told her all about Zayef. 'I have a baby now, you know. Rhabab isn't doing great but don't worry, I will look out for him and Maher's finally getting married! I expect you know all this but it just feels so good to have you to talk to again.'

I cried for all the years I'd wasted not having her in my heart, too afraid to think of her, too guilty to share my feelings and my life with her. I imagined the heat of the sun on my back as her warm prescience.

'You rest, my friend. I will come see you soon. I love you!' I blew a kiss at her name and turned towards the car. The driver opened the door on seeing me approach.

'Are you ready to go home now Madame?'

I smiled at him. 'Yes, I think I am.'

Chapter 17
New Beginnings

"Sorrow prepares you for joy. It violently sweeps everything out of your house, so that new joy can find space to enter. It shakes the yellow leaves from the bough of your heart, so that fresh, green leaves can grow in their place. It pulls up the rotten roots, so that new roots hidden beneath have room to grow. Whatever sorrow shakes from your heart, far better things will take their place."

Rumi

Curled up in the chair with Nadja on my lap my contentment was almost tangible. The gentle sighing and sucking noises she made as she drank were like a language only she and I could understand. This is what I had longed for, the unspoken communication and bond between us as she twirled my hair and our eyes locked.

I looked up to see Zayef sitting quietly in the chair across from us, the glow of the reading lamp illuminating his face in the otherwise darkened room. The paper he had been reading now lay idle in his lap. I could see the pleasure he was taking from watching us; he understood what it had taken to get to this point. It must have been a scene Zayef never thought he would see. Though through it all he stayed strong, supporting and loving me, defending my choices and my decisions. *I love you* I mouthed to him.

My return home had been an emotional one. After my visit to

the cemetery I'd headed straight for home. The car had no sooner pulled on to the driveway that Zayef came hurrying out the front door, Nadja in his arms. I couldn't help it, I burst into tears. I couldn't get out of the car fast enough. I jumped from the car and grabbed them both, hugging their bodies to mine. I laughed through the tears. 'We've missed you!' Zayef exclaimed as he took my head in his free hand and planted a kiss firmly on my lips.

'Yuk,' screeched Nadja, who was trying to escape from his arms. I swooped her up, tickling and kissing her all over, loving the sound of her giggling as she cried my name and tried to escape me.

The first week went by so quickly that after the initial exhilaration of being home my anxiety began to creep in. I worried about how much I had to prove. I had gone off and left my child for months and now that I was back I felt an overwhelming pressure to be 'better'. Would everyone now expect me to be perfect? To have come back whole? New and complete? Unfortunately, this damn illness did work like that. I was never going to be cured, I would always have days where I felt overwhelmed. Those everyday things or life events that people took for granted would, at times, be a mountain to climb. Medication, routines, strategies would always be part of my life. But I could do it; live, love, function, create. I could make friends and enemies in spite of this, not because of it. I could even make more babies if I wanted to. It was the day after I had returned home and we had gone to my mother's for dinner. I was surprised to find there was only my mother and father joining us. Once we had finished eating we retired to the garden to relax and let Nadja tire herself out. As always she had the undivided attention of the two men in her life, her father and grandfather, who were now taking turns to push her on the swing or push her along on her trike.

'She has those two wrapped around her finger,' I laughed.

'Yes, I think they will be tired long before she is,' my mother said lovingly, watching them play.

'Your father and I have been talking to a counsellor and doing a bit of research.' I sat up to speak. 'Let me finish first.' I reclined, looking at my daughter, and listened.

'We wanted to be able to support you Aalinna, plus we realised we needed to learn a bit more about this too. I'm sick of this, this thing, bipolar, messing with my family.' *Go Mum!* I thought but I said nothing.

'So we have got more insight into this and also we discussed how and what we could do to support you when you got home. We've also been talking with Zayef's parents,'she confessed. 'I know how much you value your privacy but...' She wrung her hands as she formulated her explanation. 'But we can't help if we don't know how to.' Now I did interrupt.

'Mum, why did you think I would get angry? I appreciate it, I really do,' I said reaching for her hand.

Relief replaced her embarrassment and knitted eyebrows. She gave a weak smile. 'That's why there's only the five of us today. I thought it would be best not to invite everyone because it may overwhelm you. But your face when you walked in looked so disappointed that they weren't here... I wasn't sure whether I had done the right thing or not.'

'You did the right thing,' she beamed back at me. 'How about in the future you ask me? I don't want you to be afraid to ask me things or talk to me. I just need you to accept my answer, even if you don't understand why, or if you think your way is better. I need you to accept my choices. I need you to accept me.'

'I will try,' she said, hugging me.

'That's all I ask, Mum.'

*

I was glad to be able to spend my first few days and evenings with my husband and daughter, giving me the chance to find my feet and talk late into the evening with only Zayef and a bottle of wine for company. Zayef had taken a few days off of work so we could all spend some time together. It was a kind gesture but if I'm honest, it really didn't help. I felt a bit out of my depth; he had his own routine with Nadja and his kind fussing only made me more anxious, so as much as I loved having time with him, I was excited to kiss him goodbye that morning and wave him off with Nadja in my arms. *Right young lady, let's do this.*

Things didn't go quite as smoothly as I'd hoped, our first bath time was a calamity. I manage to get soap in her eyes and frustrate her with my lack of knowledge. I could feel my resolve waver.

'Mama!' she whined, 'Do it like dada!' I became frustrated and felt tears stinging my eyes. I took a deep breath. C*ome on, Aalinna, you're the adult here. Don't fall at the first hurdle.* I kneeled down at the bath tub so I was level with her, her lip wobbling. 'Mama has a new way of doing it and it's going to be fun,' I said, tickling her. I was soon wet from her splashes – disaster averted. I'd managed to also assert myself on a few occasions, whilst feeding Nadja. I hadn't been happy with the look of her dessert. I tasted it and felt my teeth dissolve! It was laden with sugar. I swiftly replaced it with a plate, a fork and a banana.

'Madame,' one of the housekeepers protested. 'The treat is what she likes, this is what Sir gives her. You try, she will like it,' she said as she walked off.

I instantly felt embarrassed and guilty, she knew what my child liked and I didn't. I stared at the bowl. I stood up, snatching the bowl and made for the kitchen.

'She is not to have this anymore; it is not good for her or her teeth. In the future she can have fruit as a dessert and maybe this as a treat.'

'Yes Madame, of course.'

'Thank you.'

I walked back to the table. My heart was pumping but now I'd done it I felt great. Small everyday things were a challenge but the more I did them the more my confidence grew.

*

It had been organised that we would all get together at the weekend to welcome me home and celebrate Maher's engagement. I was excited and looking forward to seeing everyone there: Aunt Sabera and Uncle, Maher and Ema, Yushra and Uncle Abraham, as well as my parents and in-laws.

All were present at the restaurant by the time we arrived. I was delighted to see Yushra and couldn't wait to have a proper chat with her. I squeezed her close.

'*Come back to ours after for a drink*,' I whispered in her ear.

'Yeah great, I want all the gossip,' she winked.

We all ate heartily, the women, once finished, moved closer together all excited and wanting to discuss the up and coming ceremonials. Whilst the men feigned boredom and used the excuse to smoke cigars and talk business. I was just glad not to be the focus of attention. On the way back from the bathroom I bumped into Maher.

'Hey!' We said to each other hugging. It was the first we had the chance to be alone. 'I'm so pleased for you,' I said, squeezing his hand. 'And it's about time too!' I scolded.

'Yeah, yeah, yeah, you and everybody else,' he laughed. 'You're looking great, Aalinna. It's good to have you back.'

'Thanks.'

'I wanted to talk to you actually, about Rabab.' Taking my arm, he drew me further away from the table, you have been in touch with him recently, right?'

'Yeah, he sounded okay. I mean, you know, it's like you say. He's not right and there is obviously a lot of drinking,' I bit on my lip, 'and other things,' I said, lowering my gaze.

'It's alright, I know,' he said, rubbing my shoulder. 'You don't have to protect him.'

'But I at least got him to open up to me a bit, he's really hurting.'

'Damn, Aalinna. I feel so bad but I'm dreading having him back for the wedding. He's my brother and I love him, but shit, look at my parents. This is the first in months they've actually been getting on and mother is so happy. I don't want him to spoil it.' He rubbed his temple with his fingers. 'He's a fucking ticking time bomb. I want him by my side, but he and my father in the same room? God I feel sick every time I think about it. And I swear I will kill him if he upsets Ema at the wedding.' He instinctively looked over his shoulder at her, sitting surrounded by the women, her face glowing. Then he looked back at his favourite cousin.

'I can't leave him out, he's my brother, but sometimes I could happily choke him.' He was now red faced and sweating.

'Calm down. Go in and splash some water on your face and take a deep breath. And come out smiling. We will sort this, okay? But not here, not now.' I could see Aunt Sabera looking at us now, a worried expression on her face.

He took a deep breath. 'Sorry I didn't realise how stressed I was till I started talking about it, I shouldn't be putting all this on you.'

'Hey we're family, okay? You guys have stuck with me too.' I knew there were a few times I was the ticking time bomb in the company but they had always invited me, always protected me so now it was my turn. I kissed him on the head. 'Smile,' I said through gritted teeth. 'Your mother is watching.'

He laughed. 'Isn't she always? Thank you, Aalinna.'

I could see Aunt Sabera rising from her seat. Maher immediately made for the bathroom whilst I intercepted her half way. 'Hey, Aunt Sabera, I bet you're busy and excited,' I said, steering her back towards the table.

'Yes, yes, very much so, isn't it wonderful?' She looked over my shoulder. 'Is everything okay? Maher looked upset.'

'Upset? No he was just telling me how excited he is and my fault, I got a bit emotional.' I prayed for forgiveness in my head.

She seemed satisfied and returned to the table with me. Maher returned to the table unnoticed and the night continued without incident, with much laughter and storytelling for the bride-to-be. Uncle Abraham, as usual, received scorned looks from my mother when he inevitably gave his opinion on marriage. Even I could see the new closeness between my aunt and uncle, the way he smiled over at her when she relayed stories about their wedding day, the soft touch he gave her hand when she yawned. The excitement and planning of an up-and-coming wedding (and no doubt the prospect of grandchildren) had given them a new focus and a boost to their marriage. If only Rabab had known what he was putting everyone through he would feel so bad, I knew this because I had done the same.

Later, when everyone else had gone home. I, Zayef, Yushra and Maher went back to our place for a drink. Ema had decided to go on home, she had been tired having spent most of the day being whisked from one wedding appointment to the next. She insisted Maher come to our place with the rest of us.

Yushra poured a sauvignon and I sat with my feet up on the sofa facing her.

'Well how're you? How was America?'

'Good, really good. I sorted a lot out, I'm feeling pretty okay.' I retold my story about the bath time with Nadja, and the staff. She laughed at first before giving me a high-five. 'You told her!'

'Yeah, you know. I'm just taking each day as it comes.' I said as I refilled our glasses. 'Some are easier than others. It's crazy, sometimes it's the stupidest things that get me worked up, like wrapping a present for this birthday party I got to take Nadja to next week I swear I got in such a state. It took me about an hour, I was sweating by the end of it. And the other night, I was trying to open a can I was so pissed off. All I wanted to do was have a nice meal with Zayef but by the time he got home I was so worked up we started arguing,' I sighed.

'Hang on,' Yushra began, 'you have staff and you have a cook. Why didn't you get them to do it? Why put yourself through the stress when you don't have to?'

'Ah, I don't know. I just thought I should. I should be able to do these simple things.'

'Says who?' Yushra replied, waving her wine glass. 'For God's sake Aalinna, maybe you should be able to do it maybe you shouldn't, no one cares. You're just being hard on yourself. Don't sweat the small stuff, you've enough to contend with. You're not bloody Mary Poppins you know? Seriously, I can wrap a present I can open a tin and it's no problem for me.' She said thumbing at herself.

'Oh thanks, make me feel stupid why don't you,' I said as I gave her a playful kick.

'Look, we're in a privileged situation here, use it to your advantage. Don't use it as a stick to beat yourself with.

'You're right, Yushra.' I leaned in to hug her. 'Ah. Another wine will be great thanks,' she laughed, sticking out her glass.

*

I lay in bed going over what Yushra had said to me. I smiled. She was one of the few people who could get away with giving me a good talking to and I loved her all the more for it. Maryam's mood was much the same these days, though it was good that somehow out of this whole mess we had become truly close. I'd missed her tonight but I knew she would be home a few weeks before the wedding so it wouldn't be long to wait. We managed to talk often on the phone.

'What are you thinking about? 'Said Zayef as he came out of the adjoining bathroom.

'Yushra,' I replied. I didn't mention my thoughts on Maryam, I didn't want to get into a conversation about that yet. We hadn't had a chance to talk about it since I got home and now was not the time. I hadn't even told him about my dyslexia but I had a plan for revealing that.

He got in to the bed beside me smelling of mint toothpaste and Cuban cigars. 'Yushra is great, it was good seeing you too together,' he said.

'Yeah, but we didn't see much of you. You and Maher, you were both hiding out in the kitchen all night,' he said nothing and stared up at the ceiling.

'Hey, it's okay. I can guess what you guys were talking about. He spoke to me about it briefly at the restaurant.'

'Aalinna, he is so stressed out. I don't know. I tried to reassure him but he has a point. I've been hearing more and more about

Rabab and it doesn't sound good.'

I sat up on my elbow. 'Has Maher even told Rabab about the engagement?'

'Yes he has. Well, I should say he tried. He's called him a number of times, left messages but still no response. It's really pissing Maher off because of course Aunt Sabera keeps asking when he will be home for the wedding. I think she wants time to work on Uncle.'

I said nothing, turning off the light and taking in the darkness.

'Hey, you okay?' I felt Zayef's hand search me out in the bed. 'Come here, lay close with me.'

'Zayef, I've put you all through so much,' I said, burying my head in his shoulder.

'Hey, don't go there? No more of this. You have tried everything, worked damn hard to get well. So this is not the same, this Rabab thing.'

I kissed his cheek. 'Thanks, I'm going to call him and see if I can get through to him.'

'Maybe he will listen to you, but I'm sorry Aalinna, that man needs a good talking to.' I could feel him tense.

'Hey, let's leave it for now, okay?'

'Okay.'

A few days later, before I'd had the opportunity to call Rhabab, Aunt Sabera came to see Nadja and me. She was really worried as Maher had told her that he hadn't been able to get in touch with Rabab about the wedding. 'I've tried to call him too,' she said, tears in her eyes, 'but he doesn't answer.' She looked so upset and worried, the happy glow she had at the meal was all but gone. My heart broke for her, hadn't she been through enough?

'Yes, sorry. I spoke to him briefly last night; I was going to call you today and let you know.'

I'd said it before I thought about it. It was too late, Aunt Sabera was on her feet hugging me. 'Oh Aalinna, thank you, thank you. Is he okay?' she asked, concerned.

'Yes,' I said tentatively.

'So why didn't he answer my calls or Maher's calls? I don't understand.'

'Oh, he has been on holiday.' That seemed to satisfy her. 'Yeah,' I rambled on. 'You know what he's like, off he goes, he just doesn't think. Men, eh?' I said with a nervous laugh.

I paced the floor once she left. *Shit, how had I gotten myself into this? What if he wasn't okay? What if something awful had happened him? Damn it Rabab, you'd better be okay or I will kill you myself.* Now it was imperative that I contact him.

I'd settled Nadja in bed, it had been a hell of a day – I had taken her to the birthday party with the gift that had now been rewrapped by the staff. I'd felt sick from the moment I woke, the thought of walking into a den of vipers didn't thrill me but I had to face the other mothers sometime. I fretted about what to wear, flinging clothes all over the bedroom. Taking Yushra's advice I got the staff to bathe and dress Nadja after we'd had breakfast together. I was doing her a favour, she was better off not being around me when I was this anxious.

Finally dressed, I sat on the bed and mentally listed the stares and sarcastic comments I was likely to encounter. I rehearsed my responses, there was no stronger whip than a woman's tongue, and I knew that.

I went downstairs to find Nadja dressed in the outfit I had picked for her.

'Look at me, Mama! 'She whirled round and round, making her dress flow out around her. 'You look so beautiful!' I felt my resolve strengthen. 'Come on little lady, we have a show to put on,' I said, taking her hand to leave.

'But Mama it's a birthday party!' she exclaimed, confused. I forgot how much she could understand these days.

I laughed it off. 'Of course, how silly of me. Let's go have some fun.'

I could have quite happily stayed in the back of the car but Nadja's excited bouncing spurred me on. I rang the doorbell and was swiftly greeted by the birthday girl's mother, a woman I had always got on with. She had been at my wedding and I'd known her since Nadja was small. Our husbands were good friends.

'Aalinna, it's great to see you, come on in. 'Oh Nadja! You look so beautiful!' Nadja gave her a twirl and we both laughed. I could see the crowd of mothers milling in the kitchen, chatting and nursing smaller babies. I was frozen to the spot.

'Hey,' my friend said, putting her hand on my arm. 'They will have someone new to talk about next week. Come on, do it for her,' she said, looking towards Nadja as she ran to her friends. That was all the encouragement I needed. That woman is now a very good friend of mine. I've never forgotten her kindness.

All in all, the day had gone well and as far as Nadja was concerned it was the best party ever. For me, that was all that mattered. I did have the odd nasty comment. 'Oh, Aalinna you're back then.' Or 'Poor Nadja, she must have been lonely without her mother.' They were said with a fake smiles. I knew these two they were the gossip queens of Dhaka's matriarchal cabal. *Hi, thanks. It's good to see you. She's fine, she's loving all the attention now, and we're so close. I'm so lucky having such a wonderful husband; there's nothing he won't do for me. How's yours by the way? Is he still living out in Singapore? Bet he gets lonely.*

*

My grip cracked the shitty plastic of the phone receiver. 'Right Rabab, you listen! You answer, return my calls! I don't care what you're doing, who you're with, or what time it is.' I screamed into the answer phone. 'You pick up. I've had a shit day and the world does not revolve around you. Pick up!' It was the fifth time I'd rang in a row. Thank goodness Nadja was in bed and Zayef at a business meeting, because I was getting seriously frustrated now.

'Hey, cuz.'

I had been so busy ranting I hadn't even heard the phone click and him pick up the receiver.

'Don't you 'hey cuz' me. What's going on? Why haven't you been answering our calls?'

'Hey, chill.' He slurred. 'What's the panic?'

I could hear laughter and music blaring in the background. 'Where are you, Rabab?'

'At home, obviously. You called me, remember? Come on, come on over, I'm having a party,' he was, at the very least, extremely drunk.

'Shit, Rabab. What is with you?'

'What's with all the drama anyway?' he shouted over the din.

'Maher is getting married I expect he would've liked to tell you himself. If you'd only answer the phone or pick up your calls – your mother is worried sick. When did you last eat or sleep for God's sake?'

'Hey relax, come over, have a drink.'

'Did you hear me?'

'Yeah, Maher's getting married, great, I'm pleased, that girl of his is a hottie.'

I'd lost this one. 'Sort yourself out Rabab, we need to talk about this, I will call you tomorrow. Do you hear me?' I yelled in frustration.

'I'm sorry, Lena. Don't be angry with me, you're the only one that cares.'

'I'm not. That's the point. Please call me and soon. Oh, and be sober when you do.' I shunted the receiver down. I found myself panting. I wasn't sure whether I wanted to hug or slap him. What a mess. I'd wanted to call and coax him to come to the wedding a few weeks before even. I'd try and help with his dad and hopefully keep him on the straight and narrow, even if just until the wedding was over, but he was way worse than I thought.

I was starting to think if it might be better he doesn't show at all, or this wedding could be a bloody disaster.

Chapter 18

The Wedding

"You were born with wings, why prefer to crawl through life?"

Rumi

'Yushra, quickly. Come look at these.'

We were at Ema's aunt's home as she had volunteered to do the mehndi for Ema's wedding. The large marble table was laden with books that had hundreds of intricate designs to choose from.

'Coming!' Yushra shouted from the kitchen. She entered the living room clutching armfuls of wedding sari magazines. She flopped them onto the table.

'Oh this is so exciting! When's it going to be my turn?' She sulked, folding her arms. 'I'm going to end up a lonely old woman at this rate.' She looked at Ema and me with doleful eyes.

'Nooo.' Ema and I soothed in unison. 'Don't be silly, your turn will come soon.' We dragged her to sit between us. She spotted Ema's aunt earnestly bobbing her head in agreement and muttering about how young women of today were doomed.

This was one of the great things about being home and, dare I say, settled. Apart from the obvious benefits of being around Zayef, Nadja and my parents daily, I got to spend lots of time with Yushra. .

Ema was also fast becoming a friend. Something I was so pleased about. She was practically marrying my brother and we were the same age, I looked forward to spending time with her and Maher as a couple and hoped that one day our children would become as close as we all were in that big, three-storey house. My mind automatically went to Samama, whilst of course no one could ever replace her, I could see the pleasure it gave Aunt Sabera to have another female in the family: someone to spoil, someone to go to the salon or shops with, talk things over with or give pensive advice to. She felt valued and needed again and I knew that Samama wouldn't mind, quite the opposite. Still, I wished she could be here with us. When we were little we had often said we would have a joint wedding, I imagined a framed photograph of us both in our wedding dresses just like the one on my mother's bedside. I was able to think about her now, and often. At times like this though, it hurt. I was able to enjoy her memory but the smile soon left my face. That day it was because thinking of Samama led me to think of Rabab. I really didn't know what we were going to do with him.

Surprisingly, he, as promised, returned my call the next day. He sounded groggy but at least he was compus mentus.

'I know. I'm sorry, Aalinna. It was a one off. I was just letting my hair down.'

It was like listening to myself at one time.

'What you doing up at this hour?' he asked. 'What time of the morning is it there?'

I sighed. 'I left America weeks ago, Rabab. I told you that the last time we spoke and I left you an answer phone message with this Dhaka number on before I left.'

'Oh sorry, must have forgot. Yes, of course, now I remember.' More lies. 'So this wedding,' he continued, trying to break the silence. 'What date is it? I will check out flights.'

'I think you should call Maher and let him tell you that much. Don't you? And you need to call your mother, she's worried sick.'

I knew I was being harsh but being nice hadn't worked.

'Okay, I will.'

'No now, Rabab. Please. Whilst you're sober.'

'Em, yeah,' he said, giving a nervous giggle. 'I will call them right now.'

'Promise me, Rabab. I will be checking. And be nice to your mother, she thinks you were on holiday so that's why you didn't answer our calls, okay?'

'Thanks for covering for me Lena I knew you wouldn't let me down.'

*

I called up Maher, who confirmed that Rabab stayed loyal to his word.

'He actually sounded fine, Aalinna. And he was really good with Mum, she's so happy now, so that's a bonus. Maybe he is sorting himself out.'

'So is he coming to the wedding then?'

'He said 'yes'. I gave him the dates.'

'Okay, Maher, that's great. I'm glad it's working out.'

*

The months passed quickly, Yushra and I were busy helping with the wedding, Aunt Sabera and my mother were often there, which give me a chance to see my mother without feeling I was the focus of her attention. In fairness she was improving. Although she didn't always accept my way of doing things, she did at least manage to keep her opinions to herself, most of the time. As she had said, she was trying, and on the whole it was much the same as the average mother and daughter relationship: run-ins on how to run a house, raise children, be seen by others and other usual issues.

I had called Rabab again a number of times since he kept his initial promise but he either didn't answer or, when he did, he either made excuses about being too tired or was too drunk or high to make sense. It had started to really get me down. I began fretting when he didn't answer, over which I lost a great deal of sleep. A huge 'no, no' for me. When he did answer I would get myself so angry and frustrated I'd be useless for the rest of the day, unable to focus and dropping everything I touched. It caused a huge argument between myself and Zayef.

He had come home from work late one night to find me sitting in the living room, no lights on and my meal cold and uneaten from earlier that evening. I jumped as he turned on the light switch, I'd been so deep in thought that I hadn't even heard him come in. I saw him take in my drawn face and the plate by my feet. He exploded: 'That is it! This ends here, Aalinna.'

'What?' I feigned ignorance.

'You are not doing this to yourself! He is not doing this to you!'

'Oh, don't exaggerate,' I said, thoroughly on the defensive. It's easy kidding yourself until someone literally turns on the light and shows you up for what you are.

'Aalinna, I mean it. Who put Nadja to bed then?' he snapped, hands on hips.

'What? What's that got to do with anything?' I spat.

'You didn't, did you? And early in the week you were meant to go for dinner with Yushra but now it turns out you didn't do that either. You've been wearing those same jeans for two days.'

'Don't you dare criticise me as a mother!' I was on my feet now. 'And I don't have to go anywhere if I don't bloody want to.' I yelled scooping up the plate, red faced and breathless. I'd been caught out and I knew it. He moved to block the door. 'Aalinna don't you dare make this about me. Like I'm some crazy overbearing husband. I've always treated you with respect, so how about showing me some?'

We both stood glaring at each other. Zayef lowered his head and put his hands in his pockets.

I sighed. 'I just don't know what to do anymore to help him, Zayef. I can't get through to him.'

Zayef took the plate from my hand and steered me towards the sofa where we both sat. He lifted my head with his finger under my chin and stroked my cheek.

'He's my cousin, my friend, my brother, Zayef. I'd do this for any of my friends, you know that. I have always been there for the people I love. They've always been able to depend on me. I can't lose that as well.'

'Aalinna, this has nothing to do with your bipolar, but it's dragging you towards it. We have all tried to help him, you more than anyone, but you know what you were like when you were sick, no amount of talking or coaxing would work. It's the same with him, except he doesn't want to get better, he doesn't want to listen, and he is not you. You can't make him better, Aalinna. He has got to want to get better. You got better but you fought for it, you struggled with it, hey, you do it every day. But he doesn't want to and you can't make him, this is his failing, not yours.'

I cried. I knew he was right. So I vowed that if Rabab called me and asked for help I would be there but otherwise I had to leave it alone. I felt the weight lift off my shoulders, and I began to focus on the family and friends I had around me, as well as the wedding, of course.

I knew Rabab would be coming to the wedding anyway. Aunt Sabera was fed-up with his lack of commitment and communication and probably feared he wouldn't turn up. She'd booked him a ticket and sent it with her hopes and expectations. He was due to arrive the day before the wedding. I didn't know whether this was a conscious decision to keep him away and not take the chance that he would spoil the pre-wedding social events. I was relieved, and I think secretly everyone else was. So for now we were all enjoying the build-up and excitement, spending great times together. I was learning and growing every day.

Maryam was arriving soon and we would be spending a week together before the wedding. She was going to get my undivided attention; I wasn't going to make that mistake again.

*

'Hello, where's the princess?' my sister said. Nadja on hearing her voice immediately ran into her arms.

'What are you doing here?' I said.

'That's a nice way to greet your sister,' said Maryam, swinging Nadja around, making her screech with delight and excitement.

'But I wasn't expecting you until tomorrow,' I exclaimed. 'I have to go out; I was taking Nadja to the park, then I was going to do some final shopping and fittings for my dress for the wedding – and I haven't had anything prepared for dinner!' I ranted, wringing my hands. I absorbed into my anxiety at Maryam's unexpected arrival, Nadja's loud screeching, being caught off guard and having my routine disrupted.'

'Hey,' said Maryam, putting Nadja down on the floor and taking me by the shoulders. 'We can do all that together can't we?' She deployed the look she often gave as a child when she wanted something from me.

I burst out laughing. 'Of course, I'm sorry.' I grabbed her in a hug. 'It's so good to see you but how did you get here?'

'Simple,' she said as she sat Nadja on her lap . 'I took an earlier plane, aren't I clever?' she asked Nadja. Nadja clapped in agreement. 'Zayef organised a lift from the airport for me, isn't he a clever daddy?' Nadja clapped harder at the mention of her father. 'We thought we would surprise you,' Maryam said with her signature grin.

'Of course, I'm delighted. You know me I just get a little crazy.'

'Silly Mummy,' Yushra said to Nadja. She now clapped furiously.

'Huh, so much for loyalty,' I said, tickling her till her little legs and arms ached.

The next two weeks on the build-up to the wedding were hectic and one of the best times of my life. I finally got the time I wanted to spend with Maryam. Our days were spent shopping, playing with Nadja and having girl's lunches with Yushra. We'd spend them gossiping and sharing funny and embarrassing stories. I got to know Maryam better and she got to see the side of me I'd longed for her to know. I was delighted that she and Yushra got on so well and we both loved giving her our old women's advice on men, kids, clothes and handling parents. We often talked long into the night sometimes about the past and my condition but also about her and her life. Our bond grew stronger by the day.

My mother and Aunt Sabera meanwhile, were as always close friends, but the wedding had given them a joint venture together and they were loving every minute of it. To see her and

Aunt Sabera excited and happily heading off, dressed up and full of plans, was balm to my heart. Aunt Sabera, whether through choice or a need to live in the moment, no longer mentioned Rabab or her concern for him. She appeared content with the fact she would be seeing him soon enough at the wedding. As for Uncle, he was once again the proud father, playing his favourite role of grouchy old man.

'Do you see this? You see what I have to put up with?' He threw up his arms in mock despair. We were all once again at my mother and father's for dinner.

'She will bankrupt me this wife of mine, how many more dresses and accessories must I buy for this wedding?' He winked at my father who sat relaxing in the arm chair next to him, his face a picture of contentment. The women sat at the cleared table with coffee discussing the purchases they'd made that day.

'You watch out, son,' Uncle said, giving Maher's knee a fatherly pat. 'This is what they do once you marry them.' Zayef looked at me with raised eyebrows.

'Ah, not a word from you,' I said winking at him.

'Oh hush, ' said Aunt Sabera waving a playful hand at my uncle.

Maher, sitting next to his father, looked over at Ema. 'I don't mind, she will be worth every penny,' he said giving her a loving smile.

The women sighed and ahh'd, the men threw up their hands in despair laughing.

'I think marriage is overrated, men and women should-' Uncle Abraham was interrupted by the sound of my mother's chair scrapping along the marble floor.

'Yes, yes, we all know what you think. Now be quiet and just finish smoking your smelly cigar,' she said, waving at his spiraling smoke and making for the door with a roll of her eyes. No doubt she was off again to check on Nadja who was safely tucked up in bed. Fortunately for Uncle Abraham, she did not see the face he made behind her back. Yushra, Maryam and Ema giggled at the banter.

I sat looking at everyone. I was surrounded by the people I loved but this time I was part of it, not sitting on the outside looking in. I had a beautiful daughter a wonderful husband, a home, family, and friends.

*

It was the day before the wedding and the house was in chaos. Nadja was running around still undressed; she had Maryam wrapped round her little finger, so instead of bathing her as per their morning ritual, Maryam had yet again given in to one more game of hide and seek. My mother was giving her critique on my mehindi which Ema's Aunt had completed the night before.

'She did a good job,' she said, grudgingly. 'Though I did tell her I would've been happy to do it. I have done many more weddings,' she said haughtily. *I need this like a hole in the head.* I threw a beseeching look at my father, even he wasn't sure what he was doing here.

'Yes, dear you are so skillful,' he placated my mother. Putting a hand on her shoulder to steer her away. 'But don't forget! You have another daughter. You will soon be able to show your tailoring skills on her.' My mother was all smug smiles. I mouthed my thanks to my father as I made my escape to shower and dress myself.

In the sanctity of my bedroom, I realised how nervous I was

about Rabab coming. I was excited to see him of course but worried about what state he would turn up in. I felt bad that I hadn't called him again, but then, he hadn't called me. I would just have to wait and see. Maher was pacing the kitchen floor downstairs, his shinny brogues clicking with each step. Coffee in hand, he strategised the day with Zayef.

'So I'm going to go pick him up, I want to make sure he is fit and able before he gets anywhere near my mother.' Maher ran his hands over his face. 'Shit I could do without this.'

'Look, calm down,' said Zayef as he walked round the kitchen picking up papers to be stuffed in his briefcase. 'I will be finished by lunchtime. Any problems, call me and just bring him back here instead of your mother's.' Zayef crossed the kitchen, putting down his cup and squeezed Maher's shoulder. 'It's going to be alright. Okay?' He repeated when Maher didn't respond.

Maher sighed deeply. 'Yeah you're right, thank you for this and thank you for talking to my father.'

Zayef had agreed to talk to Uncle to see if he could smooth the way for Rabab arriving. Basically, he had lied. In as much as he told Uncle what we were all hoping would be the case. Rabab would have sorted himself out, he would be back studying and was looking forward to returning for the wedding to reunite with his parents. And all the family.

Zayef said he wasn't sure how much Uncle believed him but the thing they both agreed on was they wanted Aunt Sabera to be happy, and not to spoil Maher and Ema's day. So he agreed to let the past go in the hope that the wedding would give them all an opportunity to begin making amends. We all hoped he was right.

Once Nadja, Maryam and I were all finally washed and dressed, we had breakfast and the house was a bit calmer. Zayef had left for work, his relief evident as he planted a kiss on all the women's heads. 'Rather you than me,' he said, looking around the room as I walked him to the door. 'Yeah thanks,' I said, shoving him out into the driveway none too lightly. 'Make sure you're back by lunch or I will send them all to your office to get you.' I warned.

My mother and father were next to leave, heading for Aunt Sabera's to see what they could do to help. Maher left last, much the same as myself, he was anxious but excited to see Rabab. He was his brother after all. I made him promise to call me as soon as he picked him up, reminding him if there was even a hint Rabab wasn't right, to bring him here and I would meet them.

'Shit, Aalinna. Now you're making me nervous.'

'Sorry,' I said, walking him to the car. 'What I'm trying to say is I'm here if you need me.' 'Thanks.'

As it was, Maryam and I were still at the house an hour later, Nadja had fallen asleep. Maryam had tired her out with all the running around that morning. I was not happy and told her as much.

'This is just what I didn't need,' I said throwing a look at her. 'I've so much to do and not only am I way behind, she will be like a bear with a sore head when she wakes. You wait and see,' I said, stomping off upstairs to gather some bits I needed. I smiled, it felt good to have a normal sister argument and not get tied up in knots over it. It was the small things like this that everyone else took for granted that made me happy.

When I returned to the room a short while later, ready to make up, I was surprised to find Maryam grinning from ear to ear.

'What are you up to?' I asked laughing.

Maryam grabbed me by the arm, putting her finger to her lips, shushing me as not to wake Nadja, she dragged me to the hallway and pointed at the front door. It opened and I gasped.

There stood Rabab with a bunch of flowers. I immediately ran into his arms crushing them and him to me.

'Now that's what I call a welcome!' he said over my shoulder to Maher and Maryam who were watching and laughing, with tears welling in their eyes.

I turned to Maher, still not letting go of Rabab. 'Why didn't you tell me you were bringing him here?'

'I didn't know! He insisted on coming here first, even making me promise to stop for flowers for you. I thought they'd given me the wrong brother,' he said, punching Rabab on the arm. Once we had all moved inside I got my first proper look at Rabab. I held him at arm's length, studying him.

'Will I do?' he joked, stretching out his arms. He wore some casual, but fitted pants with a Ralph Lauren polo shirt. His belt matched his Armani loafers which were shined to reflection and his hair was cut and brylcreemed off of his face.

'Oh, Rabab, I've been so worried. You look great, it's so good to have you here.' I was daring to think everything might just be okay. Maybe this had been the wake-up call he had needed and the wedding the opportunity to come back home on good terms.

'I'm sorry, I've been a bit of an asshole.'

'A bit,' I laughed. 'Seriously, come on. I told you, I get it, but none of that matters now. You're back, that's all we care about,' I said, hugging him again.

'Who are you?' a small voice asked. Nadja had woken unnoticed.

'Hey, sweetie,' said Maryam scooping her on to her lap. 'This is your uncle Rabab.'

'Oh, Aalinna, she is so beautiful,' said Rhabab as he crouched down next to Nadja, taking her hand.

'Thank you, I know,' I said, grinning.

'I don't know who you are,' said Nadja looking up at him through suspicious eyes, everyone in the room cringed a little.

Rabab rubbed her cheek. 'I know, but we're going to change all that,' he said, looking from one to the other of us.

Maher and Rabab didn't stay long, they needed to get back and see their mother and father. I managed to speak to Maher alone while Maryam and Rabab briefly caught up.

'He is so nervous about seeing father,' Maher said, but I reassured him that Zayef had a word and that we, all of us, had his back. 'I think it will be okay, Aalinna. I think this nightmare could be coming to an end.' It was evident he was relieved. Maher looked two feet taller and ten years younger, it was only for seeing him so happy and relaxed that I truly realised what pressure we had been under for so long.

I practically skipped through my errands. Even Nadja's cranky mood couldn't bother me, I'd called and told Zayef about Rabab's visit and he sounded as relived and happy as everyone else.

That evening we all called in to see Rabab and Maher at Aunt Sabera's. We women wouldn't stay long, as per tradition we would go to see the bride before her big day.

Aunt Sabera was practically floating round the room. According to Maher, Uncle had made a huge effort as soon as Rabab arrived, he had hugged and pulled his son to him, welcoming him home. They stood side by side with Maher, talking to my father. Their faces were animated from their story telling, their body language relaxed. Aunt Sabera came up behind me putting her arm around my waist.

'Oh, Aalinna, how I have longed to see this,' she said, smiling. Her eye lashes glistened with the tears she was trying to hold back. 'God knows I'm grateful, but seeing them all together makes me miss her even more.'

I squeezed her hand, 'I know she would be so happy that you're all together, and you know she would love that you have Ema in your life.'

She raised my hand and kissed it. 'I knew you would understand.'

I was so happy I couldn't sleep, Nadja, Zayef's and my clothes were hanging ready for the next morning and the hairdressers would be coming to do our hair at 8am sharp. I couldn't wait to see Nadja all dressed up. I tossed and turned prattling on to Zayef, who tried to sleep bedside me. 'She is going to look so beautiful, don't you think?'

'Yes,' he muttered.

'Rabab did look well, didn't he?' I asked, looking for reassurance.

'Yes, Aalinna. Now shh, go to sleep,' he said throwing his arm over me. I snuggled into him and closed my eyes looking forward to the big day.

*

I loved mornings like this. We were all up early, sitting round the breakfast table, Nadja in her high chair making a racket with her cutlery. Zayef was reading the headlines to her in a sing song voice, keeping her entertained whilst Maryam and I chatted about our strategies for dresses and hair.

'Actually,' I began, looking at the clock and grabbing one last swig of coffee 'We had better get a move on, the hairdresser will be here any minute.'

'It's okay,' said Maryam. 'I will take Nadja.' She looked at Zayef, smiling, 'You two have another coffee together, I can sort her out.'

'Thank you,' I said as she reached for Nadja, whose arms had reflexively shot up the moment she stood. I would have one unhappy little girl when it was time for Maryam to leave. Zayef had put down his paper and moved to the sideboard to get more coffee. 'You want one with me?' He asked holding up the pot to me.

'Yeah go on, I have ten minutes.'

As he was pouring I looked at the morning headlines. 'That's so sad, what happened to that family, isn't it?' I said pointing at the paper, I began to read the story out loud to him as he sat down. At first he didn't notice but then as I continued (slowly at first and then louder and more confidently) I snuck a look at him. I saw the realisation dawn on his face. I stopped.

He was open mouthed; his lips were working but no were words coming out.

'I've been learning to read, well properly' I felt self-conscious now. 'I have dyslexia Zayef. I wanted to tell you but I wanted to get good at reading first,' I said with a worried half-grin.

He still hadn't said a word, I hadn't planned on telling him this way, the moment just felt right and it was getting difficult sneaking out to my classes. I wanted to be able to share it with him.

Say something. I noticed the tears come down his cheek.

'My God, Aalinna. You're amazing!' He leant over and hugged me to him. 'You're such a dark horse, when will I ever learn not to be surprised by you? I'm so proud of you.' We kissed deeply, the sound of the door knocking broke our spell.

'That'll be the hairdresser,' I said, straightening myself. We both looked pretty flushed.

'Right, that's my cue to leave,' he said, giving me one last kiss. 'Hey, we will talk more about this, but I meant it, you're amazing,' he said, winking at me.

I longed to follow him upstairs but the persistent knocking

of the door prevented me. I pulled open the door and pinned a smile to my face. There stood Rabab in his wedding outfit with his hair disheveled, his skin pale and hands shaking.

'Shit!' I dragged him in by the arm. 'What are you playing at?' I hissed. 'Get out to the balcony before anyone sees you!' Once I had closed the door behind us I turned on him . 'You look like shit, Rabab? I don't fucking believe this.'

'Aalinna wait please, I swear, I can explain.'

'Go on,' I said, shoving him none too lightly.

'I messed up, it was harder than I thought. I just thought I'd have a smoke, you know, get myself together. But you know how it is – one leads to another and now my head's all over the place.'

'What? Weed? Drugs? Let me get this straight,' I said through gritted teeth, 'You not only bring drugs through the airport, and into your parents' house, you bloody smoke it the night before your brother's wedding?' My throat was sore; I had literally been growling; I had to keep my voice down for fear we would be over-heard.

'I know, I know,' he said, his head in his trembling hands. 'I swear. No more. I just need a stiff drink to straighten me out, just one. I swear I'll be fine then.'

'You have got to be kidding me, Rabab!'

'I wouldn't ask Aalinna, but you know my parents don't keep booze at home and if they see me like this my mother will be so upset my father will be furious. And Maher will go nuts, you don't want that, do you?' he said, grabbing my wrist.

I pulled away from him, " don't you dare put this on me".

'I'm sorry, I didn't mean it like that, Aalinna, I swear, but I've nowhere else to go. Just one stiff drink to get me through the day.'

I couldn't believe this was happening, I knew he was right but I didn't want to be responsible for giving him alcohol. Still, I couldn't leave him like this.

'Damn you, come with me,' I said, coming off the balcony and leading him through to Zayef's study. He followed like an obedient puppy. 'You wait here; I will be back.'

I went to the dining room and took a bottle of *Johnny Walker* from the cabinet and poured a glass. I returned to the study. Maher jumped as I entered.

'It's only me,' I said. 'You're lucky Zayef has just gone to get ready so he will be a while.' Now drink this and pull yourself together, then get back and look after your brother. Today is about him, not you,' I said, throwing him a disgusted look as I turned to the door.

'Aalinna, I'm sorry. I swear I will make it okay.'

'I didn't look back.'

When I checked half an hour later, he was gone. *Please just let this be a blip*, I was comforted by the thought that there would be no alcohol at the wedding, so at least I knew he couldn't get any worse. Or so I thought.

Mr. Walker's amber restorative seemed to sort Rabab out. He stood smiling and confident next to Maher as we all waited for Ema to make her entrance. She looked stunning and the love and pride shined in Maher's eyes as he watched her enter. Everyone looked amazing in their best clothes, smiling and happy, the love for the happy couple was tangible in the room.

Chapter 19

All good things come to an end

"Life is a balance between holding on and knowing when to let go."

Rumi

Aunt Sabera cried the whole way through the ceremony with a huge grin on her face. The wedding was exactly what she (and we) had all hoped for, filled with love, excitement and tears of joy. And, most importantly, no dramas. Uncle stood by her side, tall and proud. He had been trying so hard since Rabab had come home, allowing him to fit back in with ease, not letting old grievances to get in the way. For such a proud man I knew this was no easy feat. He moved to stand side by side with Rabab as Aunt Sabera gushed over the couple. Their vows were complete and Rabab darted over to his brother, heartily pumping Maher's hand in congratulations. As I waited to congratulate the happy couple, I felt Zayef's hand slip into mine.

'Are you okay?' he squeezed.

'Yes,' I said with a satisfied grin.

'It all worked out well in the end,' he remarked, nodding towards Rabab.

'Uh huh.' I felt so bad keeping that morning's drama from him but I didn't want him worrying. As always, I wanted the day to be perfect for everyone and if that meant keeping Zayef and the others in the dark then so be it.

I changed the subject. 'She looks stunning, doesn't she?'

Ema sat demurely in an oak chair next to her new husband, greeting their well-wishers. Her face was radiant, the many layers of gold she wore reflected off her skin and eyes, creating an angelic effect. Her lips were set in a small self-satisfied smile of contentment as she gazed up at Maher, who held her bangled hand, caressing it with his thumb – unconsciously offering his support. They held on to each other as they were showered with kisses, hugs and words of congratulation.

'She does look beautiful,' Zayef said as he leant down and picked up Nadja, interrupting her in her quest of spinning to make her dress flow out around her like an errant UFO. 'But not as beautiful as my girls.' He looked at me longingly and kissed Nadja on the head.

'Oi, don't be mean,' I said, secretly reveling in his look and words.

'Dada I need the toilet,' Nadja interjected. She jiggled around in his arms. Zayef rolled his eyes and made for the bathroom.

I took the chance to speak to Rabab. I'd noticed while speaking to Zayef that he had moved away from the wedding party and made off in the direction of the venue's front door. I found him outside smoking, he stood a little way off with his back to the door, taking in the gardens and a few drags deeply.

'I hope that's only tobacco,' I said as I came up behind him.

He spluttered, almost dropping the cigarette. 'Shit, Aalinna, I nearly choked, you know what my mother is like about smoking, so I sneaked out while she was occupied.'

'So how are you doing, Rabab?'

He flicked his cigarette causing it to land a distance away in the grass.

'Look, Aalinna, I'm sorry truly, I am.' Now that he had turned to face me I was getting my first proper look at him since this morning; his suit was a lot less crumpled, I could imagine Aunt Sabera dragging it off him the minute she saw him. His hair was shiny and clean and swept back neatly. He had obviously showered after leaving me this morning. He did look better much better, his stature was taller and his hands were steady, even his face was no longer waxy and damp. But there was something…

'Aalinna, I'm alright. God, give me a break, okay? I messed up but I'm fine now, I've got it under control.'

I'd obviously made him feel uncomfortable under my scrutiny. He turned from me, digging his hands into his pockets, pulled out a Zippo and his last three *Camels*.

'Give me a break,' he said again. He stabbed a cigarette between his lips and pumped the lighter in frustration, dragging deeply when it finally ignited the cigarette.

He was right, I was being paranoid; like he said he had messed up, it happens, nothing worse than somebody dragging it out. After all who was I to be all holier than thou?

'Give me a drag of that,' I said, taking the cigarette from him and dragging deeply.

I slipped my arm around his waist. 'I thought you gave up,' he said, laughing. He looked behind us, keeping watch.

'I have,' I said as I threw the cigarette at my feet and stubbed it out. 'Come on, let's get in there and enjoy ourselves.'

We walked back towards the door. 'You go ahead I just want to put these back in the car,' he said, waving the cigarette box and lighter. 'I'll hide the evidence,' he grinned.

'Good idea, I'll see you in there.'

The day carried on with a beautiful meal on the lavishly decorated tables. Bride and Groom and the generation that immediately preceded them, sat along an oak slab table draped in an embroidered silk cloth as long as the window drapes. I flitted between the lesser tables catching up with family and avoiding old friends; I simply waved graciously with my best grin, never getting close enough to start up a conversation. Before long the plates were cleared and the tables moved to make room for a dance floor. The tempo of the music helped to rouse people, their full bellies now easing. As always the children were first up, Nadja was in the center twirling around with all the other little girls. Their skirts a kaleidoscope of colours and billowing hair fanning out, making the adults queasy with nostalgia. They watched, smiling and remembering, their own younger days, their children's younger days. For me I was remembering two little girls and two little boys dressed in their best, running from the kitchen chased by an angry cook.

I felt a hand on my shoulder. 'Hey, are you okay?' I put my hand up to cover Zayef's.

'Yeah, I'm fine. Just reminiscing, where does the time go Zayef? Look at her.' I said, nodding my head towards Nadja. 'It seems like only yesterday that Maryam was that age.'

'Yes and look at her now,' Zayef said laughing pointing to Yushra and Maryam who had now joined the dance floor with some of the other younger women. They were all dancing and laughing and smiling, aware of the appreciative looks they were getting from the young men.

'I feel old,' I said, looking round.

'Where's Rabab?' I thought he was with you.

'Don't worry he has just nipped out for yet another cigarette. He seems in a pretty good mood though. You know him, he's been charming the aunts and grandma.'

Zayef laughed. 'Actually he has been gone for ages, I'm going to see what he's up to. I will check in with you,' he said, kissing my head. He made his way through the tables. I caught sight of my father sitting at a table tapping his hands to the beat of the music. Uncle was talking in his ear, obviously more concerned about making his point rather than the issue of whether or not anyone was listening. This is why they got on so well, my father was happy to let him talk, and he loved to talk whilst my father simply drowned him out, nodding, smiling or frowning when the dialogue called for it. I spotted Maryam and Yushra sitting together on a sofa in the corner of the room. They smiled and waved as I approached.

'Hey,' I said, coming to stand in front of them. 'How're you two doing?'

'We're fine, just enjoying the view,' they giggled.

I followed their gaze, a group of well-dressed and handsome young men stood enjoying their admiring glances, posturing like peacocks.

'You two have no shame,' I said in mock disgust. 'Maybe there is hope for you yet Yushra.' The subsequent thump to my arm was playful but still hard enough to make me think twice about my comment.

As I leant in to sit next to them I was almost taken off my feet by a girl about Maryam's age barging past. I looked around assuming an apology was imminent only to be given a look that would have turned milk sour, accompanied by a shake of the head before she marched off to stand with a few friends who all turned to glare in our direction.

'What the hell, did I miss something,' I said, looking from Yushra to Maryam.

'Damn, that was rude,' said Maryam, what a cow.' I was pleased she was so indignant on my behalf but didn't want her getting upset.

'Whatever, you two are probably eyeing up her boyfriend,' I said with a fake laugh. I had a bad feeling about this and didn't know why. 'Right. Enjoy, you two. I'm off to see what my mother is feeding my daughter.'

My parents had insisted on Nadja sitting with them, which was great, I was always up for a bit of time out but not when it meant I'd be up half the night with a sick child that had been propelled to the dance floor by the sheer force of E-numbers.

As I made my way to their table I looked around for Zayef. He and Rabab were still not back. Moving on instinct, I made my way towards the front door. My heart stopped. I saw Zayef standing over Rabab, who had his head in his hands. I stood for a moment rooted to the spot. Rabab shot up from his chair.

Fuck off, Zayef! I'll do what I like!' he yelled standing chest to chest with Zayef. Zayef's face was twisted in disgust. I could tell by his pale face and the veins standing out on his neck he was furious. 'You're a joke, Rabab.'

Zayef must have felt my gaze, he turned to stare at me, Rabab didn't seem to notice. 'Piss off,' he said, throwing his hands in the air. He was unbalanced and immediately fell back into the lounge chair.

I went to Zayef's side as he looked down in disgust at Rabab who was bent double, hanging his arms between his legs and a trail of thin saliva between his knees.

'You need to get your ass upstairs,' Zayef said through gritted teeth, trying to keep his voice down. We became aware of the glances from the staff at reception who were taking all in while, pretending they hadn't noticed anything amiss. Rabab didn't even look up.

'Fuck you,' he slurred, spit spluttering on his shoes.

I was seeing a whole different side to him and it wasn't a pretty one.

I tried a different tact. 'Rabab,' I began, putting my hand on his shoulder. 'Come with me, let's sort this out. His head sprung up, he hadn't even realised I was there, his face a picture of shame. Zayef stood with his arms folded, enjoying Rabab's humiliation. I couldn't really blame him. Rabab shot him a look of hate as he got up and stormed towards the staircase which led to the rooms the family had booked to change in and stay if needed. I followed Rabab and my heart sank, Zayef was following us both. We all walked in silence one behind the other, Rabab swaying. He only spoke to seek directions to the correct room – wordlessly I directed, pointing till we reached the room. He marched straight in slamming the door In our faces behind him.

'Bastard,' Zayef muttered, making for the same direction.

'Wait, please,' I said, putting a hand on his arm. 'Tell me what's happened, what's going on?'

'He is wasted!' Zayef roared, pointing to the door that Rabab had since disappeared behind. 'I kept him beside me, a few times he said he was going for a smoke, fine, I thought. Then he started going more often and taking longer to come back. I hadn't seen him in over an hour that's why I went to look for him after I spoke to you. When I got out to the foyer, I knew something wasn't right. I could hear his laughing before I got anywhere near him. I thought at first he was talking on the phone, but then he looked up and saw me, he began shouting like an idiot. *'Ah, there you are I was just telling these two lovely ladies how sexy they look this evening, which one would you like?'* . Aalinna, I could have died of shame. I hadn't even noticed these young girls sitting there but when I did I could see the disgust on their faces. It was them he had been laughing and jeering at, not talking on the phone!'

'Oh shit,' I said, putting my hand across my mouth.

'Oh no, it gets better. I told him to shut the hell up and

pushed him down into the chair, the girls obviously saw that as a good time to get out of there and started to squeeze past us, but before I could stop him he was on his feet grabbing one of them by the arm and mauling at her, trying to kiss her.'

'Is he for real ?'

'I told him to get out and tried to apologise to the girl but she stormed off crying.'

The girl who had bumped into me and threw me a scathing look. She probably knew Zayef was my husband and Rabab my cousin. I felt my own face burn with shame. Zayef continued 'When I turned back to him Rabab was outside heading for his car.'

'Yeah,' I interrupted. 'Probably getting his damn cigarettes. He threw them in the glove box earlier.' Zayef regarded me curiously. 'I came out to check on him earlier today, he was smoking and when we went to go back in, he said he was going back to the car to hide his cigarettes. He didn't want his mother seeing them.' *I knew something wasn't right.*

We smiled our greetings at an elderly couple making their way along the corridor, willing them to move on without starting a conversation. They didn't.

'He wasn't getting cigarettes from the car Aalinna, he was in the back seat with a bottle of *Johnny Walker* and whatever else to his mouth, I think there were more than just *Camels* in that pack. I don't know where the hell he managed to get it.'

I'd left him in Zayef's study, he had his own drinks cabinet. Rabab must have taken it, that's why he was gone when I returned. I was furious. He hadn't run off because he was ashamed or afraid of getting me in trouble. He had stolen from me, my home, when I was sticking my neck out to help him. I realised now he had been playing us all the whole day, obviously taking swigs every time he went for a cigarette .

'Aalinna are you alright? You've gone white.'

'Yes, sorry,' I said, taking Zayef's hand as much as for support as it was to comfort him.

'Well anyway, you know the rest, he stormed back in trying to make his way back to the reception hall. I dragged him back to the foyer.'

Zayef rubbed his temples hard, instead of vocalising his exasperation. 'Aalinna, I couldn't let him in there. He would have caused mayhem, the mood he is in.'

'Thank God you were there,' I felt sick at the image of the look of shame and disappointment on his parent's faces. As for Maher, I'd no doubt he would have swung for him for spoiling Ema's day and shaming her in front of her family and friends.

'I was so glad you turned up, I didn't want to involve you, stress you out. I just didn't know what to do with him,' Zayef sighed. 'I was ready for killing him myself there is no way he was going to budge for me.'

'Thank you, Zayef. Thank you for getting him up to the room.' I held him to me and kissed his neck. He was such a kind man, a gentleman. He must have been mortified at Rabab's behaviour. I hated seeing him so upset and God only knew what he was going to say when he heard about this morning, about how Rabab really got his hands on the whiskey. *I've really let him down.*

'Look,' he said, rubbing my back. 'You see to him, keep him in that room. I need to cool down and try and smooth things over with that young girl before she complains to one of her family members.'

'I hadn't even thought of that.'

As I entered the bedroom and closed the door my stomach tumbled when I turned around to see the bed empty. It took me a moment to figure out what the pervading noise was; it was

Rabab throwing up violently in the bathroom. I couldn't muster any sympathy for him. I sat on the chair next to the dressing table and faced the bed. I tried to steady myself, I don't think I have ever been this angry or disappointed. Or hurt.

I heard the toilet flush and the bathroom door open. Rabab zig zagged his way to the bed, his shirt stained with his own vomit. His hands shook as he attempted to wipe his mouth. His skin so white it had a transparency. He fell on to the bed in a heap without looking at me. I jumped as the bedroom door flew open as Maryam burst into the room, breathless. She threw a look of disgust at Rabab on the bed as she came towards me, kneeling at my feet.

'Aalinna are you okay? You're white as a sheet,' she said, taking both my hands in hers and rubbing them.

I didn't know what to say anymore.

'Zayef came to find me,' she explained when I didn't respond. 'He told me what happened. He's managed to smooth things over with the girl I left them talking. He asked me to come up and check that you're okay.'

Rabab sat up on the bed, his legs hanging over the edge sitting in what seemed to be his normal position his head hanging down. 'I'm sorry, Aalinna,' he said to the carpet.

Maryam moved to speak, I squeezed her hand hushing her, begging her with my eyes to stay quiet. She got up and sat on the chair in the corner of the room refusing to look around at Rabab.

'Oh Aalinna, please don't look at me like that, not you, I swear I didn't mean to get drunk and I just -' he hung his head again. 'Please, Aalinna. Talk to me. You don't know what it's been like for me,' he slurred. 'All these years, losing my sister and then my family. I've been so lonely, confused, and guilty.'

I did not speak.

'So many times I thought about killing myself,' he pleaded, sniffling. Maryam shook her head in disgust.

'I've tried; you know that Aalinna. But it's been so hard.' I felt my anger dissolving, then I jumped at the sound of Maryam's voice.

'You talk to her about trying. What have you done other than think of yourself?' She snarled. She stood up against his slumped figure. 'She has been to hell and back, yes she's made mistakes but she has paid for them. She's tried time and time again, counselling, therapy hospitalisation even. Always getting back up to try again – but not for herself, but for the people she loves. The people she cares about. Have you stopped to think of them? Have you stopped for one moment to think of the loss your parents have suffered? Your brother? Your friends? The bloody rest of us? This impacted on all of our lives, Rabab. I felt like I was losing my parents until not too long ago, I thought I'd lost my sister. Are you even grateful for the fact that you still have a brother? I had no one. So yes, I know about the hell you're talking about. We all do,' she yelled. 'We understand it; we have felt it but you have got to get a grip on it. We have all tried to help you, everyone. You throw it back in our faces, it's like we're not worth the effort. You think your pain means more than all of ours. Well it fucking doesn't Rabab. It doesn't,' she was crying now. 'And I'll tell you this, I will not sit here and let you drag my sister down. I will not sit and watch you take advantage of her kindness and take advantage of her illness. She can empathise with you, she has a connection and all you can do is see it as a way to make excuses for your behaviour.

You're taking advantage of her loyalty and love you disgust me,' now she wheeled around to me. 'You need to make a choice here, Aalinna. All you worked for, all we've been through to get to where we are now, he's ruining it all. He's destroying the relationships we've all fought so hard to build, you're lying to your own goddamn husband, your aunt, your mother. He's dragging you into his web of deceit; he is an addict Aalinna and he's not ready to admit it, and you can't make him.'

She stormed from the room. Rabab sat dry eyed and open mouthed. I buried my head in my hands and cried. Unbeknownst to me, Zayef was downstairs playing the host, trying to divert people's attention from the fact we were both missing. *Oh she's gone for a lie down.*

Nadja was lying along one of the couches fast asleep, snuggled in a blanket. The evening to Zayef's relief was coming to an end. The happy couple would shortly retire to their room and once people had waved them off, the remaining guests would either leave for home or retire to their rooms upstairs.

Maryam had pulled herself together and recruited Yushra, filling her in on what had gone on. Yushra made sure she kept Aunt Sabera and Uncle busy, talking and listening to their stories. She would casually wave a hand when asked where Rabab was.

'Oh, I just saw him, didn't you? He's in the foyer chatting to the younger crowd,' she smiled.

I'd been sitting with Rabab alone for an hour and we had barely spoken. Maryam's words had sobered him up quicker than any amount of caffeine ever could. He was finally contrite..

'I'm sorry, Aalinna,' he wasn't whining or beseeching, his voice was strong. 'I've seriously fucked up. I'm such a mess. I shouldn't have dragged you all into my shit.'

I believed him. 'I'm sorry Rabab, I'm not trying to make you squirm, I just don't know what to say anymore,' I sighed.

'I know.' He caught sight of himself in the mirror, he was taking in his vomit covered shirt, his pale face with eyes so red they looked like burn tissue. He shook his head at his reflection. He walked silently from the room and into the bathroom. I heard the shower run and tried to ignore the wrecking sobs I could hear choking him. I heard a small tap on the door, I was afraid to open it. This was Rabab's room. What if it was Aunt Sabera checking where he was? How would I explain me being here?

'Aalinna, it's me.' I heard Maryam whisper through the gap in the door. I didn't know how much more I could take. I opened the door to see her with Nadja fast asleep in her arms. I thanked her and took Nadja from her arms, holding her close and headed for my room a few doors away.

What about him?' Maryam whispered as we made our way along the corridor.

I turned and looked at her, and beckoned her close. I wrapped my free arm round her. 'Thank you.' I kissed her on the head. 'He has a lot of thinking to do, it's you I'm worried about now, do as your big sister says, get to bed, you look exhausted.'

'I love you, Aalinna.'

'Me too.' I blew her a kiss and watched as she walked to her room, ensuring she was safely inside before entering my own room. I quietly undressed myself and Nadja. Ignoring the cot, I put her in my bed. I slid between the sheets and wrapped her in my arms. I held her close, listening to her little breaths and absorbing her heat. I closed my eyes and waited for Zayef. This is where I was needed. This is where I needed to be.

I woke to Nadja poking at my nose with her fingers, the smell of her hair filled my nostrils. 'Hey beautiful.'

'Hey mama,' she said, imitating me.

'Hey my beautiful girls,' I heard Zayef say from behind me.

Nadja giggled. 'Dada, where are you?' she said sitting up. I felt his strong arms encircling me. He must have crawled in to bed during the night. I felt him kiss the back of my head, neither of us moved or spoke. I wanted to stay there forever but Nadja had other ideas, she squeezed between us making us squeal as she trampled and kicked her way through. We said nothing about the night before, simply enjoying the moment. We had our time laughing and playing eventually dressing and showering.

A tapping on the door was accompanied by Maryam's voice, 'Hey are you guys up?' I had no sooner opened the door that Nadja jumped into her arms. 'I guess I'll bring her down to breakfast then,' she said, ruffling Nadja's hair.

I went to sit beside my husband on the bed. He took my hands in his own and swallowed deeply. 'He's gone Aalinna.' For some reason I wasn't that surprised, I simply gave Zayef a weak smile. 'You did all you could, Aalinna.'

'I know.'

'It couldn't go on.'

'I know.'

'I went to see him last night, I told Maher he had gone out with some old friends and that's why he wasn't there. When I got in there he was just sitting on the bed staring. He told me what Maryam had said. Zayef shifted his weight on the bed and put a few more pillows behind his back. He stared at the patterns of artex on the ceiling. 'I think it really hit home but he's just not ready, Aalinna. He said so himself.' I knew all this but I said nothing. I knew it the minute I left his room last night.

'Zayef I need to talk to you, I need to tell you something about yesterday.'

'I know, Aalinna,' he replied brushing the hair that had fallen across my face as I'd bowed my head in shame.

'How?'

'Rabab told me, he didn't want to cause trouble between us,

he admitted it was his fault he had manipulated you and he was ashamed. He reckoned he wanted to make it up to you by taking responsibility. He loves you, Aalinna. I can see that now. He said to tell you that when he is ready, he will come to you and he knows you will be there.' I fell in to Zayef's arms, we held each other for a while.

'Oh no! What about Aunt Sabera?'

'He left them a message at reception. Some story about having to get back to hand in a paper he forgot about.'

I raised my eyebrows in response. 'I know but you know what, Aalinna? I think they will accept it. I think we were all kidding ourselves and just wanted to make it alright for a little while. If only, just, for a little while. Especially for Maher and Ema's sake.'

*

As we entered the room for breakfast no one mentioned Rabab's absence. As we all chatted about the wedding and what a great day it had been I knew I'd made the right decision. I would always be here for Rabab but until he was ready to get professional help or at the least admit he needed it, there was nothing more I could do for him. The best I could do was be there for his family, my family, our family. I was where I needed to be, surrounded by my family and dearest friends. It had been a long road for us all but somehow we were still all here, all getting through each day, stronger and happier.

Zayef raised his glass of juice. 'To the happy couple.'

'To family,' Said Maryam, raising hers. 'To friends present and past but never forgotten.' We all clinked in agreement.

Chapter 20
Life Is Beautiful

"This being human is a guest house. Every morning is a new arrival. A joy, a depression, a meanness, some momentary awareness comes as an unexpected visitor... Welcome and entertain them all. Treat each guest honourably. The dark thought, the shame, the malice, meet them at the door laughing, and invite them in. Be grateful for whoever comes, because each has been sent as a guide from beyond."

Rumi

My bipolar breakdown and hospitalisation had completely caught me off-guard, forcing me into defensive mode, scrambling to piece together the shattered fragments of my life. When I was younger, I knew that the world was a beautiful, happy, secure place, a veritable garden of blossoming relationships and memories with just the occasional lethal winter. However, senseless family disagreements blew-up into full-on war. Friendships were lost. Pressures weighed hard. Death and failure introduced themselves. Lives were compared and found wanting. It was a re-birth; regaining my life taught me to walk and talk again with plenty of stumbling and confusion along the way, but little by little, I gained the strength to stand, to converse, to take care of myself. I gained confidence, built friendships and deepened relationships systematically, as I had done with Zayef and Nadja months before. I ate well, exercised more, worried less, paid attention to my needs and asked if I needed help.

I've learnt to take nothing for granted. In the first 22 years of my life, I rarely had a negative experience. Whatever I wanted or needed was given to me—always. I had everything, in a country when many have nothing, and not just material things. I had my confidence, I had my physical health and I had my loved ones. I was happy, outgoing and sociable. I could go anywhere and do anything. Even when I was growing up and not doing well in school, my self-esteem was unscathed. I could talk comfortably to anyone, about anything. I had no problem stating my opinion. I knew I was smart, even if my grades didn't reflect that. I never had problems with friends and family.

But it all went when I woke up on my mother's bed that fateful morning. If any infrastructure had remained in my life, Samama had taken it with her in her passing. I clawed it back over the course of a decade. I had to take everything, small-step by small-step; little things day-by-day that made me more confident.

More than ever now, I enjoy my children and husband. I have even entered this fascinating world of reading and I remain in love with it.

Yushra is still my best friend and to this day we see each other regularly, she did eventually find her Mr. Right and had the wedding day she always dreamed of. My parents, Zayef, Nadja and I, were all by her side, along with Maher and Ema and their two beautiful sons.

My cousin Rabab continues to waver between acceptance and denial of his illness and addictions, usually camping on the side of denial. He still cannot accept the shameful idea that something is wrong with him, that one denial is what keeps him from progressing towards a healthy, normal life. But we continue to be there for him, but now for me This Life Is Beautiful.

THE END

My readers, fellow sufferer.

I live happily in our beautiful home. Where one room is devoted to my love of reading, a vast library that is my sanctuary. My husband and I have two beautiful children, a boy and a girl. My children are my heroes, they bring so much love and happiness into our lives. It's been amazing to watch them grow from sparkly-eyed children to fun-loving, clever individuals with their own unique personalities. It hasn't always been easy, we have had our ups and downs, but doesn't everyone? We are simply a normal family.

I will be forever grateful to my children, they think I am their hero, but they are mine. They gave me the strength and motivation over the years that I have needed to stay well, they rescued me from falling into the darkest deepest hole and saved me from my illness.

A seed has to die before it can produce a bountiful harvest. And perhaps I had to experience an emotional death. All of the decay and destruction in my life was to be burned away to discover how beautiful my life really was. At first, living with bipolar disorder felt like death, but as I struggled through the years I came to see my illness differently. It was not a door that locked me in and closed me off from experiencing the world in a normal way.

Rather, it was a window, into the manic interpretation of the world and with the shutters held open and the breeze rolling in, I could acknowledge it, even admire the view and then move on.

I'd thought bipolar disorder put me ten years behind in everything. I couldn't do a lot of things that came easily to people of my age. For a long time, I felt like I was in my own world. And yet, in other ways, this illness pushed me forward, full-throttle into wisdom beyond my years. Teetering on the brink of what felt like the complete destruction of my soul and somehow tumbling out alive has taught me some invaluable lessons about life, for which I would not trade a single moment of the hell I lived through to learn them. I actually see my illness very positively because it posed important challenges for me and taught me many less. Now, today, I deeply appreciate what I took for granted before my illness. Now I appreciate every ounce of my confidence.

There are so many things just waiting to be noticed and enjoyed. If I miss them, I will miss some of the most beautiful gifts that my life can offer—simple things like having a normal conversation with a friend over a cup of tea or interacting with others without feeling anxious and lost; spending an afternoon with my own company, content and without feeling constantly restless. Reading a book, having a sit by the window, in the warm afternoon sun; having a family and a place to call home.

Having this illness has also taught me that I don't have to prove anything to anybody, a feeling that is indescribably liberating. I know who I am and I don't care what other people think.

I learned that I can't be afraid of sorrow, a natural and unavoidable part of life. Instead, I welcome it, a normal, and human, upset. Life is a journey, with ups and downs, twists and turns, gentle hills and massive pot-holes. Problems will come, without a doubt, but ultimate wisdom is in how to deal with them instead of running away.

I do not regret the struggles but take pride in how they have positively moulded my character. My illness has made me strong, patient, insightful, confident and content. It has made me a better person, a better wife, a better sister, daughter and mother. I know that I would not be the person I am today without my illness.

I now have the ability to recognize the onslaught of a manic episode. I could – *can* – identify signs and symptoms as they are happening. And instead of caving into them, I acknowledge and take control of them.

I have not let this disease defeat me. The battles were not easy but I was learning how to fight them and stay healthy. I am convinced, now more so than ever, that bipolar disorder was merely a part of me—it did not define me. Finally I am comfortable in my own skin.

For some people it takes being 'reborn' like this to realise how beautiful their life really is. At least, that's what it took for me.

When you have gotten through, and you *will* get through, you will see that every struggle, every challenge and every tear shed has only made you stronger. Life is too short to constantly ruminate over what you could have done better.

But living a beautiful life is not merely a destination – it is a choice; you don't get any marks just for turning up. I wouldn't change anything about my past. I am who I am today exactly because of the things that happened to me on this journey until the present. Now I have an inner peace, for which I have been longing for years. I know who I am and I don't care what other people think. I realise what life is all about. It's hanging on when your heart has had enough. It's giving more, when you feel like giving up. And when you do hang on, when you do give more, life has so much to give you in return: gift upon beautiful gift, just waiting to be opened by a brighter, happier individual. I am that individual, and you can be too.

Thank you for reading.
Lamia Islam